M. O'Connor Morris

Dublin Castle

M. O'Connor Morris

Dublin Castle

ISBN/EAN: 9783743418448

Manufactured in Europe, USA, Canada, Australia, Japa

Cover: Foto ©Andreas Hilbeck / pixelio.de

Manufactured and distributed by brebook publishing software (www.brebook.com)

M. O'Connor Morris

Dublin Castle

BY

M. O'CONNOR MORRIS

AUTHOR OF "RAMBLES IN THE ROCKY MOUNTAINS," "TRIVIATA," ETC.

London

HARRISON AND SONS, 59 PALL MALL

BOOKSELLERS TO THE QUEEN AND H.R.H. THE PRINCE OF WALES

1889

PREFACE.

In presenting this slight historical sketch of
Dublin Castle, which at this moment is supposed
to be somewhat in the parlous position described
by Hamlet, "To be or not to be, that is the
question," and is, therefore, invested with extrinsic
interest, the author begs to disclaim any pretence
to original research or insight, or, indeed, to
originality of any kind. He has, however,
gone to the most generally accepted sources of
authentic information, has read a great many
volumes connected with the subject, by such
writers as Bagwell, Lecky, Gilbert, Plowden,
Carte, Wraxall, Prendergast, Forster, Spencer-
Walpole, Halliday, Macaulay, Charles Greville,
and many more, and endeavoured to set forth
a fairly accurate picture of the Castle and its
Gesta, and of the more remarkable tenants of its
venerable walls, neither extenuating anything,

nor setting down aught of malice, whether pre-pense or otherwise.

To illustrate the reigns of the Castellans it was necessary to make a sort of running com-mentary on the events of Irish history—history which has been written with varying aims—with political purpose by some writers, and without the knowledge which recent work in the Record Office has made accessible ; for instance, Lingard minimises the massacre of Protestants in Ulster in 1641, while many writers exaggerate, even to the point of absurdity, that terrible calamity. Clarendon is silent as to the Glamorgan Treaty, which is a guiding light in the study of that crisis of our Constitution, while, to come to minor matters, that very clever and interesting author, Mr. Spencer Walpole, shows a nescience of the topography of Dublin when he talks of the views to be gained from that very minor mound, " The Hill of Clontarf," which O'Connell pro-posed to make his bema—when he gathered to-gether his braves at Clontarf—like King Brian Borhoime.

It is the fashion of the day to blame English misrule for any poverty, turbulence, and impatience of law that is witnessed in modern Ireland; and certainly the teaching of history confirms the *injusta noverca* argument up to a certain point; but ever since the Reform Bill Ireland has been dealt with with fair liberality—at least with liberal intentions by the English Legislature; and it may be questioned whether, if Ireland had been subjected to any other great power she would have fared half so well, while the political enmity to England which permeates a portion of Ireland, and which is sedulously fostered by a section of her Press, that has apparently adopted the *rôle* of the ancient bards, poets, and rhymers, who kept up the *odium Anglicanum* at fever heat in Wales, Scotland, and Ireland alike for so many decades, is shared in a mitigated form by Wales and Scotland, for the Welsh and Irish have been bitterer foes, though claiming kindred, than ever were English and Irish; moreover, English statesmen may claim that they have raised *the people* of Ireland to a far higher level than they would probably have attained, or ever did attain, under autochthonous chiefs, or an oligarchical Parliament, from which *they* were entirely excluded. Historical perspective requires a distant standpoint, and we are still comparatively very near to the much-debated Union; whereas Scotland, where the fires of national hatred burnt even more fiercely than in Ireland, is a long way removed from the date of her union and incorporation which is generally pronounced to have been an immense boon to both countries. Yet Scotland has not renounced one jot of her nationality or traditions : though we believe the public display at the last Glasgow Exhibition of such English perfidies as the order for the Massacre of Glencoe, or the view of the personal paraphernalia of the Bruce of Bannockburn, did not lead even to indignant newspaper leaders, or to more appeals to " Scots wha hae," &c. Protestant ascendency, the almost necessary consequence and corollary of unfortunate rebellions and revolutions in Ireland, is haply a thing of the past, ignored in theory or practice, a hatchet to be buried by both belligerents, who have each had their triumphs and reverses, and should allow Benburb to balance the Boyne, and Londonderry Limerick.

The territorial system of Ireland, which had a certain element of feudalism in it, is fast crumbling to pieces under enlightened legislation and the spread of free trade, aided by increased facilities of transport. The plausible fiction, that the landlords of Ireland were a grasping, griping, rapacious class, is dispelled by the testimony of Gladstone, and the evidence of a generous adversary, who wrote thus apropos of the famine era :—

" The majority of resident landlords really did all in their power. When the famine appeared many landowners found themselves on the verge of ruin. They had inherited property that was already heavily mortgaged. The money paid for rent did not remain in their hands, but went to pay their creditors. The loss of a year's rent brought them fatally near seizure and bankruptcy. They knew this, and yet it must be acknowledged that a great many of them who might have escaped disaster by harshness towards their tenants preferred their own ruin." It may be doubted if a fairer tribute was ever paid to the magnanimity of a body of men.

To the credit of their political consistency, if to the disparagement of their financial foresight, the landlords of Ireland rejected unanimously Mr. Gladstone's Bill for Home Rule, coupled with the magnificent compensatory offer of £150,000,000 as a solatium—

> " Gladstone has proved the landlord's friend,
>   Let truth be ever told ;
> When patriots said—let's give them lead,
>   The old man said—give gold."

The landlords, at least those of old stock, were not harsh, but they were imprudent and reckless, and made a ductile people, to whom they were examples, reckless too. Tiger Fitzgerald and fighting Fitzgerald were sure to find replicas in a lower social stratum ; and such magnificoes as " Buck Whalley," who for a bet walked to Jerusalem and played ball against its walls, or Beauchamp Bagenal, who *inter alia* fought a royal duke and

carried off a nun from a convent, raised false standards, *vitiis imitatibiles*, though we cannot forbear
some admiration of their dare-devil dash and
gallantry. Where the landlords of Ireland failed
was in the *neglect* of their own people and their
want of cohesion and *esprit de corps*. Following
the Court and Courtiers of England—Wills o'
the Wisp that led them into sad scrapes—they
grew to despise their own country and countrymen, to their own sore hurt and impoverishment. Ireland might, merely to take pastime
for illustration, have been as good a game ground
as Scotland or England; we know how bare
of game it is now generally—as a theatre for
hunting it is miles in front of England, yet
Melton was ever an irresistible magnet to hunting
Hibernians. Whether because Ulster, like Attica,
διὰ τὸ λεπτόγεων ἀεὶ ἀστασίαστα οὖσα, escaped to
a great extent the constant storm of war that
swept over richer Leinster and Munster, or
whether she got inured to industry from her
frequent Scotch infusions, we know not; but
Ulster points a moral to the rest of Ireland,

which we trust will not be lost in the general attornment of the people to ways of peace and industry. Nor would we attempt to say more than "Jam satis," to those who have been the leaders of the popular movement, that with its abominable excesses and immoral aims still had something to admire in it—" The resurrection of a nation " as an English peer styled it. Yet even these leaders, mainly hybrid Hibernians, might reflect that none, or hardly any, of the old Celtic families are with them—O'Connells, Kavanaghs, O'Conors, O'Donohues, O'Mores, O'Callaghans, O'Neils, O'Cahans, &c., &c. Paul of Tarsus was not less a patriot in that he was proud of his Roman citizenship.

I have abandoned my original intention of devoting a chapter to Anecdotes referring to the Castle and its tenants, though at first I thought that such a chapter would be the *pièce de résist-ance* of the volume ; and perhaps, if all the *bon mots* uttered in and about the Castle could be collected together, they would be very lively reading indeed ; but such a thing is practically impossible ; nor would it—to take a few samples —be worth the trouble to record many such items as that the Castle courtiers declared that Lord A. was the most hospitable Viceroy ever known, because, while others invited their guests to dine only, he asked his friends to "dine and sleep" (but then he did the post-prandial sleeping himself) ; or how the Duke of B. found that some ladies in Dublin were so hypnotised or mesmerised by their *Ponche à la Romaine* (to which it seems they were partial) that its formal use was discontinued ; nor how some mischievous maidens played a silly trick on a gallant A.D.C., who, they fancied, did not show sufficient *empressement* to join his corps in the field, by sending him an official envelope, marked "Urgent," which, when opened in a public place, revealed nothing but a cloud of small white feathers ; nor yet how a provident spinster was seen folding the wing of a cold capon in her cambric handkerchief by a Castle official, who brought her a few slices of ham to add to her little hoard. Every Court has its little *répertoire* of jokes, and why should

Dublin claim exception ? But these chronicles
of small beer hardly shine in print, though
amusing enough to listen to. The readers of
Sir Bernard Burke's Anecdotes and Reminis-
cences will learn that the splendour of the
Dublin Court was acknowledged in the days of
the Georges and Queen Anne, and that though
occasionally suffering from partial eclipse, it has
had splendid recent revivals.

I had also purposed to write a chapter on
the topography of Dublin, and to show the
great growth of the city and its environs from
the time when the Liffey was approached by
marshes, while so erratic was its flood at times
that not very much more than a hundred years
have elapsed since the Duke of Leinster's yacht
made a suburban cruise in a flood tide over what
is now the Mayfair of the capital—Merrion
Square. It would have led too far, so I gave it up.

Bishops, and Archbishops, too, played no
unimportant part on the stage of Irish politics,
from Henri de Loundres, the King's kinsman, who
almost built the Castle, to Stone and Boulter,

who were practically the rulers of Ireland for
many years, and some notice of the Church might
have been expected, but the roll of political
prelates was not a very bright one, and the non-
political divines, such as Usher, Berkeley, and
Bedell have attained a more enduring fame, even
if they did not leave fortunes of several hundred
thousand pounds, acquired by the arts of the
money changer, that in one or two cases have
become historical. The Church of Ireland has
been lately shorn of much temporal power : the
spiritual domain is beyond the power of Prince or
Parliament, and here it may be stated that one
of the difficulties of the ruler of Ireland consists
in the anomaly that in three provinces out of its
four, and partially in the fourth, the Government of the island is a quasi-theocracy, administered by a hierarchy, that has immense power for
good and evil, and has generally wielded it *pro
bono republicæ*, as all statesmen will, I think,
allow. One of the stock arguments for the disestablishment of the present state of things is
the assumed chronic misery of the island ; it may

A

be questioned whether agricultural distress has
been anything like so severe in Ireland as in
England, though there is more squalor, while Mr.
Davitt very recently testified to the buoyant
prosperity of the woollen trade, which England
sought to extinguish many years ago. Altered
conditions have, no doubt, affected a few industries most cruelly, but so they have all over
the world, especially in England. Ireland still
recognises what Shakespeare calls "degree,"

> "Take but degree away, untune that string,
> and then what follows?"

for close to the Castle is a tramcar line with
three classes, the only one I ever saw; a hint
that the aristocratic element is still strong, though
temporarily suppressed. The history of the
Castle is practically the history of Ireland. This
remains to be written, though much good work
has been done in preparation for it.

INTRODUCTORY.

THE "intelligent" foreigner (as the phrase goes)
arriving in Dublin for the first time would be
pretty sure to direct his steps to College Green
to view the al fresco Valhalla of native genius,
exemplified by Grattan, Goldsmith, Tommy
Moore, and Edmund Burke, appositely placed
near the national Alma Mater ; to see foreign conquest represented by William of Orange sitting
on a carty charger ; and the several great banking
emporia, headed by the Bank of Ireland, the ci-
devant Parliament House of the Kingdom of
Ireland, where, however, the memorial tapestries
are hardly in keeping with existing national
sentiment, while the stone-cut legend on its vis-
à-vis, the National Bank, "Erin-go-Bragh" is in

A 2

direct opposition to Sydney Smith's counsel of perfection " Erin go bread and cheese." Then in his career of curiosity and sight-seeing he would walk through Dame Street congratulating himself, if a Gaul, that even here a tribute was paid to his native tongue, till he reached the Castle of which he had read so much, not only in the insular records, but more recently in the daily diatribes of the patriotic press, in which it was represented as the "fons et origo" of the many miseries of misgovernment, and a British bastille which public indignation had long ago stormed (on paper), a Jericho against which the trumpets of " the leaders of the people" and of Joshua himself had blown blasts of defiance for many a day, which, however, from want of faith or some other cause, had proved inoperative ; but to our visitor, on passing through the portals of the upper or lower Castle yards, the first impression of this stone symbol of the might and majesty of Great Britain would be one of

disillusion most complete—a galimatias of gro-
tesque Greek, Gothic, Plantagenet, and Queen
Anne architectural styles. He had conceived
a Place d'Armes, with all its characteristics,
whereas a half dozen sentries and as many constables were the only outward and visible signs
of that *force majeure* which for centuries had
held the heroic race of Hibernia in thrall.
St. James' Palace and the Tower had seemed most
mesquin mansions to his eye in London the other
day, but here in the bureaucracy of brick buildings and the pettiness of the "palatial" apartments, at least externally, he could discover no
outward and visible sign of the wealth and power
of victorious, if perfidious, Albion! True, he
thought the chapel looked something of a fair
Gothic shrine while the Birmingham, or Wardrobe or Record tower, though all unarmed,
and without even a gun *en barbette*, seemed a
link with a most polemical past, but for the purposes of defence or aggression, or even for the
semblance of inspiring awe, the whole thing was

to his mind, a ghastly failure and imposition, far
more bourgeois than baronial! while, *pour comble*,
the Castle yards were hemmed in by a network of
mean streets, the homes apparently of a poor
proletariat. The best feature to his eye, however, was the ample space enclosed by these two
irregular quadrangles, for the upper yard was 280
feet long by 130 feet in breadth, while the lower
was 250 feet by 220

CONTENTS.

LIST OF ILLUSTRATIONS

———◆———

DUBLIN CASTLE.

CHAPTER I.

" This castle hath a pleasant seat."—.Macbeth.

VERY little is known about the Castle of Dublin prior to the Anglo-Norman Invasion, nor has it, I believe, been decided whether the Dun or Citadel of the Scandinavians is identical with what has been the *place forte* of the capital of Ireland for many centuries. The balance of probability seems to be that the fort which Milo de Cogan captured, by a *coup de main*, was on the same site, though about as much the same castle as the Norman keep—as Queen Elizabeth's famous knife, which had new blades, and a new handle, added to the old foundation at various intervals. We know that the Ostmen had been more or less

in occupation of Dublin ever since the 9th century,
and that if the Battle of Clontarf crippled them
for a period, it by no means extirpated them
from their ancient haunts, or interfered with their
supremacy at sea.

Having had our historical faith rudely shaken
by the philosophical iconoclasm of Niebuhr and
the German school, we are very apt to question
the authenticity of annals which are more or less
interwoven with legendary exaggerations, the
screeching of scalds, and the poetic licenses of local
poets laureate, whose *raison d'être* was the glorifi-
cation of the chieftains and dynasts to whose
personal staff they were attached ; but I believe
there is little more reason to doubt the fact of the
Battle of Clontarf having taken place than of that
of Borodino or Pultowa, and a chronicler gives it
the further verisimilitude of exactness by telling
us how Sitric was married to a daughter of Brian
Borhoime, and that her woman's heart went out to
her husband and adopted countrymen rather than
to her own people ; while the two-handed sword
of the Irish Generalissimo is still preserved at
Clontarf Castle, Mr. Vernon's residence — a
witness of the faithful workmanship of the
armourers of those days, and the sinewy strength
of the arms that could wield such weapons.

The excavations made for building purposes in the neighbourhood of College Green, once Hoggen's Green, where the bloody battle between Milo de Cogan and Hasculph long surged and wavered, revealed, centuries afterwards, broken weapons and human remains, faithful records of the fierce fray, and the Virgilian hexameter—

" Grandiaque effossis mirabitur ossa sepulchris" was literally exemplified.

Moreover, it is a fact that the strong strategic points picked out by the early Irish and the Ostmen have for the most part been retained by subsequent conquerors ; a corresponding fact is recognised very often on the Continent.

Thus Sadowa was erst a battlefield of Frederick the Great.

I think it is Walter Scott who complains of the general mistrust of ancient records and traditions. We often hear, says the Wizard of the North, of vulgar *credulity*, but there is such a thing as vulgar *incredulity* too, which finds the task of absolute rejection far easier, less tedious and exacting than that of examining and investigating, and so it is with regard to the Scandinavian conquests and annexations in Ireland, to which Mr. Halliday's researches have given us so good a key; but even supposing that the present castle occupies the Scandinavian site—and its position on the top of the hog-backed ridge, close to the river's edge and with a good supply of water ("jugis aquæ") within its area, would seem to confirm this idea—we know that the Normans were nothing if not castle-builders, for "the castle" was not only their fortress and defence, but their means of pushing on their conquests and annexing fresh pastures—a fact which a few drives through Meath, de Lacy's country — would confirm, ruined castles there being almost as common as cottages and cabins.

Harris, the historian and topographer, has given us documental proof that King Henry sent instructions to his representative in Dublin— Meiler Fitzhenry—to add to and improve the buildings already in existence : "The King, to his beloved and faithful subject, Meiler Fitzhenry Lord Justice of Ireland, greeting. You have given us to understand that you have not a convenient place wherein our treasure may be safely deposited, and forasmuch as well for that use, as for many others, a fortress would be necessary for us at Dublin, we command you to erect a castle there in such competent place as you shall judge most expedient, as well to curb the city as to defend it if occasion shall so require, and that you make it as strong as you can, with good and durable walls. But you are first to finish one tower, unless afterwards a castle and palace and other works that may require greater leisure may be more conveniently raised, and that we should command you so to do : for which you have our pleasure, according to your desire—at present you may take to this use 300 marks from G. Fitz-Robert, in which he stands indebted to us. We command also our citizens of Dublin that they strengthen their city, and that you compel them thereunto if they should prove refractory. It is our pleasure also that a fair be held in Dublin every year, to continue for eight days, and to begin on the day of the Invention of the Holy Cross, another at Drogheda, on St. John Baptist's Day, to continue also for eight days, with toll and custom thereunto belonging ; another at Water-ford, on the Festival of St. Peter ad Vincula, for eight days ; and another at Limerick, on the Festival of St. Martin, for eight days ; and we command you that you give public notice thereof by proclamation, that merchants may resort thereto. Witness, the Lord Bishop of Norwich, at Geddington, 21st August, 1205." There is no record of the progress made by Meiler Fitzhenry,

but we know that Henry Loundres, Archbishop
of Dublin, refounded the Castle, so to speak—
and the subsequent necessities of the age caused
an infinite number of improvements and altera-
tions to be effected from time to time, especially
by Lionel, Duke of Clarence.

The Castle, from its position and prestige, was
more than once besieged, but the most memorable
attempt to take it was in 1534, when Thomas
Fitzgerald, eldest son of the Earl of Kildare,
was created Lord Deputy by his father, who had
been summoned to London.   History tells us
how a rumour had been circulated that the Earl
had been beheaded in London, and on this his
hot-headed son, known as " Silken Thomas,"
hastily summoned the Council, and having
surrendered the Sword of State into their hands,
broke out into overt rebellion.   The plague had
raged in the town and thinned its population, but
for all that, when news was brought that the
O'Tooles were driving cattle they had captured in
their raids through " Fingall" to the co. Wicklow,
the Dubliners turned out and attacked the
reivers, but were grievously discomfited and lost
heavily.   This caused something of a panic, and
Fitzgerald, taking advantage of it, craved from
the citizens leave to march through their streets to

besiege the Castle. This leave was reluctantly
granted, and with the aid of a good citizen,
Alderman Fitzsimmons, the Castle was victualled
for the leaguer, of which supplies the Alderman
contributed, we learn, 20 ton of wine, 24 ton of
beer, 2,000 dried ling, , and 16 hogsheads of
powdered beef. He also gave 20 chambers for
mines, and an iron chain for the drawbridge,
which he had caused to be forged in his own
house that it might not excite suspicion. Six
hundred men were now introduced by Fitzgerald
under six captains ; three pieces of cannon were
planted near Preston's Inn, opposite to the Castle
Gate, and at the same time strong entrenchments,
with ramparts, were made to protect them from
the Castle fire. In addition to this Fitzgerald
threatened to place the youths of the city on top
of the trenches. While this was going on, Sir
Francis Herbert, Alderman, who had been
knighted by the King, to whom he had gone for
advice, returned with promise of speedy succour
from his Majesty, and on this encouragement the
gates of the city were closed, and many of Fitzgerald's troops surrendered.

" Silken Thomas," hearing of this disaster,
marched to Dublin, and commenced the siege
from Ship Street, but the Castle ordnance was

well served, and an engineer named White set
fire to the thatched roofs round the Castle by
means of some artificial compound, of the nature
of Greek fire probably. These vigorous measures
caused the siege to be raised, and the loyalty of
the citizens was rewarded subsequently by his
Majesty.

It may be mentioned parenthetically here
that Silken Thomas had abandoned his siege-
works to the care of a Lieutenant, when he heard
of some cattle that were on the move, and could
therefore probably be looted. He was successful
in his stock-raid though not in his siege, and he
had presently to undergo one himself in his
" Crom a boo " Keep at Maynooth. The epithet
" Silken " was applied to this Hibernian Hotspur,
or Paddyland Percy, not from any effeminacy or
softness in his composition, but from the fringes
of silk worn by his warriors on their morions.

The Castle had the narrowest escape from
being burnt by the imprudence of Dean Swift,
who *would* read in bed, a very dangerous custom,
especially when curtains were in vogue. The
Dean's backsheesh and blandishments hushed
up the mishap we are told.

The following account gives a fair idea of the
old fortress, which, in 1783, it was proposed to

supersede by a regularly planned modern citadel, designed by Sir Bernard Gomme, but which was never erected. The entrance to the Castle was then, as it is now, from the north side, but there are no remains of the drawbridge that led to it by two strong towers, called the "Gate Towers." The gateway between them was furnished with a portcullis armed with iron, such as may be seen on the Somerset Shield—this was intended as a second defence in the event of an enemy surprising and "rushing" the drawbridge. To these two was added in later times a platform surmounted with two pieces of heavy ordnance.

From the Gate tower on the west a strong and high curtain extended in a line parallel to Castle Street, till it connected it with Cork tower, so named because it was mainly the work of Richard Boyle, first Earl of Cork, of whom it might be said—

"Di tibi divitias dederunt, artemque fruendi."

This tower replaced an old one that fell in May, 1624.

From Cork tower the castle wall continued in one curtain of equal height with the former, till it joined the Birmingham tower, said to have been built either by John Birmingham, Earl of Louth and Atherlee, Lord Justice in 1321, or else by Walter Birmingham, who filled the same office in 1548; while others trace its name to William Birmingham, who, with his son Walter, endured in 1331 a long imprisonment within its walls. (Some of the cells are still to be seen.)

From the Birmingham tower the curtain goes on to the Eastern Gateway tower at the entrance into the castle—a building oblong and quadrangular, which was strengthened by a broad, deep moat, in which a *detenu*, who was making his escape, now and then spent the greater part of the night, till rescued by some marauding O'Byrnes or O'Tooles early next morning.

Beyond the Castle walls, towards the east, was a chapel, the Provost Marshal's prison, an armoury, the workhouses of the armourers and smiths attached to the artillery train, and the stables of the chief Governor. There also at one time were the quarters of the groom-porter or croupier—an office not now recognised—and the offices of the Ordnance Department, for that of War and the Treasury, and for the Registry of Deeds and Conveyances throughout the island. Formerly there were two sallyports or postern gates in the Castle walls—the one near the Bir-

mingham tower, the other affording a passage to
the Castle yard. The former was closed in 1663
by order of the Duke of Ormonde, then Lord
Lieutenant, on discovering the plot of Jephson,
Blood, and others, to surprise the Castle by
its means. The other remained for years, till
the North tower and its curtain were pulled
down.

In early times the guard of the Castle was
entrusted to a constable, a gentleman-porter, and
a body of warders, consisting of archers and
pikemen : the constable receiving £18 5s. per
annum, each warder £2 5s. 6d. In the days of
gunpowder, arquebusiers and artillerymen were
added. The two " Gate Towers " were reserved
for the constable and the State prisoners, but
their custody was not always very secure, as in
the instance of Lord Delvin, who conspired with
Tyrone, Tyrconnel, Maguire, O'Cahan, and other
Ulster chiefs to surprise the Castle, but were
frustrated by the loyalty of a Roman Catholic,
who revealed the plot to the authorities. There
was a mint in the Castle as well as at Trim in the
co. Meath ; and the importance of Dublin Castle
is shown by the fact that its keeper or constable
must be a full-born Englishman. We learn from
the letter-press of J. Rocque's map—a most

B

interesting illustrated chart—that Dublin Castle
was not converted into a regular residence
for the Viceroys till the reign of Queen Elizabeth. They sometimes lodged in Thomas Court,
sometimes in the palace of the Archbishop of
Dublin at St. Sepulchres, sometimes at St.
Mary's Abbey, and sometimes at the Castle of
Kilmainham. Thus in 1488 the Earl of Kildare
received Sir Richard Edgcumb in the King's
great chamber, in Thomas Court, and there did
homage and took the oath of allegiance to
Henry VII., in the person of Sir Richard. We
read of Kildare in 1524 taking the oath of office
in Christ Church, and proceeding thence in state
to the Abbey of St. Thomas, Conn O'Neil
carrying the sword of state before him, as the
Chief Secretary of the time being—at present
Mr. Balfour—now does. When Kilmainham
Castle had been dismantled by a violent storm,
Queen Elizabeth directed the Castle of Dublin to
be repaired and enlarged for the reception of
the chief Governor, her frugal mind discovering
this was cheaper than repairing Kilmainham. Sir
Henry Sidney put the coping stone on the reno-
vated edifice. Among the Rolls may be found
extant the Indenture between the deputy and
other officers, and George Ardglass, to do all the

keeping and maintenance of the Castle—including its clock—for 16*d*. per diem.

The Irish Parliament seems for some time to have been peripatetic, and to have had no local habitation. Thus Sessions were held at Trim in Meath, and at Kilkenny, too, and in the latter some of the most important enactments, and the most far-reaching in their consequences, were made ; but Dublin appears to have been, so to speak, the central Parliamentary station, though, judging by the attendance, the questions of the day were not often considered burning ones by the burgesses and knights of the shire, to whom attendance at the Session was often a work of great danger. A curious record remains of Parliamentary peril from the stores of gunpowder in the Castle, which latterly became the Parliamentary home, as well as a forensic theatre ; for in 1606 Chichester thus writes to the English Council :—

" To bring the Court of Law again into this Castle were to draw them just over the store of munitions which not only by practice (as formerly hath been attempted) but by using of fire, by burning of some prisoners in the hand, may be fired, to the exceeding detriment of the State, and ruin of this Castle. In which respects we doubt

not but your Lordships will think it exceeding
inconvenient ; and for our parts we know it to be
so dangerous, and at no time more than now, as
we cannot, without almost incredible hazard, ad-
venture upon it." Chichester seems to have had
the Gunpowder Plot on the brain, but his despatch
led to no result, and Dublin Castle continued
to be the ordinary hall of convocation for the
making as well as the administration of law till the
rebellion of 1641, and thence to the Restoration.

During the past century the Castle has been
almost entirely rebuilt, and the Wardrobe Tower
is almost the sole survival of what Harris saw
and described. The Viceregal apartments appear
to have been in a semi-ruinous state in 1631, and
indeed for another century were in hardly a civilised
condition. Thus the apartment under the sitting-
room of the Lord Deputy was a bake-house, while
fuel was piled up in front of the gallery windows,
and the remains of St. Andrew's Church—then in
Dame Street—served for a stable. The Gate
Towers—so salient a feature of the building—were
not finally pulled down till 1750 ; and the old
Birmingham tower would probably have remained
to the present day but for a fearful explosion of
gunpowder (such as Chichester dreaded) which
split it into fissures, and, owing to the goodness

of the masonry, it was only with much labour
demolished. The Castle is divided into two
courts, commonly called yards, and the upper
contains the apartments of the Lord Lieutenant
and his suite; " between the principal or Eastern
gate, and the corresponding one (artificial only),
the interval is occupied by a building of two
stories, exhibiting Ionic columns, or rusticated
arches supporting a pediment ; and from this rises
a circular of the Corinthian order terminating in a
cupola. This is called the Bedford Tower. It is
appropriated to the use of the master of the ceremonies and aides-de-camp of the chief Governor,
and here since the demolition of the old Birmingham tower the flag has been displayed on State
days ; and here also on the 1st January, 1801,
the Imperial united standard waved for the first
time upon the union of the two countries. The
Presence Chamber is over the colonnade, and was
formerly the Yeoman's Hall. The throne and
canopy are covered with crimson velvet, richly
ornamented with gold lace. From a richly-fretted
ceiling hangs a glass lustre of Waterford manu-
factory, purchased by the Duke of Rutland.
St. Patrick's Hall, used for the installation of the
Knights of the Order of St. Patrick, is also a
ball room, of fine proportions, 82 feet long, 41 feet

broad, and 38 feet in height. It was begun by
Lord Temple during his Viceroyalty, and contains some good paintings, among which is one
of St. Patrick converting the natives; of Henry
the Second receiving the submissions of the Irish
chieftains; and an allegory representing George the
Third as a benefactor to Ireland (with which view
contemporary Catholics find it hard to coincide).
At the back of the apartments of the Viceroy is
a small Italian garden, to which a flight of granite
steps leads." The lower court or yard, though
larger than the upper, is irregular in outline, and
built on uneven, unlevel ground. Here is the
Ordnance Office, the Arsenal, with stores for
40,000 men, and sundry offices.

In the corner is the Chapel Royal, built in the
florid style of pointed Gothic architecture, with a
rather handsome interior. This chapel was erected
in the reign of John, Duke of Bedford, 1807, as
the following tablet tells us :—

Hanc ædem,
Deo optimo maximo olim dicatam
vetustate penitus dirutam
denuo extrui jussit
Johannes, Bedfordiæ dux, Hiberniæ prorex,
Ipseque fundamenta posuit, anno a Christo
nato MDCCCVII.

The Chapel of the Castle of Dublin is men-

tioned as early as 1225, in a close roll of England,
from which we learn that William de Radcliffe,
then King Henry's Chaplain, received 50 marks
as a gift from the Crown. On an Exchequer
account of 1250 are entered payments for improv-
ing and repairing the Royal Wardrobe in Dublin
Castle, for repairs of the Great Hall, kitchen
windows by the houses, chapel, and chambers of
the Exchequer. A Plea Roll of 1728 records the
indictment of " Frigola," wife of Walter Mac-
Torkoyl, for having carried to the Castle of
Dublin linen cloths, with which he and others
made ropes to descend the walls of the fortress.

The chaplain of the Lord Lieutenant is now
styled Dean of the Chapel Royal.

The Castle seems occasionally to have been
turned into a gladiatorial arena, or prize-fighting
ring. Thus, in 1528, Connor MacCormack
O'Connor brought Teig McGilpatrick O'Connor
before the Lords Justices (Adam Loftus, Archbishop of Dublin, and Sir Henry Wallop) and
Council for killing his men who were under
protection. Teig, the defendant, pleaded that
the appellant's men had, since they had taken
protection, confederated with the rebel Cahir
O'Connor, and therefore were also rebels, and
that he was ready to maintain his plea by combat.

The challenge being accepted by the appellant, all things were prepared to try the issue, and time and place appointed, according to precedents drawn from the laws of England in such cases. The weapons, being sword and target, were chosen by the defendant, and the next day appointed for the combat.

The Lords Justices, the Judge and Councillors, attended in places set apart for them, every man according to his rank, and most of the military officers, for the greater solemnity of the trial, were present. The combatants were seated on two stools, one at each end of the inner court of the Castle.

The court being called, the appellant was led forward from his stool within the lists, stripped to his shirt, and searched by the Secretary of State, leaving no arms but his sword and target; and taking a corporal oath that his quarrel was just, he made his reverence to the Lords Justices and the Court, and then was conducted back to his stool. The same ceremony was observed as to the defendant. Then the pleadings were openly read, and the appellant was demanded whether he would aver his appeal? to which he answered in the affirmative. The defendant was next asked whether he would confess the action, or abide the trial of the same? He also answered that he would aver his plea by the sword. The signal being given by the sound of the trumpet, they began the combat with great resolution. The appellant received two wounds in his leg and one in his eye, and thereupon attempted to close the defendant, who being too strong for him he pummelled till he loosened his hold, and then with his sword cut off his head, and on the point thereof presented it to the Lords Justices, and so his acquittal was recorded. Hooker remarks, "that the combat was fought with such valour and resolution on both sides that the spectators wished that it had rather fallen on the whole sept of the O'Connors than on those two gentlemen."

The account of this Judicial duel reminds one of Voltaire's description of that between Condé and Turenne, in the " Henriade."

> " Mais la trompette sonne, ils s'élancent tous les deux,
> Ils commencent enfin ce combat dangereux."

The fitness of things, regal and vice-regal, demands that kings and vice-kings should have changes of air and scene like meaner mortals; and for this reason country and suburban palaces have ever been found for the rulers of our realms.

The Majesty of England has quite a wealth o
Royal residences at its disposal : Windsor and
Hampton Court in the semi-suburban zone,
Buckingham Palace and St. James' in the urban,
Holyrood and Balmoral in Northern Britain,
Osborne in the Isle of Wight, but unfortunately
none in Ireland ; though perhaps in that unfor-
tunate island she lives as much in the hearts of
her neglected people as in more favoured and
prosperous places.   We have seen that the Lord
Deputy or Lord Lieutenant had, in early times,
a considerable choice of lodgings besides Dublin
Castle—St. Mary's Abbey, St. Sepulchres, St.
Thomas' Court, and Kilmainham Priory and
Castle, were at his service ; but Queen Elizabeth
was the first sovereign who meditated a move
into comparative country for her hard-tasked
servants ; and, if records be reliable, the happy
thought of " Parking " the Manors of Newtown
and the Phœnix was an inspiration of hers, and
making it a sort of official " Pale."   However,
what good Queen Bess might have done had ,
Ireland been England, and Dublin London, we
know not ; but can guess that if she really " meant
it," the work would have sped on pretty fast, but
Her Majesty's proreges had to content themselves
with the Castle in Dublin ; nor was it till Charles

the Second's era that the Phœnix Park con-
ception emerged from its embryo form.

Meanwhile, Strafford, whom contemporary
Irishmen styled "Black Tom," began to build
himself a brick palace or mansion about a mile
from Naas, on the Newbridge and Kildare high
Road, and the remains of its massive masonry
are still to be seen on the banks of the "Grand"
Canal; nor am I quite sure the Kennels of the
Kildare Hunt, which abut upon the gaunt and
ruinous structure, do not occupy some of the
space dedicated to its once princely pile. In
Charles the Second's reign, the mansion which
is now known far and wide as the Viceregal
Lodge, was bought, with its curtilages, from
Clements, Earl of Leitrim. The Royal Standard
floats over it whenever the Lord Lieutenant is in
occupation—when he goes away it is taken down.
But, though this is now the sole Viceregal residence within the Park walls, it is certain that
General Fleetwood, Cromwell's representative,
lived in some lodge or other that was temporarily
viceregal, while in Ireland, and not campaigning;
and history also records that Henry Cromwell,
the Lord Lieutenant, who by all accounts was a
popular governor, retired from the Castle to this
Lodge, and adds that, so straitened was this

Liberal Lieutenant in his ways and means, that the cash necessary for his transit to England was not at the moment forthcoming.

Of the 1,760 acres that form the area of the Phœnix Park, the wall of which is said to be 7 miles in extent, 209 have been reserved for the little Park within a Park—Imperium in Imperio—that forms the Viceroy's domain. This is well planted, and laid out with gardens in the Italian style, and fenced off from the surrounding Park by a deep and broad ha-ha—a sunken fence, which would stop all cavalry permanently, and would arrest infantry for some minutes, till fascines were thrown into the fosse, or planks for crossing it were procured, to serve as a temporary bridge. The Viceregal Lodge somehow recalls the White House at Washington, U.S., the President's residence, to my memory, though the former is considerably larger and more ornate, having, like Janus' temple at Rome (and not a few public characters in Ireland), two fronts or faces—that looking to the north, built by Lord Whitworth during his viceroyalty, is ornamented by a pediment supported by four Ionic pillars of Portland stone, from a design by Johnson. The view to the northward, however, is quite *borné*, and very inferior to that to the south, which takes in

the sierra of the Dublin and Wicklow Range,
sometimes snow-capped, but more generally of
purple tints. The viceregal range helps to form
a sort of official quadrilateral, consisting of the
Parks and Pleasaunces of the Chief, Under, and
Private Secretaries' Lodges, covering an area of
about 130 acres, more or less. The Chief Secretary's is the largest in area, and has the biggest
mansion.

The Viceregal Lodge may now be considered
the permanent official home of the Viceroy, as
it is said to be more healthy than the Castle,
which, as a matter of fact, is only occupied
now during the Dublin season ; a season which
generally sets in "with extreme severity"
during the Lenten term, and lasts for some six
weeks, finding its natural close on the 17th of
March, St. Patrick's native day according to
current tradition. Then all "the courtiers" of
the season assemble in St. Patrick's Hall and
keep the Saint's anniversary jollily, if not absolutely holily (according to some standards),
and baptise their shamrocks in something
stronger than the pure lymph from the holy
well honoured by his venerable name. It is a
spacious mansion and can put up a number of
guests, while the gardens and grounds form a

charming and ample theatre for the little
comedies that are created by afternoon garden
parties, the largest of which, and perhaps the
most promiscuous, was given by Lord and Lady
Aberdeen, during the Viceroyalty of the former,
when Irish manufacture in costumes and toilettes
was absolutely *de rigueur*. I have already mentioned that a large sunken fence or ha-ha
demarcates the viceregal ground from the
Phœnix Park. On the day of Lord Spencer's
second formal entry into his Dublin dominions as
Viceroy, just a little more than seven years ago, the
assassination of Lord Frederick Cavendish and
Mr. Tom Burke, the permanent Under-Secretary,
was perpetrated, before the windows of the Lodge,
at a distance of some 300 yards or less from them.
It is said that Lord Spencer, who had only
entered the Viceregal Lodge a few minutes previously, having been engaged in looking at a
game of polo played on the All Ireland Polo
Ground, a part of the " 9 acres " on the verge of
the Viceregal grounds, and almost under the
shadow of the Chesterfield Avenue of elms, was
with one or two officials gazing out of the windows of the sitting room that looks southwards,
when they saw what they took to be a drunken
brawl, but something by-and-bye, whether it was

the flash of steel or not, opened their eyes to the true
character of the foul fray, then they rushed through
the French windows to the ha-ha, and some of
them scrambled down it, but too late to avail, as
the murderers had driven off; curiously enough
the foul murder was viewed by a young cavalry
officer from a little tope of trees about as far
off as the Lodge, and he too thought it was a
mere brawl or fight for several seconds. It
seems strange to reflect that there was a guard
of soldiers within hail of the spot where the
assassination was perpetrated, and constabulary
barracks less than 600 yards distant, not to
speak of park-keepers and rangers. Reverting to
the Viceregal Lodge, it may be mentioned that
Lord Hardwicke, in 1802, during his Viceroyalty
added wings to the building. Between the house
and the Chief Secretary's Lodge is the racquet
court, and just beyond that, in a delightful glade,
is the cricket ground, where many a good match
has been played since Lord Carlisle's time, who, I
think, first associated the Lodge with this great
Pan-Anglican summer pastime. Lord Carlisle did
not play himself while Viceroy, but took the
liveliest interest in the matches and scored them.
Lord Spencer also relaxed the tension of the
official bow by a little mild play, but the

strongest eleven that the Viceregal grounds
have known for some time has been got together
during Lord Londonderry's reign. His Excellency plays a good deal himself, and is the
cause of much play in others, as he always has the
I Zingari men over in August, and puts them up at
the Lodge, and is equally hospitable to their Irish
imitators, the " Na Shulers." Half way between
the Viceroy's Lodge and that occupied by the
Chief Secretary is the column erected by Lord
Chesterfield during his reign, on the top of which
is a stone presentation of the fabulous Phœnix,
the bird which took such a hold of Herodotus'
fancy, and that possibly may have suggested to
the Aryan mind the *rite* (or wrong) of " Suttee ;"
the Phœnix on the column is in the act of fanning
with its wings the pyre that is the source of succession for future Phœnixes. On one side is the
inscription :—

> " Civium oblectamento
> Campum rudem et incultum
> Ornari Jussit
> Philippus Stanhope
> Comes de Chesterfield
> Prorex."

On the other the tablet declares that—

"Impensis suis posuit
Philippus Stanhope
Comes de Chesterfield
Prorex."

We need not pause to offer conjectures on the
curious title to the Park, namely " Phœnix ;"
certain it is that the manor that formed a large
portion of it was early styled as " Phœnix,"
though there is a spring within it known to Irish
scholars as Fion Uiske, which pronounced rapidly
has some similitude of sound to " Phœnix." In
1787 that most social satrap, the Duke of Rutland,
died at the Lodge, and very prematurely too. Lord
Lifford was his chancellor, and, according to the
precedents, he issued a summons to the Privy
Councillors in Ireland to attend, for the election of
a Lord Justice ; but prior to their assemblage the
Duke of Buckingham received the appointment.

In 1783 Sarah, Countess of Westmoreland, died
in the Lodge, of what was called a "*miliary*" fever,
possibly now it might be called a *military* fever,
from the comparative proximity of that military
nest of the typhoid plague, the Royal Barracks.

The records of the Irish House of Commons
tell us how that Mr. Thomas Conolly of Castle-
town brought in a bill to settle the Viceregal
Lodge on Grattan and his heirs. The bill, how-

C

ever, did not pass, as might have been anticipated.
Passing to the history of the Phœnix Park, most
of it appears to have originally belonged to the
Templars, from whom it was taken at their
degradation and disestablishment, and transferred
to the Knights' Hospitallers of St. John, located
at Kilmainham Priory. The lands of Chapel Izod
(or of La belle Isolde or Isode) were acquired from
Sir Maurice Eustace, those of Upper Castlenock
from J. Warren of Corduff, Ashtown from Corcan
of Pelletstown, and so on as to the other portions.
Certain it is that the Manors of Newtown and
Phœnix were annexed by the Duke of Ormonde,
(by command) for £3,000, which must be considered cheap for 467 acres near a city. The
whole area, it seems, cost the Government some
£40,000. Sir John Temple built the wall round
it, and Lord Palmerston's family hence derived
their droits of park pasturage. The Lord Lieutenant originally derived 100 guineas from the
pasturage, a right waived by the Duke of
Devonshire while Viceroy. The Duchess of
Cleveland was said to have had a settlement of
£1,000 a year out of the undisposed lands round
the Park. This was during the reign of Essex.
The house where William III., the Irish William
the Conqueror, sojourned after the battle of the

Boyne, is still pointed out by the banks of the Liffey, but it is not now within the Phœnix Park.

Just now, owing to the mysterious prevalence of enteric fever in the Royal and Richmond Barracks, which seems to baffle sanitary engineering science so far, the garrison of Dublin is living under canvas in a southern corner of the Phœnix Park, and not far from the powder magazine, which provoked one of the last flickers of Jonathan Swift's most mordent wit. But prior to giving his quatrain, we may remark that the storage of powder near the Castle of Dublin had nearly shaken that part of the city to its foundations when an order went forth from the Cæsar of the day to store the gunpowder in the new magazine. Swift's impromptu ran thus :—

> " Behold a proof of Irish wit,
>   Here Irish sense is seen,
> When nothing's left that's worth defence
>   They build a magazine ! "

Close by it are the remains or outline rather of the fort projected by the Duke of Wharton, who, during his tenure of the sword of State, took into his head that an attack would be made on the Castle, and proposed to build this fort and entrench

C 2

himself therein.   It is known as "Wharton's folly."

It is curious how history repeats itself ; in 1788 the Marquis of Buckingham, then Lord Lieutenant, ordered a camp to be formed in the Phœnix Park, and nine years later Lord Camden formed another on the same ground.   It must be recollected that the Curragh had not then been annexed by the Crown for military purposes and made an Hibernian Campus Martius.

I have searched and searched but have been unable to find any trace of Irish Kings as domiciled or *habitués* in Dublin Castle, or even in Dublin itself ; for though Dublin has been for centuries the capital of Ireland, its heart, and to a certain extent its *ville de lumière*, like Paris, there is no reason whatever why it should have been a place of primary importance in the ante-Norman era, when the sons of Heremon and Heber, according to the tradition, were monarchs of all they surveyed.   Indeed, there is every reason why it should not have been so esteemed, for the Irish do not seem to have been a ship-building or commercial race of men, in spite of the legends of Niall of the nine hostages, and Dublin was but one of many hundred ports equally adapted for their petty enterprises on the ocean and by the coast.

They were a race of cattle-rearers and dealers, and their descendants understand this business as well as most men, and can buy and sell and get gain where animals of all kinds are concerned, from horses to hogs. Their kings and dynasts were merely glorified graziers who had more stock of all kinds than their clansmen, and who occasionally let out these herds, or parts of them, to their poorer dependents, very much as the modern salesmaster undertakes to stock a farm of pasture-land for a grazier of slender capital and little credit. Kinkora, illustrated by Moore's ballad-notice, " He returns to Kinkora no more," was the palace and farm of the Munster monarchs. Galway or Galvy, well known in the days of Strabo and Ptolemy, was probably a far more important place than Dublin ; at any rate, only a few hundred years ago, a writer described it, if I recollect right, as the third city in the king's dominions, and from its petty port there was much trade to and from the Iberian peninsula. It probably divided with Croghan, Athlone, and Roscommon the patronage of the Kings of Connaught. Ardmagh, the Primatial city, probably was the capital of the O'Neils, of Ulster. Killeigh, or Geashill, was probably the chief town of the O'Connors of Faly ; Birr of the O'Carrolls, of

Ely ; Campa, now changed to Maryborough, of the O'Moores, and so on ; but it was not so with the Ostmen, styled Danes in Ireland, including the white and the dark Gaels. Dublin was to them a port of great price, connecting their chain of harbours along the eastern coast, still recognisable by their names—such as Wexford, Carlingford, Waterford, Strangford, &c., and very handy for the Isle of Man, their great stronghold, and the Hebrides, as well as for the Welsh coast. They were traders and pirates, a combination as common as in early Greece, when, according to Thucydides, piracy was anything rather than discreditable ; so to the Danes Dublin was very dear, and after fighting for it with the Anglo-Normans, they bargained with them for certain rights and privileges, when they were beaten. To the Danes the interior of the country was comparatively valueless, though we know that in both England and Ireland they had won their victorious way much more extensively, probably with a view to trade, than was generally estimated. In point of fact, the Scandinavian element is far stronger in the inhabitants of both islands than we imagine. In the 10th century we have Malachy, the monarch of all Ireland, winning a golden torque or collar from one Danish champion, a

sword from another—a fact that Moore alludes to
—" When Malachy wore the collar of gold, which
he won from the proud invader."

This Malachy was deposed by Brian Borhoime, or " Boromy," as Warner calls him, the
Alfred of Ireland who for some 50 years fought
them constantly and beat the Danes consecu-
tively in 29 battles ; in the great fight at Clontarf,
Leinster and its legion was arrayed on the
Danish side, but victory at last inclined to Brian's
braves, though it cost the gallant old warrior the
remainder of his span of existence. He was said
to be 76 when he died.

Brian, as the King of Ireland, was bound to
attend the Tara Wittenagemot when the provincial dynasts and chiefs of septs met together
with their bards and musicians to take sweet
council together (and perhaps something stronger
too) as to affairs of State.

From the total absence of masonry or brick
round Tara it would appear that the Royalties held
a sort of Feast of Tabernacles, and dwelt in
" boolies," or wicker houses similar to those put up
in Dame Street when Richard II. feasted " the captains and great estates " of the island in Dublin ;
but the record of the contributions paid in annually
by the men of Munster to Brian at Kinkora

(independently of provincial tributes) is interesting, as showing something of the manners and
customs of the age—these were : 1,450 oxen,
3,650 cows, 4,800 hogs, 2,600 wedders, 100
horses, 1,150 mantles, a fleet, well manned and
equipped, besides guards, foot and horse soldiers,
&c., when required. The Dalgais seem to have
been a kind of corps of Janissaries for special
services.

In addition to these supplies we read that
the Danes of Limerick sent him 325 hogsheads
of claret per annum ; the Danes of Dublin,
150 pipes of wines of various sorts. We
learn, too, that " the Book of Rights of
Munster " is, with the exception of the histories of
Greece and Rome, the oldest historical record
extant.

That gold was not wanting at the Court of
Kinkora we learn from the fact that King Brian
offered 20 ounces of that metal for the shrine at
" Ardmagh ; " while Malachy's torque was but
one of many similar ones to be seen at the time,
in a perfect state, as they are now to be viewed
in an imperfect condition, in museums. The
Danes had, while still Pagan, a habit of plunder-
ing abbeys, churches, and monasteries where
records were kept, and then setting fire to the

buildings by way of a *feu de joie*. Hence the
difficulty of painting anything like a picture of
that past period with such scanty materials to
hand. The English captains, too, were not
quite free from this species of sacrilege, and
we read that the Abbey of Killeigh, in the
King's Co., of which only a gable or two and
some arches survive, was burnt down by the
Elizabethan soldiery, with all its wealth of painted
glass.

These observations have been made to dispel
the erroneous impression that Ireland was wholly
uncivilised and barbarous before its annexation
by the English Crown, and to show how there was
no continuity of Government and institutions in
Ireland as in England.

The fatal arrow that tore through Harold's
armour at the Battle of Hastings and robbed him
of life may be said to have achieved the conquest
of England. London, the Tower, and West-
minster Abbey were adopted by the victors as a
Royal fane Castle and City, where the functions
of the Crown were held. In Ireland it was
wholly different. Kinkora and Tara sink into
insignificance, and the Castle of Dublin, with the
subsidiary ones at Trim and Kilkenny, rise into
importance and note ; yet it would be a great

mistake to depreciate bye-gone grace and greatness
because the erosion of time and the storm of war
have left little trace of their existence and importance. The Cinque Ports are very tiny towns now
—a few hundred years ago they were strong
points on our southern coasts, and keys to
England, more or less. Cashel of the Kings, in
the same way, is little more now than an historic
landmark and beacon ; even the Tower of London
owes its grandeur to association alone. Apropos of
the Abbey of Killeigh, in Offaly, the historian
gives us in his pages a presentment of the
Lady Margaret O'Connor at a great function
held there in March, 1447, which certainly
indicates a fair amount of civilisation and
refinement, in mind as well as in manner and
costume.

" Rich and rare were the robes she wore" as
she appeared seated in queenly style, and in
raiment of cloth of gold ; and we learn that she
opened the Congress by presenting two massive
chalices of gold on the high altar of the church
as an act of duty towards God, as the chronicler
points out, and then she took two orphan children to rear and nurse, an act of charity to her
neighbour. Moreover, one of the Elizabethan
Viceroys records that in his progress from Clare

to Connaught he was with his suite very handsomely entertained by a country gentleman of
the period, Sir John O'Shaughnessy, whose style
of living made a considerable impression on the
Deputy's mind—possibly it may have been *le
bonheur de l'imprévu*, the less expected the more
welcomed !

We have noticed one or two escapes from
the *duresse* of the Castle, probably due to the
disloyalty of some of the warders to their
Sovereign (or loyalty, if it may be so called,
to their own race), just as Stephens, the
Fenian "Head-Centre," was allowed to escape
from Richmond State Prison, and, after remaining *perdu* for a considerable time in
Dublin he made his escape in disguise to the
Continent.

A more dangerous rebel, or patriot (from
whichever standpoint you judge), than any we
have noticed was allowed to make his escape
from Dublin Castle, to deal death and destruction
by-and-bye to the English and Scotch who
were arrayed against him. " This enterprising
chieftain," says a writer in the " Dublin Penny
Journal," date 1832–33, " was the son of Hugh,
Chieftain of Tyrconnell ; his mother's name was
Inneen Duff (dark Ina), daughter of Macdonnell,

Lord of the Isles. He was born in the year
1571 ; in early life he not only displayed considerable genius and independence of spirit, but
he made these qualities acceptable to his countrymen by the noble generosity of his manners and
the matchless symmetry of his form. In former
times the O'Donnels of Tyrconnell and the
O'Neils of Tyrone were often addressed by the
English Monarch as equals, and sometimes called
on for aid against foreign foes, and occasionally
written to as Kings, and it was therefore natural
that young Hugh should desire to substantiate his
independence, so often acknowledged. He made
no secret of his intentions, which were soon the
subject of conversation all through Ireland, and,
reaching the ears of the Lord Justice, created no
small alarm at Dublin Castle. Sir John Perrot,
then the head of the Irish Government, instead of
endeavouring to gain over the young chieftain by
honours and concession, laid a plot to seize him,
which, though successful for the time, was as
unworthy as it afterwards proved injurious. In
the year 1587 a ship was fitted out and stowed
with Spanish wine, and directed to sail to one of
the harbours of Donegal. Accordingly the vessel,
fraught with the merchandise most acceptable to a
Milesian Chief, put into Lough Swilly and cast

anchor off the Castle of Dundonald, near Rath-
millan.

"The captain, disguised as a Spaniard, proposed to traffic with the people of the fortress, and
they, nothing loth, bought and drank until they
became intoxicated. The people of the adjoining
district did the same, and all the surrounding septs
of O'Donnel, McSwiney, and O'Doherty entered
into jolly dealings with the crafty wine merchant.
It could not be supposed that when all were laying
in stores of Sack and Alicant, the young prince
of the county should stay back. No! as was
expected, he arrived with his followers at
McSwiney's Castle, who sent the captain notice
that his chieftain had arrived, and that, therefore,
he must prepare to send some of his very best
vintages in store for his use. The captain replied
that what he purposed to sell was already disposed
of, but if the young prince would come on board
he would let him taste some of his choicest sack,
intended as a present to the Lord Deputy. This
invitation was accepted ; the young chief went on
board, and he and his followers drank of wine and
strong liquor as Irishmen used to drink. When
they were all intoxicated, their arms were stolen
from them, the hatches were shut down, and next
morning saw the vessel clear of Lough Swilly, and

on its way for Dublin. Thus was the base design accomplished, and Red Hugh, in his 16th year, round himself a captive in Birmingham Tower, where he remained for 3 years and 3 months, a long period for a fiery impatient spirit at such a period of life.

"In the year 1591 he and some of his followers descended by means of a rope on the draw-bridge, and getting safe off from the fortress they escaped towards the Wicklow Mountains, and reached the borders of O'Toole's country. There O'Donnel was obliged to stop—his shoes had fallen off his feet, and passing barefooted through the furze and heather that covered the hills he soon broke down, and his companions, consulting their own safety, left him with the one faithful servant who had assisted him and them to descend from the Tower.

"This man, secreting his master as well as he could, proceeded to the residence of Phelim O'Toole, who also had been a prisoner in Birmingham Tower, and while there had entered into bonds of friendship with O'Donnel, and a solemn pledge of affection had passed between them.

"But the O'Toole betrayed his friend ; and the young chief, heavily chained and under a stricter

watch, was again consigned to his apartment in
the Tower. A second time he effected his escape,
having by means of his trusty servant got down
through a shore funnel into the Poddle, and
creeping along the muddy stream, again took
refuge in the Wicklow Hills. He did not again
trust himself to the O'Tooles, but continuing right
on over these high and desolate hills endeavoured
to reach the fastnesses of Feagh McHugh
O'Byrne, in Glen Malur. In the early period of
their flight they were separated from Henry
O'Neil, who had escaped with him from the
prison, and as the night advanced, Arthur O'Neil,
another of his companions who had also escaped
from prison, being a heavy and inactive man,
was obliged to give over, and he laid down
drowsily, and slept the sleep of death. Young
O'Donnel got a little further and stationed himself
under a projecting rock, in order to shelter himself from the snow hurricanes that swept the
hills, and sent his servant to Glen Malur. Feagh
McHugh, on the arrival of the servant, sent his
servant provided with all possible refreshments
and clothes for the relief of the fugitives. O'Neil
was found dead, O'Donnel's young blood was still
circulating, but his feet were dreadfully frost-
bitten. Every hospitality that the O'Byrne

could show to him he did, and when he
was able to ride he forwarded him and
his faithful servant, Turlogh Boy O'Hagan,
on good horses towards the province of Ulster.
On their arrival at the Liffey they found its
usual passes guarded, for the Government were
on the watch to prevent O'Donnel's escape to his
own country. But the Liffey is in so many places
fordable that he found no difficulty in passing it
and getting through the plains of Meath. On
coming to the Boyne they were obliged to throw
themselves on the patriotic fidelity of a poor
fisherman, who not only faithfully ferried them
over, but also, with no small courage and address,
drove their horses before him as cattle he
intended to sell in the north country, and so
driving them to where their owners were lying in
secret, he furnished them with the means of
reaching the hills of Ulster, thus regaining, after
five years' absence, their own principalities. On
Red Hugh's arrival, all the different septs of the
country — the O'Donnel, the O'Doherty, the
O'Boyle, and McSwiney — elected him as *The*
O'Donnel, in the room of his father, who was
now much advanced in years and willing to resign
his government to a bolder and a steadier hand.

" It would completely go beyond our limits to

recount all the adventures of Red Hugh O'Donnel after he became the head of the various septs of the country. His long imprisonment had given him a cordial hatred of the English, and for a series of years he was the scourge and terror of the Government. He kept his mountain territory of Donegal in spite of Elizabeth's best generals, carried his incursions even to the remotest parts of Munster, and made his name be respected and his power feared to the very mouth of the Shannon. At last a fatal error—the only military one he was known ever to make, caused by a rivalry between him and O'Neil about leading an onset—was his ruin ; he was totally routed by Lord Mountjoy at Kinsale, fled to Spain, and died in Valladollid in the year 1602."

CHAPTER II.

"Oh, sir, it is a dolorous country, a very dolorous country."
DR. JOHNSON.

THE story of the annexation of Ireland to the
English Crown by a few semi-French fillibusters,
introduced by Dermot MacMorrough, King or
Dynast of Leinster, is too like a thrice-told tale to
attempt to vex the public ear by its repetition ;
Macaulay's typical school-boy knows it well, and
so do probably most of the historically crammed
candidates for Civil Service employment.　It
reads like a page from Pizarro, or a chapter in the
Cortez conquests, and we only allude to it here
apologetically as a necessary preface to a recital
of the earlier Viceroys in Ireland who occupied the
Castle, and administered the Government of the
country, "tam bene quam male," as the " Baillis,"
Deputies, or Viceroys of the Sovereigns of
England, during what we may term the Plantagenet period, when the garrison or colony planted
in the island by strong arms and stout hearts,

dwindled and waned so perceptibly that by the date of the accession of the first of the Tudor kings, Henry VII, the Lordship of England had become a mere *nominis umbra*, unsupported by wealth, power, or prestige, till—so history repeats itself—the Crown had the utmost difficulty in finding great noblemen or men of position to accept the thankless and dispendious position of Viceroy. Lord Salisbury found himself in a similar plight in the present year 1889.

A few remarks may, however, be made before the long list of Castle tenants is submitted to the reader's notice, of which the first will be that the assumption, often made, that Ireland was in a condition of civilisation very inferior to that of neighbouring countries at the time of the descent of the Norman knights on her eastern coasts, is quite erroneous, though it must be admitted that the Church monopolised much of that culture and civilisation. Dermot MacMorrough cannot be placed on an historical pedestal as a patriot prince, a moral monarch, or a compendium of the cardinal virtues. But he was a strong Sovereign. His wealth absolutely dazzled, by the received accounts, the needy Normans ; and while he had great influence with his lay subjects, he was by no means banned or " boycotted " by his subjects

D 2

spiritual ; moreover, his close connection with
Edward the Confessor showed that his position
was recognised as a right royal one.   No doubt
his aid greatly facilitated the Norman conquests,
and if it be objected that the Irish were very
feeble folk to yield to such slender forces, it must
be recollected that the latter had no combination
to resist, and that whereas the conquest of
England was achieved by a single battle, that of
Hastings, the conquest of Ireland has occupied
some seven centuries.   Moreover, the spiritual
puissances were arrayed against them, seeing
that Henry II. was the ally and executant
of the Pope, and that his title was confirmed by
the Bull of a second Bishop of Rome.   Looking
now to the past through the glasses of experience,
we could wish that the invading force had been
stronger, or equal at least to the estimate made
by Agricola for the conquest of the island, namely
a legion, or 10,000 men.

Hugh de Lacy, then, was the first holder of
the Sword of State, and wearer of the Cap of
Maintenance, which are the outward and visible
signs of Viceroyalty.   He was a great castle-
builder, and having extended his dominion into
what is now the King's County, Faly, or Offaly,
he began to build a castle at Durrow, but in the

midst of his work he was beheaded by an angry
Irishman not far from the place where the Earl of
Norbury was assassinated in the "forties." He
had married a daughter of Roderick O'Connor,
and thus paved the way for the assimilation by
the Celts of the Norman adventurers, the consequences of which were most disastrous to the
English Raj.

Strongbow, or Richard Fitzgislebert, Earl of
Strigul, the reputed conqueror of Ireland, was the
second Viceroy ; he was married to Eva, King
Dermot's daughter and heiress. He died in
Dublin, and was buried by Archbishop Torean
O'Tuathal, generally known as St. Lawrence
O'Toole, in Christchurch Cathedral, where his
tomb remains to this day, preserved with extra
care, perhaps, because rents used to be payable
upon it.

The third Viceroy was William Adelm de
Burgh, who was the ancestor of the Earls of Ulster,
the Earls and the Marquises of Clanricarde. The
de Burghs, till they degenerated, were the most
powerful subjects of the Crown in Ireland, their
precedence was recognised, and they intermarried
with Royalty.

Next, Prince John (afterwards King) occupied
Dublin Castle as " Dominus Hiberniæ," and we

are now within the historic pale, for in his suite
was Giraud de Barri, generally known as Giraldus
Cambrensis, whose account of Ireland is very
interesting, if slightly inaccurate.   Then came:
Hugh de Lacy the Second ; William le Petit ;
William, Earl Marechal ; Pierre Pipard ; Hamon
de Valoques ; Meiller Fitzhenri, a bastard son
of King Henry I. ; John de Gray, Bishop of
Norwich, who built Athlone Castle, on the
Shannon ; Geoffroi de Marreis, the Justiciary ;
and Henri de Londres, a great-grandson of
Dermot MacMorrough, and brother-in-law to
Henry III. of England and Alexander II. of
Scotland.   He was a powerful Governor, and in
his reign the Castle of Dublin was greatly im-
proved, and almost rebuilt.

Then Walter and Hugh de Lacy administered the Government, followed by Geoffroi de
Marreis, in 1226.   In his time the stipend of the
office was fixed at £580 per annum, a sum
seemingly very small, yet not so entirely incon-
siderable or disproportionate when measured by
the pay of a knight, namely, 2s. a-day ; but for
this stipend he had to find 19 fully-armed or
panoplied horse soldiers, himself the 20th.
About this time the great Norman families of de
Lacy, de Ridelisford, and Gislebert, Marechal,

Earl of Pembroke, became extinct in the male
line. The five daughters of the last-named
nobleman were great-granddaughters of Dermot
MacMorrough, and co-heiresses. They married
into the most powerful families of England, so that
the best blood of England is largely infused with
Irish ichor, and the process of interfusion has gone
on steadily ever since.

We have, then, in the list of Governors—

> Maurice Fitzgerald.
> Prince Edward, nominated Lord of Ire-
> land.
> Alain de la Zouche.
> Etienne de Longue Epée.
> Guillaume le Dene.
> Sir Richard la Rochelle.
> Jean FitzGeoffroi.
> Davide de Barry, 1st Viscount of Butte-
> vant.
> Sir Robert D'ufforl.
> Richard d'Exeter.
> Jaques d'Audeley.
> Sir Jeffroi de Joinville.
> Sir Robert d'Ufford.
> Estevene de Foleburne, Archbishop of
> Tuam.

Jean de Saundford, Archbishop of Dublin.
Guillaume de Vesci.
Guillaume de la Haze.
Guillaume d'Odingselle.

Then Fitzmaurice, father of the first Earl of
Desmond, who took an ape for his cognizance,
having, when a baby, been rescued in a marvellous manner by sympathetic Simian.

Sir John Wogan.

In his reign the Templars were disestablished in
Ireland, and their temporalities handed over to
the Knights Hospitallers of St. John of Jerusalem,
who thus acquired Kilmainham Priory. He was
succeeded by

Sir Guillaume de Burgh,

and he by Piers de Gaveston, Earl of Cornwall.
Then came Sir Edmund le Botiler, of the present
"Ormonde" family (though Ormonde is but
eponymous of the title), who caused such peace
in the country that it was said he could travel from
Arklow to Limerick with an escort of three horse-

men, a distance of between one and two hundred miles. Then—

Theobald de Vaudun,

and Sir Edmund le Botiler again. He was unable to cope with Robert Bruce, of Scotland, and was succeeded by Roger de Mortimer, who also suffered defeat; nor was Bruce arrested in his career of conquest till encountered by Jean de Bermingham, who shattered his power and killed him in battle, but not till the Scots had practically ruled most of Ireland for three years. Thomas Fitzjohn Fitzgerald was the next Viceroy, followed by Jean de Bermingham, Earl of Louth. Next came—

Sir Ralph Gorges.
Sir Jean D'Arcy.
The Earl of Kildare.
Roger Utlaugh, Prior of Kilmainham.
William de Burgh, killed by R. de Man
    deville.
Sir Antoine de Lucy, Baron of Cocker-
    mouth.
Sir Jean D'Arcy.
Sir Thomas de Burgh.

Sir John de Cherlton, Baron of Powys.

Thomas de Cherlton, Bishop of Hereford.

Roger Utlagh.

Sir Jean D'Arcy.

Sir John Moriz (Deputy-Governor).

Sir Raoul D'Ufford.

Sir Roger D'Arcy.

Sir John Moriz.

Walter de Bermingham.

John de Carew.

Thomas de Rokeby (a strong Governor).

Maurice, first Earl of Desmond.

Thomas de Rokeby, who died at Kilkea
    Castle.

Almaric de St. Amand.

Prince Lionel, Earl of Ulster, Duke of
    Clarence.

Gerald, fourth Earl of Desmond.

Sir William de Windsor.

Maurice Fitzthomas, fourth Earl of Kildare.

Prince Lionel added considerably to the Castle
of Dublin and its armament. In virtue of his
high rank he was allowed 13s. 4d. per day. He
married *en seconde noces* (his first was the de Burgh
heiress) Violante, daughter of Galeazzo Visconte,
and received with her a dowry of £200,000, but

died soon after his wedding. Gerald, fourth Earl
of Desmond, known as "the poet," succeeded to
the Viceroyalty. Then—

> Sir William de Windsor.
> Maurice, fourth Earl of Kildare.
> James, Earl of Ormonde.
> Edmund de Mortimer, Earl of March and
>   Ulster. (He died at Cork.)
> Dean John de Colton.
> Roger de Mortimer.
> Philip de Courtenay, of Powderham Castle.
> Robert de Vere, Earl of Oxford, Duke of
>   Ireland.
> Sir John de Stanley.
> James, third Earl of Ormonde.
> Thomas, Duke of Gloucester.
> Roger de Mortimer.
> Reginald Grey de Ruthyn.
> Thomas Holland, Duke of Surrey.

Then we have—

> Alexander de Bascot.
> Prince Thomas of Lancaster.
> Sir John de Stanley.
> Thomas Cranley, Archbishop of Dublin.
1413. Sir John Talbot.

James, fourth Earl of Ormonde.

Edmund de Mortimer, Earl of March and Ulster (killed by the Plague).

Sir John Talbot.

James, fourth Earl of Ormonde.

Sir John de Grey.

Sir John Sutton, fourth Baron of Dudley.

Sir Thomas le Strange.

Sir Thomas Stanley.

Sir Leon de Welles, sixth Baron of Welles.

James, fourth Earl of Ormonde.

Earl of Shrewsbury and Waterford.

Archbishop Talbot.

Richard Nugent, Baron Delvin.

Richard, Duke of York.

Earl of Wiltshire.

George, Duke of Clarence.

Tiptoft, Earl of Worcester.

John de la Pole, Duke of Suffolk.

Richard, Duke of York (and of Carlow).

Earl of Kildare.

Edward Prince of Wales.

Earl of Lincoln (John de la Pole).

During the 300 years and upwards covered by the Plantagenet puissance in Ireland, there seem to have been some hundred deputies, lieutenants or viceroys, baillies or justiciaries, most of whose names and titles I have inserted.

Of the majority it might be said, as of Colas in the French epigram—

> " Colas est mort de maladie
> Tu veut que je t'en plains le sort,
> Que diable veut tu que je t'en dit ?
> Colas vivait ; Colas est mort ! "

These " Colases " played their part on the Irish stage for the most part without any great display of purpose, principle, or energy. A few shine out conspicuously on the pages of history— "velut inter ignes Luna minores."

Such were the great Talbot and Sir John Rokeby, who said he preferred to eat from wooden dishes and pay his debts, to supping from silver and neglecting his creditors. But the majority were either *rois fainéants*, extortioners, and oppressors, or else, owing to the alliances and connections they had formed with the chiefs of " the Irish enemy," they were divided in their allegiance to their sovereign, and illustrated in their public conduct the impossibility of serving two masters, or even three, for the mastership of Mammon must not be ignored ! Great numbers of the chief vassals of

the Crown had, by adopting Irish customs and
costumes, become more Irish than the Irish.
" Hibernis ipsis Hiberniores."

In Munster there was not much to distinguish
the Desmonds from the O'Briens, their kinsmen.
The loyal corporation and burgesses of Waterford had no worse plague than the Poers or
Powers. In the west and north the de Burghs
had so utterly degenerated that they had even
assumed the composite name of " MacWilliam,"
and, unmindful of their royal race and English
connection, had thrown themselves into the Irish
side ; while merely to mention another historic
house, the Berminghams, had openly cast off their
loyalty and opposed the action of the Crown
where it interfered with their own views and
interests ; in fact, every baron had become a petty
prince more absolute than his own sovereign.

The causes of the decline of British power in
Ireland in this period may be traced to several
sources—first, to maladministration and malversation ; secondly, to the constant absenteeism of the
great feudatories ; thirdly, to the bickerings and
jealousies of the local lords who called in the Irish
to redress the balance of power, and thus established a caste, so to speak, of native "Free Lances,"
or wandering warriors, ready to take sides at the

shortest notice. Then the diversion of Robert
Bruce of Scotland, who was virtually King com-
mandant in most of Ireland for upwards of three
years, gave a great blow to the English power
and prestige, while the wars of England in Scotland and France absorbed much of the resources
of Ireland in men and money, and if Irishmen
shared in the glories of Cressy and Poictiers, they
gained nothing solid thereby ; but the great
depletion and diminishing of the Imperial Exchequer arose from the waste of lands by constant
" hostings " and reprisals, and the barbarous custom of quartering horse and foot soldiers on the
farmers of the country for lengthened periods, a
custom known as " coyne and livery," which had
its origin in the dishonesty of the Barons, and led
to exactions and spoliations worse than a state of
actual warfare. Then religion, instead of being a
salve to the sores of the State, proved rather a
blister, for the *Norman* version of the Catholic
faith was not the *Irish ;* and in point of fact, there
was nearly as wide a gulf between the English
Catholic and the Irish, as between the Irish Protestant and the Irish Catholic in later post-
reformation days.

Meanwhile the Irish chieftains, or dynasts, had
grown in power and importance. The O'Connors

of Faly, or Offaly, had frequently worsted the
English in the field, and their chieftain, or king,
was now regularly subsidised, or "black-rented,"
by the Government, while the O'Byrnes, O'Tooles,
and Kavanaghs, brought home the horrors and
harryings of real war to the citizens of Dublin—
reiving, killing, and carrying off their prey to
their mountain fastnesses from under the very
walls of Dublin and its Castle, like the modern
brigands of Attica or Italy. The remedy for
this state of insecurity was to "pale in" the
portion of territory that remained in Leinster to
the Crown—hence the term "English pale." But
a glance down the Viceregal List shows that the
Plantagenet Kings endeavoured constantly to
face the evil, not to *fly* from it. Many of their
Princes were appointed Viceroys of Ireland, and
several of the kings graduated in the school of
Irish Politics—for instance, Henry II., King
John, and Richard II., while Mortimers, De
la Poles, and Clarences were Proreges or
Viceroys. The royal choice of "good men and
true" for this office was very limited; for if they
sent English officials, or "English by birth," to
fill it, their ignorance neutralised their honesty and
thoroughness. If they selected "English by
blood," they too often found that the Celtic

surroundings of their families had impaired their loyalty and fettered their freedom of action, and that instead of furthering the interests of their sovereign, they were bent upon self aggrandisement.

" The Castle," which had on several occasions been repaired and fortified, seems, during this period, to have been not only the citadel or *place forte* of the English garrison, for which its situation on the crest or summit of the ridge running from east to west, and defended on the north by the river Liffey and its marshes, while the Podder, or Poddle, one of the tributaries of the Liffey, filled its fosse to a great depth on the opposite side, qualified it, but was the Treasury and Bank of the Government, as well as its Mint—the Master of the Mint being styled " Percussor Monetæ." Here were lodged " the political prisoners " of the day, as well as the hostages taken for the good conduct of State officers— or native chieftains. Here were the offices of the Government Departments, so that " the Castle " was then a very important and populous place.

We have glimpses every now and then of the superior knowledge of cookery possessed by the Normans, who even then had their *chefs* and

E.

cordons bleus, and astonished the more simple-
stomached Celts by their splendid entertainments,
varieties of plate, and costly raiment; witness the
feastings of "the natives" with Richard II.
That good cheer was not lacking to the Viceregal
staff even on their journeys is shown by the writ
(1393) addressed by the Viceroy, James third Earl
of Ormonde, to the Seneschal of "the Liberty"
of Wexford. "By this instrument the Seneschal
was ordered, under penalty of £100, to have provided at Ross, where the Earl meant to pass
Christmas, all needful supplies for the Viceregal
housekeeping, including 40 crannocs of pure flour,
60 crannocs of oats, 60 good bullocks, 4 boars,
80 large and 60 small pigs, 100 geese, 100 ducks,
200 pairs of rabbits, 100 trusses of hay, 6,000
poultry, 6 lambs, 5 meases of herrings (a mease
means 500 fish), 100 cod and ling fish, and 100
salted salmons."

The Irish "Hobbies," meanwhile, were the
wonder and admiration of the English knights,
as Giraldus tells us. Irish falcons were in the
very highest esteem; while Edward III. drew
largely, we may conclude, on his Irish resources for
the means of hunting and hawking in his French
wars. He had 60 couples of hounds with him;
just as Arthur Wellesley, in the Peninsula,

varied actual war with what Somerville styled
its " image."

The halo of romance and remoteness begins to
disappear with the accession of the Tudors to the
throne of England. No longer can the page of
history be illustrated by such marvellous *hauts faits*
as the conquest and annexation of the Province
of Ulster by such peerless Paladins as John de
Courci, and his brother in *law* as well as in *arms*,
Almeric Tristram St. Lawrence. " That vile "
saltpetre and murderous muskets began to displace
chain armour and cloth-yard shafts, and the power
of the Crown to assert itself over the shattered
ranks of the great feudatories whom the Wars of
the Roses had decimated and depleted. Of strong
will and earnest resolution, the Tudor Sovereigns
governed as well as ruled, and admitted no *maires
de palais* to share their sceptres and undermine
their authority. For the most part they had a full
share of business capacity, and preferred efficient
commoners, or middle-class men, who knew their
work, and had shown a faculty of organisation and
administration, to the proudest of peers ; and if
the spirit of parsimony, carried to the verge of
meanness, had not been the conspicuous characteristic of the Tudor tenants of the throne, the complete conquest of Ireland, and its reclamation from

E 2

the tyranny of its chiefs, Anglo-Irish and native, would probably have been effected by the vigorous and faithful lieutenants who occupied the Castle, and wielded the symbol of power—the Sword of State. But the want of pence, which has vexed public men (as well as private), more or less, in all ages, completely paralysed the arms of such deputies as St. Leger and Sidney, who, in addition to Viceregal duties, had to become *defenders* of that faith which the great *offender* of the Faith of Christendom—Henry VIII.—had substituted for the ancient creeds and forms of ritual ; to act as Leaders of the Parliament, Commanders-in-Chief and Commissary-Generals, Treasurers, Presidents of the Council, and Inspectors of the Provinces with quarters in more than half-a-dozen Posts and Garrisons ; while, through their spies and instruments, they had to keep an unremitting surveillance over traitorous chiefs and rebellious vassals, who were in constant correspondence with the enemies of England abroad, and never lost an opportunity of conspiring against her peace and welfare! The Tudors were well served by their Lieutenants, but the latter had few to second them ; for the subordinate officers in Church and State were, with rare exceptions, of the worst

type—ignorant, incompetent, and very often dis-
honest and disloyal.

The battle of Bosworth, won after two hours'
hard fighting, hurled Richard III.—so cruelly
caricatured by Shakespeare—from the throne of
England, to be replaced by the victor, Henry VII.
The Wars of the Roses were thus practically ended,
and though the Anglo-Irish nobility had not
suffered to the same extent as that of England,
it had lost several gallant representatives, more
especially the House of Butler (Botiler), or
Ormonde, who were Lancastrians, while their
great rivals, the Geraldines, of Leinster and
Munster, were staunch Yorkists. The Pretender
Lambert Symnel found a strong following in
Ireland, who were aided by Margaret, Duchess of
Burgundy ; but the battle of Stoke, a Ronçevalles
to Irish chivalry, disposed of the question finally.
Jasper of Hatfield, Duke of Bedford, was
Richard's Viceroy. After the accession of Henry
and the battle of Stoke, Sir Richard Mount
Edgcombe was sent as Commissioner to Ireland
to grant an amnesty to the conspirators, including
the Deputy Kildare, who was confirmed in his
office. Perkin Warbeck now appears as a second
Pretender, and gained adherents in Ireland ; but
his influence was transient, and Henry nominated

his youthful son Henry (afterwards the Eighth) to
be Viceroy, with Sir Edward Poynings for Deputy.
His much quoted Act, which placed the Parliament of Ireland under the control of the King of
England, his Council and Viceroy, was the death
blow to nascent Irish liberty (and license); moreover, it made English law of force in Ireland, and
had memorable consequences.   The Battle of
Knockdoe, fought in 1504, between Kildare and
the Lords of the Pale, against de Burgh and his
Irish allies, in which the latter were signally
defeated, was the last great event in this reign.

At the close of the reign of the 7th Henry,
the real English Raj was contracted within the
narrow limits of the four semi-obedient counties,
Meath, Louth, Dublin, and Kildare.   The Kings
of England still styled themselves " Earls of
Ulster," a title derived from the de Burgh
alliance ; but instead of gaining any revenue from
that now fertile and rich province, they were put
to considerable expense by the maintenance of
garrisons and outposts there, and the insane
policy of not recognising the facts of the case, and
contemporary circumstances, still obtained in the
Royal Councils.   The statutes of Kilkenny were
still renewed in spirit if not in letter.   By these
statutes a gulf was established on parchment

between the ruling race of Englishmen and the
alleged inferior race of Irish-born men, on whom
the brand of Cain was stamped, if they did not
comply with the sumptuary and capillary ukases
emanating from Dublin, that proscribed Irish
customs and clothes, and made the ordinary mode
of Irish equitation (*i.e.*, without stirrups, a custom
William of Orange is depicted as having adopted
in his statue in Dublin) absolutely penal—but *quis
custodiet ipsos custodes?* At this time marriage was
not honourable in all, for polygamy was more the
rule than the exception among many of the
dynasts and their followers. It was a case of
Utah, without the clever commercial code of
Brigham Young, who made Utah an earthly
paradise. Peculation prevailed in official circles.
Diogenes might have been puzzled, even with the
brightest of lanthorns, to discover *the* honest man
of the community, while the three great leaders of
men and manners, the representatives of the
Kildare, Desmond, and Ormonde families, were
mostly steeped in Irish vice and prejudices, and
were largely allied with Irish families. A hand-
full of strong Saxons and Celts have held an
Indian Empire against external foes, and internal
rebellion, but these Celts and Saxons had never
degenerated or become Orientals in mind or body

like the Roman legionaries of Consul Crassus or the Anglo-Normans ; and, as a rule, their authority was strengthened by the exercise and display of the chief cardinal virtues. In Ireland it was wholly different. " The natives" became strong as the invaders grew weak, and when Celtic acumen became allied to the superior learning and civilisation introduced by the conquerors, it had not much trouble in practically casting off the foreign yoke and emancipating itself from a tyranny that almost denied it the heritage of a common humanity, treating the " Irish enemy" as Helots or perioikoy.

It would be impossible in this abstract or brief chronicle to follow the windings and intricacies of Irish politics and polemics minutely. As a sample, however, of the lawlessness of the men who administered the King's Government in this lawless land we may cite the case of the Earl of Kildare, who, when summoned to England to account to the King and Council for his eccentricities of conduct, more especially in the matter of burning the Cathedral of Cashel, whose Archbishop was a Butler partisan, at once acknowledged the sacrilege, but added the justificatory plea, " By Jesus, I would never have done it had it not been told me that the Archbishop was within." So

much for *burning* zeal! When told to select a
" counsel " to defend himself, his answer was, that
he would select His Majesty, "as he saw no
better man in England." When Payne, Bishop
of Meath, averred that " all Ireland could not rule
this Earl," Henry, who seems to have been
fascinated by this man of ready hand and ready
reply, declared that "this Earl shall rule all
Ireland." A warrant is extant, in which Henry
directs the Keeper of his Great Wardrobe to
deliver for the use of Gerald, the son and heir of
the King's cousin, the Earl of Kildare, "8 yards
of black velvet for a robe, furred with white lambs'
wool ; 2½ yards of a tawney medley for a gown,
lined with white lambs' wool ; 2 doublets, one of
black velvet and the other of tawney satin :
2 pair of tawney hose, and another pair of crimson ;
a hat and two bonnets, one of crimson and the
other black ; 2 yards of silk ribbon for girdles, and
3 dozen of silk point."

This well-dressed young Geraldine married
Elizabeth, daughter of John, Lord Zouch of
Codnor, and returned with his father to Ireland in
1503. Like many more well-dressed dandies in
our insular story, this Gerald fought gallantly with
his father and Lord Howth at Cnoc-Tuagh, or
Knockdoe, against the de Burgh levies. Curiously

enough, in the whirligig of time, Lord St. Lawrence, now Earl of Howth and Knight of St.
Patrick, a nephew of the Lord Clanricarde of the
day, represented the borough of Galway for
several years, and instituted annual races not very
far from this sanguinary spot. It is also somewhat
of an historical curiosity that the St. Lawrence
family, founded by the Conquistador Almeric Tristram, never once swerved in its loyalty to the
Crown—"among the faithless, faithful only they;"
for the far greater and more historic house of
Ormonde—another pillar of the State—produced,
among a cloud of loyal leaders and splendid
soldier-statesmen, a few defaulters and waverers.
Both families, too, amidst the seismic shocks of
civil discord, and the clashings of civil and religious
warfare, have preserved their ancestral lands and
homesteads, keeps, and castles. We read that
the miserly and mean Henry VII. was so
taken with the straightness and loyalty of the
Lord Howth of his day that he made him a
present of 300*l.*, chiefly, perhaps, for his suspicion
of the spuriousness of Symnel, " the Pretender."

CHAPTER III.

"Oh hapless nation ! hapless land
Oh heap of uncementing sand."

HENRY VIII. was proclaimed king in 1509.
Kildare remaining his Viceroy, and when the
latter was killed by the bullet of an O'More,
near Kilkea Castle, his own residence (the castle
is still inhabited by the Leinster family), his son
Gerald succeeded him in an office, the chief payment of which depended on the lands recovered
from rebels—a style of salary that suggested
action and vigour if not strict justice or impartiality. Meanwhile, Thomas, the seventh Earl of
Ormonde, died, leaving an immense fortune in
money and manors to two daughters, to one of
whom Sir William Boleyn was married, while
Sir James St. Leger claimed the other. To Sir
William Boleyn the king granted the Ormonde
title of Earl of Wiltshire. Sir Piers Butler was
heir apparent to that of Ormonde as well as to
the Irish settled estates. He was ultimately
forced to accept that of Ossory, Ormonde being

added to the honours of the Boleyns, whose court
star was greatly in the ascendant. At last, or
perhaps after marriage, Henry awoke to the
folly of entrusting the government of Ireland to
Kildare, and it was handed over to Thomas, Earl
of Surrey, of Flodden fame. This soldier-states-
man swept the country, but he had no means of
holding his conquests, and at his own request was
relieved of office in 1521 to the universal regret
of "the Pale." Sir Piers Butler was then named
Deputy. The Ormonde family had the misfortune
of being more scrupulous than the Geraldines,
and their estates were sandwiched between those
of the Desmonds and Kildares—a prey to both.
After a year or two of Butler rule, Kildare was
once more restored to office, and the war between
Butlers and Geraldines broke out anew and à
outrance. Kildare and Sir Piers were, in consequence, both summoned to London, and the
former was sent to the Tower, Lord Delvin
being appointed Vice-Deputy. He was, however,
presently captured by O'Connor Faly, and held
to ransom. In 1529 Henry appointed his son,
the Duke of Richmond, Viceroy, with Sir William
Skeffington as Deputy. Kildare, on his release
from the Tower, superseded Skeffington, but
public opinion was against the selection, and

Kildare was again summoned to England and committed to the Tower, where he died, and "Silken" Thomas, his son, broke out into overt rebellion, one of the first acts of his followers being the murder of Archbishop Alen. In such a plight was Dublin that the Castle was plundered by the O'Tooles, prior to its siege by "Silken" Thomas. Meanwhile, Skeffington was sent over from England with troops. The Castle siege was raised. Maynooth was taken, and in a few weeks Kildare was forced to surrender, to be sent to the Tower.

In Munster Desmond was negotiating with the Emperor Charles V., whom he acknowledged as his Sovereign. At his death the succession was disputed, but an English force was well received all through the south. Skeffington was again invested with the Viceregal power, with Lord Leonard Grey as Marshal. On the former's death the latter became Deputy, and a Parliament was held in 1536. The Act of Royal Supremacy in church matters, and that forfeiting the estates of absentee landlords to the Crown, were its chief performances.

Coyne and Livery having been discountenanced and vetoed, money payments to the troops became absolutely necessary ; but money was not forthcoming, and the troops mutinied in Dublin. However, Lord Leonard Grey adopted palliative measures, and led his victorious little army through the south and north-west, but sustained a check in " Faly." Having seized on the Earl of Kildare's five brethren somewhat treacherously, he sent them off to the Tower, whence they were taken to Tyburn and executed, together with " Silken " Thomas. The family, however, were not extinct in the male line, for Gerald, after a series of adventures, found his way to the court and camp of Cosmo de Medici in Milan, and Lady Kildare (a sister of Lord Leonard Grey's) brought up the second boy at Beaumanoir, in Leicestershire.

Lord Leonard Grey's government of Ireland was, if nothing else, energetic and vigorous; his raids and " hostings " were short, sharp, and successful, but led to no permanent results. He was accused of a very decided leaning to the Geraldine faction, through his marriage, to the injury of the Butlers ; and soon after his recall to London he was executed. In 1540 James Fitz-maurice, Earl of Desmond, was murdered, and was succeeded by James Fitzjohn. Cromwell, the famous Minister, next fell into disfavour, and was executed, and Sir Anthony St. Leger was made

Deputy in 1541. One of his first acts was to conciliate Tirlogh O'Toole, and to send him to London, where he was well received by Henry, who granted him Powerscourt. From this time the O'Tooles cease to be a chief factor in the politics of the Pale. Desmond and MacWilliam also made their humble submission. In a Parliament held in Dublin Henry VIII. was proclaimed King of Ireland—a sovereignty hitherto claimed by the Pope. This Kingship required a supporting revenue, and as a condition precedent, St. Leger's policy created a general, if temporary, peace. O'Neil was made Earl of Tyrone, MacWilliam of Clanricarde, and O'Brien of Thomond; but the pay of the army was still sadly in arrear. France and Scotland were hostile, and Irish soldiers were required for both countries. After a short absence in England St. Leger returned to Ireland as Deputy, but he took offence at the growing power of Ormonde, who, after a short campaign in Scotland, went to London to confront St. Leger. Here he was poisoned, and St. Leger returned to Ireland as Deputy.

It may be a matter of some surprise that the compulsory *volte face* made in ritual and religion in Ireland led to such slight excitement and

agitation ; the island had been the isle of saints,
in name, at any rate ; for some centuries it had
become the isle of sinners, of which not a few
churchmen were like the unregenerate St. Paul,
the chief. Contemporary chroniclers have declared
that the Mendicant Friars alone preached the
Gospel of the kingdom, and as the petty plunder
of the religious houses was pretty generally distributed, the greedy Gallios of the day readily
acquiesced in the State arrangement—just as the
Russells and Cavendishes did in that Godliness
which *to them*, at least, was "*great gain*"—while
ecclesiastics found as little difficulty in conform-
ing to the religion of "Rimmon," as Theodore
Hook did, when asked to sign the Thirty-nine
Articles at his Oxford matriculation : "forty, sir,
if you choose," being, according to the *Ana*, his
free-and-easy reply.   No one proved a more
zealous iconoclast than Lord Leonard Grey—Our
Lady of Trim, who numbered pilgrims by the
hundred, and St. Patrick's celebrated crozier,
wherewith, according to popular tradition, he had
banished the snakes from the island, counting
among his *spolia opima*.

On the death of Henry VIII., Edward VI.
succeeded to the throne, *par droit de naissance ;*
and St. Leger continued Lord Deputy.   In 1547

he was superseded by Sir Edward Bellingham, to whom the unwontedly large salary of £2 per diem was given. He was a strong and honest governor, ever "in harness," and his attention was fully occupied by piracy on the coasts, and the necessity for almost ubiquitous "hostings." Against O'Connor Faly he was signally successful, and riding with a small company from Leighlin into Munster he surprised Desmond, and carried him off to Dublin, where he taught him some lessons in lip loyalty that were not forgotten. On his departure from Ireland in 1549, Sir Francis Bryan, Lady Ormonde's husband, was made Lord Justice, but ere a year was over he was poisoned, and Lady Ormonde married "the Desmond." Sir Anthony St. Leger was again sent to Ireland, which was honeycombed with conspiracies promoted by religious difficulties and foreign spies.

Sir James Croft succeeded St. Leger. His attempt to dislodge the Scot settlement at Rathlin Island proved abortive. St. Leger was recalled in 1552. Meanwhile King Edward's death led to general risings against the English power. The revenue of Ireland at this time was about £10,000 a year, the cost of government about £50,000. The Viceroy's salary £1,000 a year.

F

The great curse of English Government in
Ireland has ever been its lamentable lack of continuity! It seems, like the faith of some pro-
fessors denounced by the Apostle, "driven about
by every wind of doctrine," and to "one thing
constant never." It was so in Henry VIIIth's
time, who declared that his plan of conciliating
the Irish was by "sober ways, politic drifts, and
amiable persuasions of law and reason." His
success with the O'Toole tribe, who infested the
spurs of the Dublin and Wicklow Range, and
swooped down on the environs of Dublin whenever opportunity availed, was most conspicuous
and signal, and might have been tried on a larger
scale in the case of the more distant Earls and
feudatories. His "plan" bore little fruit, and his
niggardliness in the matter of means and men
prevented the spread of loyalty to the Crown, as
the loyal seemed to fare worse than the rebellious.
" Parcere subjectis et debellare superbos," was a
motto of Imperial Government apparently forgotten or ignored. Nevertheless, exhaustion
was coming on the native chieftains, and the
O'Mores and O'Connors Faly must have
seen the prospective period to their gallant
struggle against huge odds in the absorption of
their territory into the shires of the King's and

Queen's County; while Dangan was named Philipstown, and Campa, Maryborough—Offaly, Fercal, Ely, Leix, and Ossory becoming mere historical names. The circle of fire was pressing the natives all round.

Mary succeeded her half-brother in 1553, and St. Leger was Deputy. With true Tudor instinct the new Queen bated not a jot of her Father's claims to supremacy in things ecclesiastical; though zealous for the ancient faith and ritual, reversing the recent policy. " Et antiquum documentum novo cedat ritui." St. Leger describes himself as a Tantalus condemned to forego the due maintenance of the government from want of means, and at his own request he was superseded by Sir Thomas Radcliffe, Lord Fitzwalter, afterwards Earl of Sussex, while Sir Henry Sidney came with him as Vice-Treasurer, with £25,000 in hand. A raid was made into Ulster, and the O'Mores were granted " reservations," like Red Indians under the American Government. When Sussex went on leave, Sidney took his place as Lord Justice, but he was paralysed for want of pounds and pence. In 1558 Sussex returned, and a " spirited policy " was inaugurated ; for the army had been increased, and so had its pay ; and the Deputy's honorarium

F 2

was raised to £1,500 a-year. An expedition
against " the Lord of the Isles " proved a failure.

Meanwhile, Mary had entrusted a commission
to Cole, Dean of St. Paul's, to persecute the
Protestants of Dublin and Ireland, who had
hitherto been overlooked, perhaps on the *de
minimis* principle. The ready wit of his landlady
at Chester, where " he lay," averted this horror,
for she substituted a Pack of Cards in the Dean's
wallet for the Mandate. Ere another could be
procured Mary had died, and Elizabeth had been
proclaimed Queen. Sidney, as we have seen,
was Lord Justice, and his initial difficulty was in
arranging the O'Neil succession. Shane, the
Tanist, claiming the Earldom, *vice* Matthew
O'Neill, Lord Dungannon, who was decidedly
illegitimate. Law, usage, and common sense
seemed on Shane's side as well as the *vox populi*,
but his rival was preferred before him by the *vox
proregis*—hence much bloodshed.

Elizabeth *insisted* on Sussex's reassuming the
Irish Viceroyalty ; he acquiesced unwillingly, and
held his first Parliament in 1560 in Dublin.
Kilmainham Hospital or Priory having been
dismantled by a storm, the Viceregal residence
was retransferred to the Castle, and was occupied
by Lord Justice Fitzwilliam, who had come over

as Treasurer-at-War, in Sussex's temporary absence in England. When the latter returned it was as Lord Lieutenant, a title disused since the Duke of Richmond's time.

Shane O'Neil now occupies all the canvas. He was a semi-savage, full of lust and lubricity. He had some—nay, great—brains, and much cunning, few scruples, and intense overweening pride. To women he proved a sensual savage, as cruel as a Kurd, and his clay was habitually moistened with wine or usquebaugh to such an extent that, to get rid of the fumes, he would bury himself in earth up to the chin for hours. He certainly had the gift of government, and Ulstermen looked upon him as their chief. Sussex's first expedition proved abortive, and it was agreed that Shane should go to the Queen to state his case and claims; there he was confronted by Sussex, but the Queen rather sided with Shane, the specious and the stalwart.

In Sussex's absence Fitzwilliam occupied the Castle, while Desmond and Ormonde went to the Queen. When the Lord Lieutenant returned to Ireland he made raids on O'Neil, which cost much treasure, but were barren of results, and, at the mediation of Kildare, a peace was made with Shane. On the retirement of Sussex, Sir

Nicholas Arnold, who had been on the Financial
Commission, took up the Government. Sussex,
with all his vigour, had been a failure. " Imperii
capax, consensu omnium, nisi imperasset."

The jealousies and incursions of the Desmonds
and Ormondes led to a pitched battle at Affane,
the last great *private* battle, or faction fight, of the
kind, save one, in Ireland. Desmond was beaten,
wounded, and captured; and the Earls were
ordered to London. Meanwhile, Shane O'Neil
defeats the Macdonnells, takes Dunluce, and
reigns supreme in Ulster. Sidney is now urged
to accept the Viceroyalty, but endeavours to make
his own terms, in which he partially succeeds.
He landed in Ireland in 1566, after a long deten-
tion on the borders of Wales, of which he was
Lord President, and after losing part of his outfit
by casualties at sea. Shane O'Neil's pretensions
were now so overweening, that a winter campaign
against him became a State necessity. Randolph,
with a small force, encamped by Londonderry, on
Lough Foyle, where he was attacked by Shane,
who was badly beaten, however. Randolph was
killed (the only man on his side), and the
Foyle garrison became demoralised from the
want of a general, and was subsequently broken
up, owing to the explosion of their powder maga-

zine. Meanwhile, Sidney made a tour round Ireland, and for the time being brought it to submission ; and Shane O'Neil, after a bloody defeat by the O'Donnels, was killed by the Scots in a drunken brawl. His death caused a temporary lull in the tale of raids, rapines, and rievings. Desmond was now in London, and *pro tanto* safe ; but a confederacy between Tirlogh Luinach and O'Donnel with the Scots mercenaries boded ill for peace. In 1557, the Massacre at Mullaghmast, by Cosby and Hartpole, whereby some 70 O'Mores were murdered, recalls the ghastliness of Glencoe in later times.

While Sidney was in London, and Fitzwilliam administered the government, the country began to relapse, and the English garrisons to grow weaker from neglect. " The well affected," quoth Maltby, "*gaped* for the Deputy's return ;" nor were matters mended by the extraordinary decision of the Law Courts in favour of Sir Peter Carew's claims to vast territories in Munster and Carlow ; regardless of the prescription of 170 years against them, and the faultiness of his own title, Sir Peter was adjudged Idrone. This set the younger brother (Edward) of the Earl of Ormonde in open rebellion, as the decision about Idrone affected his title to his Castle of Clogrennan, in Cather-

lough, or Carlow, and with James Fitzmaurice
(who had been defeated by Fitzmaurice, Lord of
Lixnaw) and the Southern Geraldines for allies,
the flames of civil war and rapine were rapidly
rekindled. But the return of Ormonde and Sidney
to Ireland smoothed matters; the rebel Butlers
submitted, and James Fitzmaurice was driven to
the woods and glens of Aherlow, while Colonel
Humphrey Gilbert brought the Munster malcontents to their knees.

The plan of placing Presidents in the Provinces, long discussed, now took shape, and Sir
Edward Fitton was sent to Connaught, with Ralph
Rokeby for a Chief Justice. In 1570, Sidney's
Parliament met in Dublin, and passed Acts of
Attainder against the rebel Butlers, but the Queen
respited and forgave them. Diocesan schools
were established, and some Protective Acts were
passed for Irish produce, to encourage the growth
of manufactures. Sir John Perrot was named
President of Munster.

The materials for a religious war were now
not wanting, nor adventurers such as Stukeley
to fan the flame, but though no Foreign Office
then existed in England, her diplomatic agents,
such as Walsingham, unravelled and counteracted
the intrigues on foot. James Fitzmaurice still

stirred up strife in desolated Munster, and, after
some protocols, Perrot agreed to fight him on his
own terms. The wily Geraldine, however,
backed out of the engagement.

The scheme of " Plantation " in Ulster had
long been entertained; it was now put or
attempted to be put in practice by the grant of
" Ards " in the co. Down to Sir Thomas Smith.
The plan, however, was a failure from the first,
and cemented the Ulster chiefs in the face of a
common peril. The Savage family still own
most of it as they have for centuries. In Galway
and Connaught Sir Edward Fitton fared badly.
Clanricarde showed his loyalty by a holocaust
hanging of his son, his brother's son, his cousin
german's son, one of the captains of his gallow-
glasses, and 50 followers, but his sons were in open
rebellion and besieged him. Perrot, however, was
victorious in the south-west, though impeded by
the mutiny of his moneyless troops. Fitzwilliam,
the Deputy, was in sad straits for money, when a
new project of Plantation in Antrim was started
by Walter Devereux, Viscount Hereford. It led,
of course, to a counter-combination of Ulster landowners, and failure was inscribed on its banners
from the start. Meanwhile Desmond was suffered
to leave London, but managed to escape from

Dublin, where he had been detained in the Castle ; while Perrot having gone to England under stress of ill health, the south and west threatened to rise, for the Geraldines " knew no God, no Prince but the Earl, no law but his behests." As a sign of recrudescent lawlessness, Sir Barnaby FitzPatrick's wife and daughter were carried off by the Graces to Kilkenny and Tipperary for ransom ; there was brigandage on land—piracy at Sea ! Some of the deeds done at this time were a foul blot on the fair fame of England and her high officials. It is not disguised that Sussex essayed to get Shane O'Neil murdered more than once. The Cosby-Hartpole massacre of the O'Mores reads like Pelissier's smokings and suffocations of Arabs, or the whole-sale murders of Red Indians (counted "pison") by the Western Pioneers of commerce and "civi-lisation ; " and their infamy is the more conspicuous by the contrasting brightness of men like Sir John Perrot, who was beloved by the harried poor, ever "entre le marteau et l'enclume " of native chiefs and English rulers, or Cowley, the Governor of Philipstown, whose religion was something more than a lip litany (he was ancestor of the Iron Duke). And now comes the murder by Essex of Sir Brian MacPhelim O'Neil, and numbers of his clan and race. In a few months more Essex and his troops were no more a menace to Ulster, as the latter were disbanded. His last feat was taking Rathlin Island from the Scots with the aid of Drake and Norris.

Fitzwilliam's ill health and infirmities of body and mind called for a successor, who appeared in the perennial Sidney. The Lord Deputy soon started for a tour. He found Leinster in a wretched state, but Waterford was fairly prosperous, while the Lords Power, or Le Poer, had administered Curraghmore to good advantage. No pessimist, Sidney found much to admire in the MacCarthys of Muskerry. Sir John Desmond and his brothers James and Sir Thomas Roe waited on him, as did also some "mean whites," originally well conditioned, such as the Arundels, Rochfords, Barretts, Flemings, Lombards, Terries, &c. James Fitzmaurice was, meantime, active in France. From Thomond Sidney went on to Connaught and was well received by MacWilliam (Clanricarde), a man of ability, though unequal to the control of his bastard sons, who overran the country, having levelled Athenry, unmindful of the fact that here was their mother's tomb. In Connaught five English families claiming to be " barons of family " had adopted Irish names and customs, but so reduced were they, says the Chronicle, "that they have not three hackneys to carry them and their train home." In Meath at this time so lax was church discipline and doctrine that Sidney believed "the very sacrament of baptism had fallen into disuse." The see of Meath, we may remark, has ever been cathedralless.

Sir William Sidney, whose son Philip appears on the scene for the first time now, appointed Sir William Drury President of Munster, who began an active career. The death of Sir Peter Carew, an Elizabethan magnate, occurs about this time, and soon afterwards Essex, who had recovered his favour with the Queen by a visit to Whitehall, died of dysentery. Hardly a very great man, certainly not a very successful one, but a great man *manqué*, and "nothing in his life became him like the leaving." Sidney now devoted himself to finance and revenue, and met his greatest opposition from the sturdy *Palemen*, with whom he had to compromise, but "the Army" was placed on a rather better pay footing.

Gerard the Lord Chancellor now becomes a prominent figure, while Maltby in Connaught ravaged the property of two Clanricardes, though he failed to secure their persons, while Rory Oge

O'More, who seemed to flit about like an aurora borealis, ravaged Leinster and burnt Naas, the capital of Kildare. In 1558 he was killed by the Fitzpatricks. Sidney's term was drawing to a close; his government was expensive, and the Queen objected to expense. Gerard succeeded him. No brighter name in the roll of Viceroys is to be found than Sidney's. In those days the Lords Deputies did not receive £5,000 for outfit, as now. Sidney's, valued at £1,500, was lost in crossing the channel, besides which his losses while in office were estimated at £9,000; and so "casually" did Britannia rule the waves of the Channel then, that he had to run the gauntlet of pirates in crossing it.

We have seen how the Lords Deputy were expected to further the cause of the Reformed faith; that that faith did not spread and increase among the people cannot be a matter of surprise, when we find that the new ritual was nowhere printed or read in Irish, and Irish was then the vernacular tongue, whereas the English was not, save in a small area. Even the Earl of Clanricarde conversed with Sidney in Latin, being probably more at home in that tongue than in that of the Saxon. But that a good deal of the morality of the Vicar of Bray was abroad is

shown by the somewhat pregnant fact that the
mitred Meiler Magrath was at one and the same
time *Protestant* Archbishop of Cashel and *Papal*
Bishop of Down and Connor, a supremacy in
mony not often reached. It is recorded that
the greater part of the Chapter of Armagh, the
primatial seat, were " temporal men and Shane
O'Neil's horsemen." The Jesuit David Wolfe
was the most diligent workman in the Pope's
vineyard. Another sign of the versatility and
adaptability of the parsons may be seen in the
manner in which, after that the ecclesiastical law
or its expounders of the time being had declared
that marriage might be dignified in all laymen, but
not in the priest, these clerics confided their *caras
sposas* to the fiduciary care of friends, receiving
them back generally a plus rather than a minus
quantity ("love's usury," as styled by the wits of
the day), once the celibate tyranny was overpast.
I should also have mentioned that another purpose
of the Castle was to serve as a *quasi* Temple Bar
for a frame for rebel heads which the English
then preferred entire, while the Indian braves were
satisfied with scalps ; it was also a place of torment,
though it was for some time, at any rate, unpro-
vided with the fashionable instruments of torture
such as the rack, thumb-screw, or boot, as we read

that the only means of questioning a recusant was
by toasting his toes before the fire, which was
actually done in the case of an ecclesiastical
" suspect."

" E pur si muove " was the muttering of
Gallileo when the Pope and his Council, who
arrogating *infallibility* in things celestial, showed
their utter *fallibility* in the diagnosis they made
of the planetary system. Ireland, too, moved,
though slowly and hardly perceptibly, under the
sway of the Elizabethan rulers. We read that
juries could be got to condemn malefactors in
some few towns, however obstinate and contuma-
cious they might prove, in the case of certain
families who were almost *sacrosanct* and *supra
legem.* It is true that the land in the track of
raids and hostings was as bare and desolate as
Germany after the requisitions of Tilly and
Wallenstein, but wherever the war chariots had
not passed there seemed to be peace and plenty,
and good store of corn, milk and butter, and if the
conquest of Ireland and its reduction seems a slow
process to us in the 19th century, it must be
recollected that the means entrusted to the
Deputies were generally wholly inadequate to the
end proposed, while those who have read about
the Maroon War in Jamaica, where a handful of

refugee slaves or their descendants, aided by
jungle and rough country, mocked the might of
England for a long time, till *dogs* effected what
man could not, will understand the situation.

It should not be forgotten that the best of the
English officers acknowledged that *only first-rate
men were of any avail in Ireland,* whereas the
rank and file sent were very inefficient, and con-
ceit and ignorance are often found in close
combination! Wherever the Irish "enemy"
picked up its education it was not deficient, some
of the chiefs being bi-lingual, some tri-lingual,
and perhaps they could write Latin in many cases
nearly as well as a public schoolboy of modern days.
All authorities bear witness to the fertile beauty
of many parts of the island, which Body styles
"an earthly paradise," a combination of mountain
and mere, rich woods and prairie-like pastures.

Insularity of position often tends to insularity
of mind, and both English and Irish were very
insulated; but in addition to narrowness of mind,
the English were painfully Procrustean in their
methods, and would insist on moulding the Irish
at once into their own ways and customs, dress and
deportment—hence hatred and recurrent rebellion.
But the few larger minded Englishmen, who
added observation to experience and were not

enslaved by prejudice, insisted that the natives had the makings in them of good farmers, as well as first-rate soldiers, and that their power of lying was not, on the whole, much superior to that of other peoples; but the men who said these things were the wiser of their party and people, and the voices of the wise have too often been condemned " clamare in eremo." It is curious to trace how often history repeats itself. The tenure of land then, as now, was the *teterrima causa belli*. The same impatience of taxation was to be seen in the denizens of the Pale, who resisted " cessing," while the detestation of " landgrabbing " was evinced by the odium against those who occupied confiscated estates.

The conquest of Ireland during the reign of Queen Elizabeth was infinitely more important to England, and more effective, than the annexation of the island by the Anglo-Norman adventurers in the reign of Henry II. The latter was writ in water, the former in blood, and to the former we owe the possibility of the real incorporation of Ireland into the Empire. Great minds illustrated this long reign. The world acknowledges but one Shakespeare, and in the galaxy of great men who lent splendour and power to the Court were Burghley, Walsingham, the Sidneys, Drake,

G

Hawkins, Raleigh, Gilbert, and scores more, too numerous to mention, many of whom were interested in Irish affairs, like Sir Walter Raleigh ; but English and European politics engrossed the major part of the attention of statesmen, and Ireland was comparatively neglected in the daily administration. She was placed " en parergou," as the Greek historian styles it. The few soldiers in garrison were half starved and in such constant arrears of pay that they had *to pawn their arms* to maintain themselves, but whenever they were effectively led they did wonders.

If this reign taught nothing else, it ought to have stamped one lesson deep on the minds of all English statesmen, namely, that Ireland is *the* vulnerable point in England's mail—the heel of Achilles that can be easily pierced—and that no nation, or chain, or fortification, can be stronger than its weakest point.

At the commencement of the reign of the Tudors, the English were almost cooped up within their Pale, to which their real realm was contracted. At its close they were the actual rulers of Ireland, powerful against all external combinations, though liable to disintegration from within. Nearly the whole area of the island was now shire land, with sheriffs and English Courts of Law.

CHAPTER IV.

"Let Erin remember the days of old
E'er her faithless sons betrayed her,
When Malachy wore the collar of gold
Which he won from the proud invader."

That time must have been very different to the present, for the faithless sons have long abounded.—O'CONNOR.

IN July, 1579, the result of the plottings of James Fitzmaurice and others was seen in the landing at Smerwick of a Spanish force. Their first exploit was the murder of two English officers—Henry Darvell, and Carter, the Marshal of Munster. Sir Nicholas Maltby attacked the Desmonds, who had risen *en masse*. Fitzmaurice was killed, his adherents routed! Sir William Drury, on the other hand, was badly beaten in the wood between Mallow and Limerick. He died soon after this in Cork. Lord Ormonde was now sent over from London as Governor of Munster, while Sir William Pelham and Sir Henry Wallop

G 2

co-operated with him. In the month of March,
Sir W. Pelham and Ormonde marched in two
columns to attack the invaders in their Castle of
Carrigafoyle, which they took by assault, and
killed the garrison. Meanwhile, Lord Grey de
Wilton came over as deputy to Dublin, and to
signalise his advent attacked the rebel O'Byrnes
in Glenmalure, but with terribly disastrous results.
Another party of Spaniards and Italians occupied
Smerwick and fortified themselves. They, too,
had to surrender, and were massacred (while the
officers were reserved for ransom)—600 in all.
Strong stern measures were now necessary, and
a conspiracy to seize the Castle and liberate
Kildare and Delvin, hatched in the Pale, was
punished on the scaffold, and Kildare was sent on
to London. The end of the Desmond conspiracy
was approaching; for the Earl, left with but
a few followers, who were plucked off like the
leaves of an artichoke, was presently betrayed
and killed, and his head sent to moulder on
London bridge. Hurley, sent over by the Pope
to occupy the see of Cashel, was caught and
extra-judicially hanged, and on the retirement of
Lord Grey, Sir John Perrot resumed the Sword
of State. His first act was to cause the word
"churle" to be suppressed in favour of franklin,

yeoman, or husbandman; he fell under royal suspicion and died in the Tower.

The condition of Southern Ireland for some time after the crushing of the Desmonds was even worse than in the potato famine of 1847-48, according to the testimony of such witnesses as Edmund Spenser! Cannibalism is said to have largely prevailed, and if this seems incredible it may be replied that the *ci-devant* cannibal, by force of circumstances, was not wholly unknown in the best English society even during the present generation. Two acts of attainder were passed, and arrangements were made for the partition of the Desmond's inheritance, nearly a million of statute acres! Sir John Perrot was ordered to repair to London, where the gallant officer died in the Tower, and was succeeded by Sir William Fitzwilliam, a grasping rather than a gracious governor. He was followed by Sir William Russell in 1594, and the executive soon became embroiled with Hugh O'Neil (Tyrone) and Red Hugh O'Donnel, with whom sided nearly all the aggrieved natives in Ireland, till, so powerful grew the Celtic coalition, that the Queen sent over Essex with 20,000 foot and 1,300 horse to crush it! His career was calamitous, and Charles Blount, Lord Mountjoy, super-

seded him, forcing the Spaniards, who had fortified
Kinsale, to evacuate it, and Tyrone to sue for
peace.   Meanwhile, the cleavage lines of creeds
and parties were increasing fast, and when Mountjoy the meritorious retired to England, as Earl
of Devonshire, a successor, cast in somewhat
similar mould, was found in Sir Arthur Chichester
(1603), who was to carry out King James I.'s
behests as to the devolution of land on the
English system.   Conscious guilt or fear for the
future now forced Lords Tyrone and Tyrconnel
to fly the country—the act was known as "the
flight of the Earls."   This " new departure " left
the coast clear for the Ulster Plantation, in which
the land grants were made on a far smaller scale
than in Munster.   However, the letter of the law
was not carried out, and many natives remained
on the land as labourers or squatters.

In the reign of James, first of the ill-starred
Stuarts in England (the sixth of that name in
Scotland), the Viceroys were Lord Mountjoy, Sir
George Carew, Sir Arthur Chichester, Sir Oliver
St. John (Lord Grandison), and Lord Falkland,
who retained office during the earlier years of
Charles I.'s reign.   Ireland was prostrate at the
conquerors' feet, and the division of the spoils by
Act of Parliament and legal chicane was the most

pressing business. The plantation of Ulster, as we have seen, was organised on a more frugal scale than that of Munster, but the "magnum opus" of the plantation "in these unreformed and waste countries" was the establishment of the Irish Society, which divided the greater part of Londonderry into twelve great territorial guilds, known as the Mercers, Grocers, Drapers, Fishmongers, Goldsmiths, Skinners, Merchant Tailors, Haberdashers, Salters, Ironmongers, Vintners, and Clothworkers. Three of these companies have lately sold their lands to their tenants, at about half a million sterling, under the Ashbourne Act, a proof of the magnitude of the interests involved. The confiscated area covered nearly four million acres! In the Parliament convened in 1613, obstruction was most prominent, but it gave the initiative to the fusion of the King's subjects in Ireland, and putting all on a common footing with a common charter of rights. In Leinster an inquisition into title caused further confiscations, and it was proposed to carry out a similar system in Connaught. It was at this time that the Boyles, Earls of Cork; Parsonses, Earls of Rosse; Loftuses, Marquises of Ely; Wingfields, Lords of Powerscourt, rose to territorial and titled greatness.

It seems to have been the curse of the Stuart
mind to fail utterly to perceive the signs of the
times as their Tudor predecessors had done.   In
1632 Sir Thomas Wentworth took over the office
and duties of Lord Deputy from Lord Falkland,
and collaborating with Laud, the Archbishop of
Canterbury, they raised a storm in England and
Ireland that cost the King his life and crown, as
well as forfeited their own lives.   James had left
Charles, his son, an inheritance of debt.   Money
had to be raised, and the landlords of Ireland
were willing to purchase at the price of £120,000
the civil and religious rights to which they were
de jure entitled.   Charles took the first instalment
of £40.000, but no "graces" were granted.   In
Ireland Protestantism had crystallised into a sort
of modified Puritanism, and with the exception of
official Dublin, and the planters and undertakers,
the inhabitants were, nearly all, not only *Catholic*,
but Papistical.   On these materials Laud and
Wentworth went to work ; the latter cajoled the
Parliament out of a large subsidy for the King,
but granted no corresponding "graces."   He
raised an army in Ireland, increased the revenue
many fold, and if he discouraged the woollen
trade, he fostered the linen industry greatly,
embarking much capital in it.   The King made

him Lord Lieutenant and Earl of Strafford. His
palace near Naas—at Jigginstown—was nearly
completed, but as he was going to take the field
against the Scots, he found the King had made
peace, and attainder and death awaited him. On
the death of Strafford, Sir William Parsons and
Sir John Borlase became justices, and they had
but 2,000 troops wherewith to confront a general
Catholic rising, headed by Rory O'More and Sir
Phelim O'Neil. The Castle of Dublin it was
intended to take by a *coup de main*, but the
scheme failed. However, Ulster, excepting a
few towns, was in the power of the rebels,
and, instigated by Sir Phelim O'Neil, a barbarous and bloody massacre of planters and
Protestants ensued. In a few months a few
forts and towns alone represented English power
in Ireland.

The Irish troops were, however, little better
than a mob till unexpected succour came from
the continent under Colonel Owen O'Neil and
Colonel Preston, who soon changed their fighting
condition. Meantime, Ormonde commanded the
royalist forces in Ireland, and when war was
proclaimed between the Long Parliament and the
King, a curious coalition took place between the
rebels and royalists, a measure which widened the

breach between the King and people in England. Ormonde was now made a Marquis and Lord Lieutenant, and Kilkenny was the headquarters of the rebel-royalist Parliament and council. The latter, however, was divided into two factions, of which one, led by Rinucini, the Pope's Nuncio, insisted on Papal supremacy; while Ormonde and his friends were content with toleration and certain restitutions and reforms. Meanwhile O'Neil had gained a decided victory at Benburb, but the King was in the hands of the Parliament —his cause in England lost. However, the disunion in the rebel camp led to curious complications, and Ormonde, who had returned from Versailles, joined with Prince Rupert, who had sailed with a fleet of sixteen frigates to Kinsale, in making a stand, aided by Lords Inchiquin, Clanricarde, and Castlehaven. Soon after the King's execution, the successes of the royalists in Ireland forced the Parliament to counteract them by sending over Oliver Cromwell, as Lord Lieutenant of Ireland, to Dublin with 8,000 foot and 4,000 horse. Here he found Ormonde had been routed and forced back to Kilkenny. The sieges and massacres at Drogheda and Wexford were the preludes to Cromwell's triumphant progress. Ireton and Coote completed his work, and in 1652 Ireland was subdued and Ormonde again in exile.

Ireton was Cromwell's deputy in Ireland; on his death the office passed to Fleetwood; and in 1652 a new shuffling of the cards, or the land of Ireland, commenced. *Transplantation*, which had before been attempted by sending "rebels" into Kerry, was substituted for *Plantation*, for the migration of the magnates into Connaught prescribed by 1654, was postponed or prolonged for a couple of years. The soldiers and subscribers to the war loan were paid in land debentures, and, according to Sir William Petty, nearly five millions and a half acres were confiscated. Henry Cromwell, the Protector's son, was now Lord Lieutenant, but most of the records of his brief reign have perished by fire. Then came the Restoration—a re-shuffling of the cards, and a quasi-settlement of the land question. Ormonde was made a duke, went to Ireland as Lord Lieutenant in 1662, but he was soon superseded by the more facile Lord Robarts, who again in turn made way for Lord Berkeley, a slave of the "Cabal" Ministry. Like the restored Bourbons Charles II. seemed to have learned little in exile, for his policy was a close alliance with France, and a restoration of Roman Catholics to power.

This led to the reaction of Titus Oates, and the
judicial murder of Dr. Plunkett, Lord Fingall's
brother. Ormonde was again appointed Lord
Lieutenant, but was recalled on Charles's death,
and after an interregnum Lord Clarendon was
named Viceroy, who in turn made way—when
the pear was ripe—for Dick Talbot, Earl of
Tyrconnel, with the title of Lord Deputy.
Catholic "ascendancy" was now universal in
Ireland, and James landed at Kinsale from
Versailles, with a French fleet, some men, and
munitions. A Parliament was held, and proscrip-
tions made. But the siege of Derry was raised,
and at Newtown-Butler the Enniskilleners routed
the Stuarts and their Celts, and Schomberg stood
boldly at bay at Dundalk.

William of Orange, who landed at Carrick-
fergus in June, fought the battle of the Boyne on
the 1st July, and then occupied Dublin. James
fled to France, and the sieges of Limerick and
Athlone were attempted, the latter successfully.
At Aughrim St. Ruth was killed, and his army
defeated with considerable slaughter. Limerick
was now the last hope of the Stuart party.

De Ginkel made a tremendous attack on
the town from the Clare shore ; it was re-
pulsed, but with great slaughter on either side,

and then came overtures for peace, which were accepted.

The articles of the Treaty were only kept in part, and the city of the violated treaty has become an historical bye-word. 20,000 men of the garrison migrated to France to form the nucleus of the Irish Brigade ; 3,000 joined King William. The rebellion was followed by the customary confiscations and the cruel Code of Penal Laws, inoperative from their mere severity. The commercial jealousy and intolerance of England was now directed to the ruin of the staples of Ireland—wool, provisions, corn—and the impoverishment of "the English garrison." Of course this led to universal smuggling and the defeat of iniquitous legislation, whose motto was "Viæ victis" all over the world then.

The Lords Lieutenants during this inglorious period were Henry, Viscount Sydney, Lord Capel, the Earl of Rochester, James Duke of Ormonde, the Earl of Pembroke, the Earl of Wharton, James Duke of Ormonde again, Charles Talbot, Duke of Shrewsbury, the Earl of Sunderland, Lord Carteret, Lionel Sackville, Duke of Dorset, the Duke of Devonshire, the Earl of Chesterfield, the Earl of Harrington, the Marquis of Harting-ton, the Duke of Bedford, the Earl of Halifax, the Earl of Northumberland, Lord Weymouth, the Earl of Hertford, the Earl of Bristol, Lord Townshend, Lord Harcourt, the Earl of Buckinghamshire, the Earl of Carlisle, the Duke of Portland, Earl Temple, the Duke of Rutland, the Marquis of Buckingham, the Earl of Westmoreland, the Earl of Fitzwilliam, the Earl of Camden, the Marquis of Clanricarde. These noblemen carried out, as best they might, the policy of the Prime Minister of England. They originated next to nothing, and their official headstones, with very few exceptions, require neither chronicle nor inscription.

Lord Westmoreland succeeded Lord Buckingham, and his reign bridges over a most interesting period, when the Catholics claimed some participation in the Constitution and a partial reversal of their sentence of outlawry. They were backed by Pitt and Dundas in England, by Grattan and Langrishe in Ireland, but there was danger obviously in offending the " Junto of Jobbers" who monopolised political power in that island, while there was also peril in denying the just and clear claims of the Catholics, who accentuated their arguments by arms, and pointed their propositions by parks of artillery, while France was intriguing for their support, and the concessions

to Catholics in England through Mitford's Bill cut
the ground from under the opponents of relief
and emancipation. The Relief Bill was passed,
Fitzgibbon being its ablest opponent, and the
Session of 1793 was a long and memorable one ;
but the north was in staunch sympathy with the
French Revolutionists, and there was a strong
party of " Irreconcilables" forming among the
United Irishmen, whose ranks were deserted by
the Patriciate. The most remarkable circumstance of the time was the non-intervention of
the Catholic clergy in the politics of the period,
for Burke writes of them, "Though not wholly
without influence, they have rather less than any
clergy I know." The Viceroy of the period, it is
evident, though representing his Sovereign, was
little more than the Secretary of the Prime
Minister in London.

From the vast welter of corruption, class
legislation, favoritism, and oppression, a few great
great names emerge conspicuously—" rari nantes
in gurgite vasto." Such were those of Swift,
Molyneux, and Lucas, who initiated the reaction
in favour of purity, Roman Catholic restoration
to citizenship, and Constitutional Government,
that bore fruit by-and-bye. Meanwhile absenteeism, tithes, middlemen, and agents were driving

the country towards that awful precipice—the wild
justice of redress by revenge and crime, and
"Whiteboys," "Hearts of Steel" boys, and
"Oak boys" sprung up to point the protests
of the poor. Parliamentary Government in Ireland had become a mere mockery. One Parliament, for instance, lasted thirty-three years.
In Lord Townshend's time an Octennial Act
was passed, but still Parliamentary Government
meant Government by place and pension. The
Nemesis came from America, to whose shores
numbers of the Protestant farmers of Ulster had
emigrated. Paul Jones was ravaging the coast of
Ireland. Volunteers started up to defend their
native shores, English aid not being available.
Arms now accentuated arguments, and *Free
Trade* was conceded to Ireland in 1779. This
was followed by the emancipation of the Irish
Parliament from the fetters of Poyning's Act and
its practical freedom, and the "Nation" granted
Grattan £100,000, of which he only accepted half.
Pitt now became Premier at the age of twenty-
three, and tried to liberate Irish trade more fully,
but English opposition proved too strong for him,
and Catholic disabilities were still unrepealed.
Naper Tandy and Theobald Wolf Tone now
appear prominently on the political proscennium,

partial Catholic emancipation was granted, and some partial reforms made. Further and fuller emancipation seemed imminent now. John Beresford was dismissed from office, Lord Fitz-william was sent over as Lord Lieutenant, but George III. obstinately vetoed all progress in this direction. One result was the reappearance of the " United Irishmen." Meanwhile, Tone and Arthur O'Connor had moved Carnot to make a descent on Ireland. Hoche had the command, but a storm prevented the landing. Duncan's victory at Camperdown in 1797 again prevented the diversion. General Lake commanded in Ulster, Lord Carhampton in chief, and martial law was proclaimed.

We are now nearing the goal of " '98," which, though poets and poetasters may profess to regard it with cynical indifference or a light heart, —

> "Who fears to speak of '98,
> Who blushes at the name?"

was a revolting episode of civil and religious war, in which atrocities of the most fearful type were perpetrated on both sides. Meanwhile Lord Camden was the Viceroy of the hour ; Sir Ralph Abercromby the Commander of the Army, which was in a state of the greatest indiscipline. The

11

latter was superseded presently by General Lake, but it was written that a man's foes should be those of his own household, and by an expenditure of nearly £400,000, the Government learnt every move of the conspirators. Lord Edward Fitzgerald, unwarned by the fate of his ancestor, "Silken Thomas," was in open rebellion. He was wounded in the act of arrestation, and died from the effects of his hurt. Without competent leaders, the rebels overpowered some scattered garrisons, as at Prosperous, in the Co. Kildare, but the Militia regiments soon rallied. In the north the rising was very promptly put down by Nugent and Barber. In Meath Lord Fingall and Colonel Preston routed the rebels at Tara Hill, but in Wexford the insurgents took possession of the county town, and two columns were commanded by those militant Priests, Father J. Murphy and Father Philip Roche. The barbarous massacre of women and children at Scullabogue has been often described and often viewed in engravings. With reinforcements, however, Enniscorthy and Wexford were soon recovered, and "the rising" stamped out in blood.

Lord Cornwallis now succeeded Lord Camden, acting as Lord Lieutenant and Commander-in-Chief. His conciliatory policy bore good fruit and restored confidence. Hoche at Killala now occupies attention. Lake's militia at Castlebar ran away from the foe, but Cornwallis and Lake hemmed him in, and made him surrender at Ballinamuck. General Hardi's ship, " the Hoche," was taken off Lough Swilley, and in it Wolfe Tone ; he cut his throat in prison.

The necessity of an incorporating union with England now commended itself to the mind of Pitt and his colleagues, and on the meeting of Parliament in Dublin, the Government brought in a resolution affirming this view, but after a protracted debate of twenty-two hours, had but a majority of one. The next time that the Bill was brought in it was carried by a larger majority of forty-two, the burrough owners having been compensated at the rate of £15,000 for each seat in the meantime, and strong arguments having been used to convince the recalcitrant.

The Parliament of Ireland—a nest of corruption, and representing extreme oligarchical narrowness—though leavened by some liberality, and not without its share of talent, may be said to have suffered the happy despatch to save its own life, just as sick cattle are slaughtered every day "to save their lives" (for their owners) ;

H 2

it must have been swamped entirely by the
Roman Catholic electors and members, for the
right of voting having been granted to the
Catholics in 1793, membership must have followed, as a necessary corollary, in a year or two.
That the Government put pressure on the members is quite true, but it was a State necessity,
and pressure nearly as strong, perhaps even
stronger, in money bids, was brought to bear on
the Opposition. Judging by petitions and movements outside of Parliament, the measure had
something akin to a *plebiscite* in its favour, and
nearly the entire Catholic population. Arrayed
against this were the representatives of Protestant
Ascendancy. Much has been written about the
bribery and corruption by which the Union was
carried, but there is little or no positive evidence
adduced in confirmation of these loose assertions,
and there is much negative evidence on the other
side. If it was corruption to take money for seats
in a house that represented nobody but the patron,
then were the anti-unionists most corrupt. For
instance, the Marquis of Downshire took £52,000
for his seats! Lord Cornwallis, a man of the
highest integrity, public and private, wrote,
" This country could not be saved without
the Union." Peerages were given with a free

hand, but not nearly so freely as on many other occasions.

Much, we repeat, has been said and written about the corruption that carried the Union. Sir Robert Walpole was styled " the Grand Corrupter ;" but he was the engineer hoist with his own petard, for he was *overtrumped*, as Mr. Glover tells us in his Memoirs.

" Don Carlos" (Frederick, Prince of Wales) " told me that it cost him £12,000 in corruption, particularly among the Tories, to carry the West-minster and Chippenham elections in 1742, and other points, which compelled Lord Orford, at that time Sir Robert Walpole, to quit the House of Commons."

Wraxall tells us how " Roberts avowed without reserve, that while he remained at the Treasury there were a number of members who regularly received from him their payment, or stipend, at the end of every session, in bank notes. The sums, which varied according to the merits, ability, and attendance of the respective indi-viduals, amounted usually from £500 to £800 per annum. This largess I distributed, added Roberts, in the Court of Requests, on the day of the Prorogation of Parliament. I took my stand there ; and as the gentlemen passed me,

in going to, or returning from, the House, I
conveyed the money *in a squeeze of the hand.*
Whatever person declined the Ministerial bounty
in the manner thus related, I entered his name
in a book, which was preserved in the deepest
secrecy; it being never inspected by any human
being except *the King and Mr. Pelham.*"

Other suasions were tried in other cases, as
we learn from a curious proposal made *in the
House* by Lord Nugent, with a view of bringing
Fox and Pitt together. " He stated that he
had accomplished, more than 30 years before, a
similar undertaking, by means of a personal inter-
view between Lord Granville and Mr. Pelham,
which took place at his own residence. These
two candidates for power, said Lord Nugent,
came to the appointment disguised. I introduced
them to each other, and then left them alone—
a good supper and excellent wine, which I had
provided, soon banished mutual reserve. They
spoke freely, became friends, and so remained.
Thus was the *Coalition* effected in a single night.
I am not much acquainted with the two gentlemen now sitting opposite each other, but if they
will meet at my house, they shall have a delicate
supper, with the finest wines. *They may even,
if they please, get gloriously drunk;* and I will

answer for it, over the bottle, their punctilios and distrust will vanish ; while confidence will spring up where difficulties previously existed."

'Ημεῖς τοὶ πατέρων μέγ ἀμείνονες εὐχόμεθ' εἶναι.

At any rate, our bribery and corruption is done more discreetly in the few places where it is possible to do it at all.

Once the Union became an accomplished fact the separate history of Ireland ceased to exist ; the greatness of the Empire to which she contributed immensely, was her greatness, Imperial disasters were also her misfortunes. Henceforward, and for nearly nine decades, she has had no separate life and no independence ; Ireland being in one sense England, and England Ireland. To be sure, there were not wanting many among her sons who deemed the marriage a miserably Mezentian one, and considered that—

> " Freedom's battle once begun,
> Bequeath'd from bleeding sire to son,
> Tho' often lost at last is won,"

and spasmodic, ill-directed efforts have been made to burst away from the bondage and thraldom ; but these efforts hardly attained even local

success, and only tended to consolidate the
Union by showing its necessity. Since the
Union thirty-two Lord Lieutenants have administered the affairs of Ireland with varied
success and unsuccess. Among them were not
a few able, earnest, and conscientious Governors,
but their ability was not equal to their will.
They were the slaves, or servants if the term
be preferred, of a party. "A vote could mar
them as a vote had made," to paraphrase the
language of a national bard, for their tenure of
office was dependent on a division, and during
office their duty was to observe and report rather
than inchoate reforms or devise measures of
amelioration; while latterly this *rôle* has been
almost entirely taken out of their hands by the
preponderating influence of the Chief Secretary,
who represents *the Department of Ireland* in the
House of Commons, where he can gauge popular
feeling and keep his fingers on the pulse of the
people, and having his own brief filled in by the
official and topical knowledge of his permanent
Under Secretary, who is generally selected for his
business and official capacity, and may be, as in
the case of Thomas Drummond and Sir Robert
Hamilton, a man somewhat *hors ligne.*

Thus the constitutional fiction, "le roi règne

mais il ne gouverne pas," is extended to Western
Britain, and the Lord Lieutenant, Prorex, Viceroy,
or Deputy as he may be, has the smallest possible
share in moulding the destinies of the country
over which he presides; having little left him
save the task of "entertaining" (which, to their
credit, many Viceroys have accomplished in right
royal fashion) or leading a small section of society
that makes the Castle its focus, and acting, in fact,
as the Master of the Ceremonies and "Arbiter
Elegantiarum" in Ireland, a *rôle*, which with its
corresponding *corvées*, has become so utterly
anachronistic and half ridiculous that the Prime
Minister, even with the bait of £20,000 a-year,
some patronage, and the glamour of a great
position, finds it hard to procure a Viceroy for
Ireland, though no chief of the Foreign Office
has ever, I believe, had the smallest difficulty in
finding a representative of England at any great
foreign port. Hence for some time social talents,
a sounding name, a pleasant presence, a liberal
hand, and a power of pleasing have been more
sought for in the selection of Viceroys than
commanding talents or great gifts of eloquence
and argumentative power, and it redounds to the
credit of the Peerage of England, no matter to
what party they professed allegiance, that noble-

men have been found to fill the anomalous
position adequately, and even well, sacrificing, in
many cases, their own predilections on the altar
of Patriotism (party patriotism, if you will), and
making sacrifices of time and money that were
by no means light ; while, as a rule, the atmosphere of Dublin Castle and Court has been as pure
as that of the Court of Queen Charlotte, Queen
Adelaide, or their greater successor, the Empress
Victoria ! Of Wm. de Windsor we need not speak.

In the Pre-Union period the chronicler's
theme was mainly of war—wars external and
internal ! Since the Union the chief area of contention has been the House of Commons ; and
the bitterness of this contention was intensified
a thousand-fold by the bigoted and obstinate
defence, by a privileged oligarchy, of monopolies
in Church and State, which were at once a peril
to the Empire, and indefensible in themselves.
The denial of Catholic Emancipation for twenty-
nine years, partly through the unfortunate mental
aberration of the Sovereign, raised up an
O'Connell, who shattered the pretentious fabric,
and taught the people, whom he led like sheep,
the power of organisation and constitutional
agitation. No one now disputes the justness of
O'Connell's claims, or denies the peerless powers

of persuasion by which he gained their tardy
concession. But the arrogant and selfish spirit
which, under Lord North (a minister who never
lost his jocosity, though he lost a continent to our
Empire), had stung the North-American colonists
into rebellion, widened the breach between the
citizens of a common country, and left scars
which are not yet healed. It is true that Ireland,
though visited by two out of the three divine
scourges—the Famine and the Pestilence—while
spared the sword—has made wonderful material
and intellectual progress during these decades.
India, which, though, in some measure, won for
England by Irish brain and bone, was rather a
Scotch stronghold and close borough, has been
opened out to Irishmen, where the Lawrences,
the Goughs, the Bourkes, the Blackwoods,
Montgomeries, Gillespies, the Fitzmaurices, and
many others, have won fame and treasure. In
Parliament the Irish voice has been more po-
tent than the Irish vote; but the country has
seen the levies of the Empire led to victory
by a Wellesley, a Wolseley, and a Roberts;
while the pioneer ship, the " Teutonic," lately
launched from a Belfast dock, and the Brennan
torpedo, show that even in ruling the waves Irish
co-operation is a useful ally to Britannia. Possibly

owing to the want of subterranean treasure in
coal and metals Ireland cannot boast of such a
port as Cardiff, with her miles of docks and
affluence of commerce; but Belfast has sprung
into commercial greatness within the last fifty
years, and annihilated by the persevering enter-
prise of her sturdy sons the niggardliness of
nature, till the Lagan has grown into something
like a Celtic Clyde! Is the Union a failure?
(As is asserted by some of Marriage.) Decidedly
not! Let those who are still sceptical on this
point read Arthur Young's Tour in Ireland, and
judge for themselves. Let them turn over the
pages of " Ireland 90 years ago," and read the
record of habitual bloody battles in the streets
of Dublin, the maiming and mutilation of men
there in open day, and the insecurity of life and
property, even in the capital, and then let them
draw their conclusions. Hundreds, if not thousands, whose grandfathers were in the humblest
condition are now affluent and independent in
Ireland, and if no bloody revolution has effected
this, "la carrière est ouverte au talent" in this
island.

Much is said about the cruelty of coercion—
always a misfortune—but, for all that, foreigners
are filled with admiration at the practical freedom

of the country and its inhabitants; while it is forgotten that the Habeas Corpus Act has been suspended in England, while still operative in the smaller island, and that Peterloo and Bristol are vividly recollected by living men. It is certainly a pity that the Victorian eye does not oftener see the triumphs and progress of the Victorian age in Ireland.

Little remains to be said about the modern history of Ireland that is not referred to in the sketches of Viceroys and Secretaries. One of the finest passages in our Church Service is the text brought into the offertory—" Not grudgingly, nor of necessity, for God (and man too) loveth a cheerful giver." English Kings gave their "graces" grudgingly to Ireland. Parliament seems willing and eager now to repair this fault, and " Justice to Ireland " seems its motto; but the Nemesis of giving grudgingly is seen in the success of agitation, and the organised resistance of the masses to legal enactments. Englishmen in many cases detested O'Connell; now they laud him, and extol the patriotism that erected a statue to his memory—

> " A leur dresser une statue
> Pour la gloire du genre humain !"

To all political parties the word " Irish

enemy" has ceased to exist, and "Irish friend"
is substituted for it, and we may see "laborantes
in unum Penelopen vitreamque Circen"—say Mr.
Gladstone and Mr. Balfour. Political triumphs
are empty things if they do not bring prosperity
in their train. Ireland has been nauseated with
politics. She wants prosperity, and Lord George
Bentinck saw that when he proposed a vote of
£16,000,000 for covering the island with a network of railways ; but a far smaller sum than that
would convert Galway into a "statio bene fida
carinis," with a ship canal to convey the raw
material to the western ports of England, while
much of it would probably be worked up in
Galway where there is ample population and
cheap labour for factories. An Irish regiment
of Guards would be a sentimental yet solid concession.

There are many simple-minded people in
England to whom the history of Ireland presents
little but a series of enigmas. They cannot
believe that their countrymen could ever have
been guilty of the most flagrant atrocities, or been
parties to enormous injustice through a series
of long years. The high-handed proceedings of
the Israelites towards the Canaanites are explained
away to our educated and reverential under-

standings by the fact that the Jews were ordained
by Providence to be the instruments of a terrible
retribution on those nations for their breaches of
written or unwritten laws; we bow our heads
in reverence, but we confess our inability to
fathom the dispensation, and can only re-echo the
Patriarch's words, " Shall not the Judge of all the
earth do right ?" When we read Irish history we
cannot help being struck by some analogies
between the English and the Irish "nations," and
the Jews and the pristine occupants of Palestine ;
the conquerors swept away the natives from the
fertile grassy valleys, and relegated them to the
hills, woods, and morasses; building castles and
forts and strong towns to maintain their conquests,
but consenting to leave a fraction of the sons of
the soil to act as their hewers of wood and
drawers of water, their herdsmen and farmers—
their charter and license for these proceedings
being an alliance with one of the Kings of Ireland
and a Bull of the Pope of Rome. The little leaven
of Irishmen left in these plains and valleys acted
precisely as the contaminating influence of the
Canaanites did in the sacred story ; the Jews had
been commanded to extirpate the natives root
and branch ; they disobeyed the precept. The
Anglo-Normans did the same thing, and in the

course of a few generations degenerated from their
ancient standard, and adopted the manners and
customs of the Celts.   All this seemed an infamy
to their kinsmen in England, who every now and
then pulled them up very sharply and made the
line of demarcation between English and Irish
wider than ever.   Native customs were denounced
as deadly sins, and even the natural bond of a
common faith, and a common baptism into one
church, was powerless to effect any reconciliation
of races.   The Irish "enemy" was to get no
quarter if he did not conform to the Saxon
standard, but the Irish enemy was very numerous,
and " malo assuetus."   It began to wax while the
English element, depleted by intestine feuds,
foreign service, and a Scottish invasion, waned
perceptibly.   The fine farms which the conquerors had seized began to revert to their
ancient owners, and the descendants of Strongbow were cooped up in a corner, which they had
some difficulty in defending.   The Canaanites
were more or less triumphant and the chosen
race was in sore straits, though it still bated little
of its arrogance and tone of superiority.

The absurdity of these pretensions to be
Lords of Ireland, which they were able to ravage
chronically but not to keep, became patent to the

Tudors. of whom the greatest, Queen Elizabeth, may be said to have really brought both the Anglo-Irish and the Celts themselves to submission. This monarch really ruled. She did not hearken to the reports of interested subjects but had several Irish chieftains over to London, and if Her Majesty had had a freer hand the subjugation of the island would have been completed in her reign, but Her Majesty had foes, many abroad and at home, and the Irish question was often left in abeyance from want of time and means.

It was not till the reign of James I. that citizenship was accorded to the Irish, who for nearly five centuries had been the victims of anarchy, tempered by tyranny.

That the analogy of the pretensions of the English and those of the Jews is not altogether fanciful or far-fetched may be seen in the admirable memorandum or " discoverie of the true causes why Ireland was never entirely subdued," &c., by Sir John Davis, " His Majestie's Attorney Generall of Ireland," wherein, after rehearsing the causes which had made the island the land of *Ire*, he indulges a hope that " it will hereafter be as fruitfull as the land of Canaan, the description whereof, in the 8 of

I

Deuteronomic, doth in every part agree with Ireland."

It can hardly be imagined that such a thing as patriotism existed in Ireland at the time of the conquest. Patriotism, such as it is in Ireland, means a sort of ignorant abhorrence of England and her customs, which for the most part is hereditary, but which is kept up to a certain extent by what is called religion, and also by the rankling of some unredressed wrongs ; but in all ages we may be assured that a nation of graziers and cattle and horse rearers felt it to be a very sore and immediate grievance to be forcibly expelled from their ancient and hereditary feeding grounds, and relegated to comparatively bare tracts, where life for man and beast was hard to sustain. Then it was hardly conciliatory to have all the laws and ordinances and customs of one's race denounced as damnable and demoniacal, while the more excellent way was not made accessible. Granting that the Brehon law was not a wise or edifying code, that it made crime common by the facility of expiation, still it was the law of the land, and was more or less a terror to evil doers, and a praise to them that did well, and *pro tanto* useful till a purer and wiser system was introduced. Under the old tribal system every kerne, or clansman, was a joint tenant with his chief of the common stock of land, and shared with the royal family the plenty and prosperity of "the nation," whether in war or peace.

The chief who accepted land under the feudal tenure introduced by De Lacy and Strongbow, was simply a traitor to his race and "nation," as, for his own private aggrandisement, he consented to waive the rights of his subjects and followers of the sept; and the title of the Norman Strongbow and other knights to vast tracts of country acquired by marriage was purely fictitious, and only sustainable by the strong arm—in fact the Irish in Ireland were bound by interest and policy to extirpate the English invaders if possible—

"Conjurata tuas rumpere nuptias
Et regnum Priami vetus."

It is impossible to understand Irish history unless these things are taken into full consideration, but it may be said that the conquest of Ireland delivered the natives from a worse tyranny and a more unsettled existence. This is hard to confirm, and bad as was the *ancien régime* we may be sure it commended itself to the natives—"A tyrant, but our tyrants then were at the least our countrymen," and so it was probably with the Milesian

I 2

Miltiades of the day. To make men outlaws and then expect them to behave like law-abiding citizens and respecters of pacts and treaties, is rather unreasonable; to condemn men to lead a life of squalor in "boolies," and then to blame them for the savageness of their habits and customs, is somewhat inconsistent, and to expect a crop of cardinal virtues when the seed sown is murder, theft, and rapine, is a somewhat hyper-sanguine hope.

The land question was then as now the primary one, and evictions were as little relished in those days as in the present. When Shylock declared that taking away the means of living was much the same thing as taking a life, he stated the case of the Irish. Of course the Lord Lieutenant had to foster the English interest, but to the credit of many, be it said, they recognised the evils of the system, and gave the natives credit for not a few good qualities, cultivated with difficulty in such an uncongenial soil and atmosphere! The words of Sir John Davis, an Englishman, are indeed a signal tribute to the surviving sense of justice among the Celtic Canaanites: "For there is no nation of people under the sunne, that doth love equal and indifferent justice, better than the Irish; or will rest better satisfied with the execution thereof, although it be against themselves; so as they may have the protection and benefit of the law, when uppon just cause they do desire it."

Perhaps the following sketch will illustrate to a certain extent the fearful condition of Ulster even in the comparatively peaceful reign of King James I. Sir Cahir O'Doherty had broken out into rebellion, and had burnt Derry and murdered Sir Amias Paulett. O'Neil was expected at the head of Spanish troops, and in the meantime the rebels and their chief were lurking about the Rock of Kilmacrenan. "The plantation of Ulster had not yet taken place, but already many Scots had settled themselves along the rich alluvial lands that border the Loughs Foyle and Swilly, and it was Sir Cahir's most desired end and aim to extirpate these intruders, hateful as strangers, detestable as heretics. He was the Scotsman's curse and scourge. One of these industrious Scots had settled in the Valley of the Lennon; Rory O'Donnel, the Queen's Earl of Tyrconnel had given him part of that fertile valley, and he there built his bawn. But Sir Cahir, in the midst of night and in Sandy Ramsay's absence, attacked his enclosure, drew off his cattle, slaughtered his wife and children, and left his pleasant homestead a heap of smoking ruins. The Scot, on his return home, saw himself bereaved, left desolate in a foreign land, without property, kindred, or home, nothing but his true gun and dirk. He knew that 500 marks was the reward offered by the Lord Deputy for Sir Cahir's head. He knew that this outlaw was the foe that had quenched the fire on his hearth with the blood of his wife and little ones, and with a head maddened by revenge, with hope resting on the promised reward, he retired to the wooded hills that run parallel to the hill of Doune. There under covert of a rock, his gun resting on the withered branch of a stunted oak, he waited day by day, with all the patience and expectancy of a tiger in its lair. Sir Cahir was a man to be marked in a thousand ; he was the loftiest and proudest in his bearing of any man in the Province of Ulster. His Spanish hat with the heron's plume was too often the terror of his enemies, the rallying point of his friends, not to bespeak the O'Doherty. Even the high breast-work of stone, added to the natural defences of the rock, could not hide the chieftain from observation. On Holy Thursday, as he rested on the eastern face of the rock looking towards the Abbey of Kilmacrenan, expecting a venerable friar to come from this favoured foundation of Columbkill to shrive him and celebrate mass, and as he was chatting to his men beside him, the Scotsman applied the fire to his levelled match-lock, and before the report began to roll its echoes through the woods and hills, the ball passed through Sir Cahir's forehead, and he lay lifeless on the ramparts. His followers were panic struck ; they thought that the rising of the Scotch and English was upon them, and deserting the lifeless body of their leader, they dispersed through the mountains. In the meantime the Scotsman approached the rock ; he saw his foe fall ; he saw his followers flee. He soon severed the head from the body, and wrapping it in his plaid, off he set in the direction of Dublin. He travelled all that day, and at night took shelter in a cabin belonging to one Terence Gallagher, situated at one of the fords of the River Finno. Here Ramsay sought a night's lodging, which Irishmen never refuse ; and partaking of an oaten cake and some sweet milk, he went to rest with Sir Cahir's head under his own as a pillow. The Scotsman slept sound, and Terence was up at break of day. He saw blood oozing out through the plaid that served as his guest's pillow, and suspected all was not right ; so, shifting the tartan plaid, he saw the head and hair of a man. Slowly drawing it out, he recognised the features well known to every man in Tyrconnel. They were Sir Cahir's. Terence knew as well as any man that there was a price set on this very head, a price abundant to make his fortune, a price he now resolved to try and gain. So off Terence started, and the broad Tyrone was almost crossed by O'Gallagher before the Scotchman awoke to resume his journey. The story is still told with triumph through the country, how the Irishman, without the treason, reaped the reward of Sir Cahir's death." The chronicle declares that Sir Cahir was killed in battle by Marshal Wingfield. I have given the tale because it illustrates the age. It is ghastly enough for a transpontine theatre; but it shows how strong the motives for hereditary hatred were, and how legal lawlessness, so to speak, could warp and estrange the best impulses of human nature. Ramsay, finding his eviction a sentence of death to himself, made it one to his spoiler.

CHAPTER V.

"Plus ça change plus c'est toujours la même chose."
FRENCH PROVERB.

1360.

So many of the leading organs of public
opinion—by which periphrasis we mean the daily
and weekly press of London and the provinces—
have so lately advocated in their columns the
experiment of a royal residence in Ireland, and
its tenure for at least a portion of the year by a
royal prince at any rate, if not by the Empire's
heir himself, that it may be well to point out now
that the Viceregal throne has already had for its
occupant more than one royal prince, who apparently wielded the "gladius authoritatis," as the
sword of State was termed, by no means ineffici-
ently. King John seems to have been an active
Lord of Ireland, travelling long distances, and un-
daunted by difficulties on sea or shore. Henry V.
was an Irish Viceroy, or Dominus Hiberniæ, long

before he was King of England. He occupied
part of Trim Castle in his youth— but there is no
need to multiply instances to prove an admitted
historical fact. It is only since the Stuarts came
to the throne of England that Ireland has lacked
the rays of royalty, and been forced to accept
instead the Viceregal sunshine and subdued
splendour! No people in the world were ever
so liable to suffer severely from this protracted
eclipse of royalty, for none are more sensitive to
slights, or more naturally monarchical by education, faith, and instinct; to none does personal
presence and prowess more strongly commend
itself or appeal to national sentiment, and the
fountains of loyal devotion; and Irishmen can
point to history in confirmation of their fidelity to
their sovereigns, shedding their blood like water
for Charles I. and James II., whom, like Mary
Tudor, they held to be their rightful monarch,
while they recall the pregnant fact that the Queen's
life was never attempted in Ireland or by Irishmen,
as it was in England by Englishmen; and that
the Irish press, however viciously virulent against
Viceroys and ministers, never spoke disrespectfully
of Her Majesty, while she herself was almost as
warmly welcomed to the shores of Green Erin
as her uncle George IV. had been. Whether

the experiment would prove operative again, after
the long years of neglect and absence, may be
problematical, but it might be worth a trial. The
Prince of Wales carries popularity with him, and
his Princess is an idol in most parts of Ireland, in
spite of the misleading of the popular mind ; and
the mere fact of Irishmen loyally clinging to their
self-elected chiefs shows how faithful they might
be to their legitimate authorities, if the latter would
but appeal in person to their suppressed sentiment!
It may be that the burden of the general cry
would be "too late, ye come too late ;" but, at
any rate, it may be no harm here to record the
happy results of the government of Ireland by the
Duke of York, who fell in 1449, and whose epitaph,
written in a French doggrel couplet, ran thus—

"En Errlande mist tal gouvernement
Tant le pays vygla paissiblement."

While a contemporary poet thus writes of him,
speaking *in propriâ personâ*—

"And maugre him (Somerset) so choyse, lo! was my chaunce,
Yea tho' the Quene, that all rulde, took his part,
I twice bare rule in Normandy and France,
And Lord Lieutenant in Irelande ; where my hart
Found remedy for every kind of smart :
For thro' the love my doings there did breede
I had their help at all times in my neede."

This Duke of York was followed by Geraldines and Desmonds. The Ormondes adhered to the Lancastrian banner.

Moreover, the Duke of York, who rejoiced so greatly in having gained the love and affection of his Irish subjects, was married to Lady Rose Nevill, daughter of the Earl of Westmoreland, who was popularly known as the "Rose of Raby." She seems to have captivated the Irish by her beauty, charm, and grace, as we read of Brian O'Byrne, chief of his sept in the co. Wicklow, in addition to an offering of 400 beeves, giving her two "hobbies" for her special use. Now a good hobby was often an animal of some value then as now ; for we read of MacMurrough's having paid 400 cows for his, wherewith he bewitched the camp of Richard II. with his noble horsemanship and spear-throwing. The "Rose of Raby" probably contributed considerably to the Duke's success in Ireland, if all Moore wrote about his countrymen be true. She was the mother of Edward IV. and Richard III. The historian tells us "that so beloved was this Duke of York in Ireland that it was reputed in England that the wildest Irishman would, in less than twelve months, be sworn English."

Something like this enthusiasm was shown in

the West of Ireland when H.R.H. the Duke of
Connaught, who was serving in Ireland with his
corps, the Rifle Brigade, spent a week or two in
the co. Galway, the guest of the late Mr. Burton
Persse, of Moyode Castle, for men came from
immense distances merely to get a glimpse of him
at a meet of the county hounds.

In the Lieutenancy of one of the earlier Earls
of Ormonde, a circumstance occurred which will
seem so curious to many readers, and at the same
time illustrates so well the wildness of the wars in
Ireland and the semi-savagery of the septs, not
unmixed with much native kindness and courtesy,
that we give it here in brief. Henry de Crystède
told it to Sir John Froissart, the chronicler, whom
he met at Eltham in the palace of Richard II.,
the conversation originating in his accounting for
his intimate knowledge of the Irish language!
Crystède, it seems, was on a " hosting " with the
Earl of Ormonde, and riding one of his chargers,
a fast galloper, if a bit of a puller; the Irish
having been put to flight, the Ormonde party
pursuing, Crystède's horse ran away with him,
when, presto! an Irish kerne jumped up behind
his saddle, and, without attempting to kill him,
bound his arms, and steered the horse for two
hours from his perch on the croup till they came

to a town or village called "Herpelipin," where
his captor, Brian or Brin Costence, claimed his
captive, treating him well, and giving him his
daughter in marriage! Two girls were born in
the course of seven years. Brin Costence was a
follower of Art MacMurrough, King of Leinster,
and in one of the border frays he took Crystède
with him. Both were taken prisoners by Lionel,
Duke of Clarence, or his captain, and Brin was
only ransomed by the surrender of Crystède's
wife and one child; the other was retained by
the grandfather. Crystède and his family subsequently settled near Bristol. His identity was
established by the recognition of Lord Ormonde's
old charger. This reads like a page in one of
Cooper's Indian romances.

1639.

The character, career, and the personality of
Thomas Wentworth, Earl of Strafford, Baron
Raby, of Wentworth Wodehouse, stands out so
conspicuously among minor men and ministers,
and had such an influence on the destinies of the
kingdom, that they merit something more than the
transient notice we have been able to give it in
summarising the *gesta* and policy of the Viceroys
of Ireland. By Royalist writers he is bracketed

with his master, Charles I., as a martyr! By
Whig and Radical writers he is described as the
foe to freedom and the panderer to privilege and
prerogative, who expiated an evil career on the
scaffold! All sides, however, combine to do
honour to his great talents and powers of organisation, wherein, according to the latter category
of chroniclers, lay his danger to the State and to
freedom. Certain it is that few princes have ever
had so able, so devoted, so zealous a servant and
councillor; few have ever proved so unworthy of
such faithful loyalty and love! Macaulay calls him
an *apostate*, never stating how he had been driven
into the ranks of opposition and "patriotism"
by gross injustice and persecution. On the death
of the Duke of Buckingham the *raison d'être* of
his opposition ceased, and the Court party claimed
him. He was now a peer and privy councillor,
and was next made President of the Northern
Council, where his arbitrary authority soon became
absolute. Retaining this office he was sent over
to Ireland as Lord Deputy, and Carte, the
chronicler, tells us how the Proconsul proceeded
forthwith to his province, landed at " Lousie*
Hill," and rejecting the splendid escort offered
him by Lord Howth and the other nobles of the

* Lazar Hill, probably.

neighbourhood, walked quietly to the Castle,
where he took the oaths, &c., &c. In Dublin
he met an old friend, Miss Rhodes, the *veteris
vestigia flammæ* were rekindled, and he made
her his third wife, being almost the only Deputy
who was married at the Castle, with the exception
of his successors the Earl of Eglinton and Lord
Fortescue. Here Lord Strafford initiated the
social side of Viceregal rule in Dublin with much
state and splendour. The finances of the island
were in hopeless confusion when he arrived ; in a
few years they were comparatively flourishing.
Piracy was swept from the coasts ; the Church
was in wretched want of money and *morale*—
he re-endowed and made it efficient for good.
The customs increased nearly four-fold. The
King had a good standing army of nearly 9,000
men, and there was a balance of £30,000 to the
King's credit in the exchequer. All this was
not done without some despotism and high-
handedness ; but, while he flouted the great and
arrogant, he was very good to the poor, and was
beloved by them. He made hosts of enemies,
and the King his friend betrayed him. He died
with dignity and composure.

According to the Chronicles, Lord Strafford
found out early that the Irish were *not* to be

governed by lenity, but could only be kept in subjection by severity.

It is worth observing that Lord Strafford soared infinitely above the littleness of despising anything *because* it was *Irish.* His own genius could appreciate genius wherever it cropped up, and as the wits say in Ireland, " He never judged the book by its *binding, but by its con·tents."* Therefore, we find Turlough Carolan, said to be the last of the Irish harpists or bards, knew his way to Jigginstown, Strafford's castle in Kildare, where he ever found a warm welcome, as he has himself recorded in a poem, of which the initial stanza runs thus (in translation)—

> " When by sickness or sorrow assail'd,
> To the mansion of Strafford I hied,
> His advice and his cordial ne'er fail'd
> To relieve me, nor e'er was denied."

Carolan could resent rough treatment or inhospitality ; for, like Archilochus, whom *"proprio rabies armavit iambo,"* according to the satirist, he denounced one Mr. O'Flynn, who had been discourteous to him, in a couplet that has survived the erosive centuries—

K

> " What a pity hell's gates were not kept by O'Flynn,
>   So surly a dog would let nobody in."

Probably Strafford encouraged national dances, for we read that James II. was much entertained by a real Irish figure dance (not a jig), in which each partner held the ends of handkerchiefs, showing that kerchiefs had come into vogue since the time of Grace O'Malley or Gran Uaille, that piratical Princess of the West, who appeared at Queen Elizabeth's Court with a bad cold and a primitive fashion of nose-blowing that offended Queen Bess's sense of the τὸ πρέπον so much that she ordered a maid of honour to hand Grace a cambric kerchief. Grace used it, but threw it directly into the fire, and repeated the process several times to the intense amusement of all the fine lords and ladies of the Court.

The feebleness of England on the sea at this period is evidenced by the circumstance that Strafford was detained in Wales for some time by dread of pirates, who actually plundered his servants.

1642.

The great house of Ormonde may be said to have reached its zenith in the person of James, Duke of that ilk, who filled the office of Lord

Lieutenant for thirteen or fourteen years, some of which were so troublous and distracting that loyalty to King and country were anything but synonymous or convertible terms. He was the son of Viscount Thurles, eldest son of Walter, eleventh Earl of Ormonde, and of Elizabeth Poyntz, daughter of Sir John Poyntz, of Acton, in Gloucestershire. Recenter historians and chronologists than Carte (who wrote many volumes, long enough for a life of Methuseleh, about his career), made out that he was born in 1607, and not in 1610, as stated. Archbishop Abbott looked after his early education, but, subsequently to his marriage with Lady Elizabeth Preston, the Earl applied himself to improve a mind that had been left rather fallow. A decided difference with Satrap Strafford, who had issued an order that swords were *not* to be worn at his levée, which Ormonde disobeyed, stating that he was summoned to appear " Cinctus gladio," or " per Cincturam gladii," led to a warm friendship and co-operation in sustaining the Royal prerogative and power in Ireland.

The Irish rebels were obnoxious alike to King and Parliament, and from both powers he received a commission as Lieut.-General for the purpose of stamping out the rebellion, and in the field he was

K 2

very successful against Colonel Preston.   When
it became evident that Ireland was the focus of
fidelity to Royalty, Ormonde was sent there by
the King as Lord Lieutenant, and held office for
three years, surrendering it to the Parliamentary
Commissioners, and retiring to France to watch
events, as he would not go all lengths with
Rinucini and the rebel party.   In 1648 Ormonde
returned to Ireland, but failed in an effort to surprise Dublin.   He had previously joined Rupert
at Kinsale and rallied the shattered Royalist
forces, causing Charles II. to be proclaimed King,
but the Cromwellian advance was irresistible, and
Ormonde, owing to his uncompromising Protes-
tanism, becoming an object of strong suspicion to
the Irish army, again went to France, only to
reappear at the restoration and coronation of
Charles II., when he officiated as Lord High
Steward.   He became subsequently Chancellor
of Oxford, and was presented with a sum of
£30,000, but Carte and his contemporary chroniclers calculate that his loyalty cost him no less
than £900,000 from first to last—a large sum in
those days ; but the Ormonde family was among
the wealthiest in the Peerage of England !   From
1667 till 1685 he for the third time filled the
office of Lord Lieutenant of Ireland, with his

son, Lord Arran, for Deputy. In 1688 he died, and was buried in Westminster Abbey, having maintained through a long life the famous motto of the De Burghs :—

" Ung foi, ung loi, ung roi."

He probably will never be accounted a great strategist or even first-class captain ; but the greatest general, after all, is the man who commits the fewest blunders, and Ormonde steered clear of them for the most part, as well as of " the falsehood of extremes." He must ever rank among the great Viceroys of Ireland ; the most conspicuous tenants of the Castle.

The Ormondes were Princes Palatine of Tipperary. Carte tells us how both the poetaster and publisher of a libel on Ormonde were publicly flogged, " pour encourager les autres."

1649.

In the " Liber Munerum " we find Oliver Cromwell inscribed as Lord Lieutenant of Ireland in 1649, and his task was to defeat the combination of English Royalists and Irish Royalists, and rebels, who refused to acknowledge the supremacy of Parliament ; like Lord Cornwallis, in a somewhat similar emergency, he was invested with dictatorial powers, and history has told us how effectually he wielded them. In less than a year Ireland was subdued, and he was enabled to leave it in the hands of Ireton, to prosecute even greater enterprises in England and Scotland, which he subdued even more completely than Ireland. The history of Cromwell is the history of the greatness and glory of England on land and sea, when

> " the wave,
> Sonorous witness to his Empire gave."

He was certainly the greatest Lord Lieutenant that ever set foot in Ireland—perhaps the most liberal and tolerant. In 1658 we find Henry Cromwell installed at the Castle, General Fleetwood having been the Lord Protector's deputy during part of the interval, and having bated nothing of the pomp and pageantry of his predecessor, Strafford, as we find in a record of his official progress from Dublin to Cork, through Naas and by Jigginstown. " Upon their entering the town of Carlow the four trumpeters, bareheaded, kept sounding, then ten of the men in livery, by two and two. The third the High Sheriff, the fourth the Governor of the town, with his officers, all bare-headed. The Lord Deputy, Mr. Corbet (afterwards Chief Baron Miles

Corbet), Colonel Tomlinson, the Major-General
(the Lord Harry Cromwell), and Colonel Sankey,
were in the coach, and were conducted to the
Castle, when the Sheriff gave them gallant treatment." "Three months afterwards," says Mr.
J. Prendergast, "Henry Cromwell, the Lord
Harry, the rising sun, was received on a 'progress' to Kilkenny, with even greater pomp!"
Four miles from the town of Carlow he was met
by Major Bolton, with Colonel Pretty's regiment,
and a mile further by Colonel Pretty himself, in
his civil capacity as Sheriff, with thirty servants
in rich liveries. In no point did the Cromwells
omit to keep up the splendour of the Castle
festivities. Even to the ancient and not very
Puritanical custom of sending the gentlemen, on
festival days, down to the Castle cellars to broach
such casks as they would, and to drink their fill—
for one, giving the Duke of Ormonde intelligence
in 1663, at the time of the Protestant plot to
seize the Castle and restore the Cromwellian
rule, has the following concerning the Earl of
Kildare.

"Lord Kildare carried the sword before
Henry Cromwell that day Dunkerke was taken,
and that night he in the cellar drank a confusion
to the family of the Stuarts."

The records of Henry Cromwell's brief reign are said to have been consumed by fire ; but there is a general concensus that he was a popular Prorex.

One of the curiosities of the history of Ireland is, that the memory of Cromwell, the tolerant tyrant, is still held in universal execration by the Roman Catholics of the land, while the oligarchical Parliament that imposed and enforced the Penal Code is looked back to with fond (national) remembrance as patriotic and racy of the soil.

1686.

Richard Talbot, Earl of Tyrconnell, may claim this *signalement*—that he was the sole representative of the Catholic Creed who filled the office of Viceroy, or held its symbol, "gladium authoritatis," since the Restoration, as Oliver Cromwell and his son Henry were the only Independents who ever acted as Lords Lieutenants. Since the Revolution of 1688, and the Act of Settlement then made, the office has only been tenable by a Protestant, though such Protestant need not necessarily be an Episcopalian or of the churches of England or Ireland, witness its tenure by the Earl of Aberdeen.

James II. had, to paraphrase a common expression, "abjured the errors of Protestantism, and embraced those of Rome," but he greatly miscalculated his own powers of persuasion, or enforcement of the Royal wishes by stronger measures, as well as the ductility of the English nation, if he seriously considered that he could draw them like a flock of sheep, as Henry VIII. had done in his day. The zeal of convert or pervert is generally great, and King James spared no pains or energy in his campaign of propagandism, with its sequences, penalties, and premiums. The faithful were to fill the high places, the recusants to be removed. With this view he selected Tyrconnell to carry out his royal behests in Ireland, where his pliant but still Protestant brother-in-law, Lord Clarendon, had displaced the Duke of Ormonde in the Lieutenancy, while Tyrconnell filled the office of Commander-in-Chief, with all the substance of power, of which Clarendon retained but the shadow or semblance, but even this shadow was obnoxious to Tyrconnell, who had the poor protesting Protestant removed from his path.

Something of what Strafford did for Charles I. Tyrconnell attempted to do for James, and in a few months' time. Nor is there any historical doubt about his movements or measures, for if Macaulay's picture of Dick Talbot be somewhat black, Lingard confirms his statements to a great extent.

The colonists, planters, and undertakers now learnt practically that there was a reverse side to " Protestant ascendancy," and that Popish ascendancy, well plied, was a powerful political factor. One thousand five hundred families were said to have left Ireland in a single week. Tyrconnell was a tyrant, and did his spiriting well, and without much scruple. The Army was made Catholic— the Bench very nearly. Fitton, said to be a forger, was made Chancellor ; Tom Nugent, Chief Justice of the Queen's Bench ; Nagle was Attorney-General ; Keatinge, who filled the Common Pleas was, 'tis true, a Protestant, but his two assessors were of the Catholic faith ; and Spring Rice presided over the Exchequer, the Court most used, as from it there was no appeal to England. The Corporations were made to send in their charters by writs of "quo warranto," and new ones were granted, in which the faithful were predominant ; in fact, Church, State, and Army were Catholicised, so far as offices and employments went. But for all that, victory was not on the side of the big battalions, even with

French auxiliaries and the countenance of the
Grand Monarque. French authorities impugned
Irish valour, but undisciplined levies under
moderate captains are seldom efficacious, and
France and Spain had ere long good reason to
change their tone, when they learnt the stuff the
Irish Brigade was made of; the same sort of
soldiers who had erst gained name and fame in
France, under English leaders, of one of whom
it is recorded that when a valiant Gaul challenged
any Englishman to fight him in single combat, an
Irishman stept forth, swam across the harbour,
and brought back the champion's head; and thus
was a Gallic Goliath overcome by a Celtic Kerne
—if records can be relied on.

The events of the campaigns that found their
close in the capitulation of Limerick need no re-
capitulation.

Tyrconnell was, it would seem, no general or
strategist; in opposition to Sarsfield, he held
with Lauzun that Limerick was indefensible.
We know the gallant stand made there, and its
results. Tyrconnell, after this, disappears from
history, from the Viceregal scene at any rate.
He had the merit of "thoroughness," if few
others. Macaulay has gibbeted him as an un-
paralleled liar, and braggart too, for he throws

doubt on the story of the pearl necklace, a sort
of companion to the more famous diamond necklace legend of the de Rohan family. It is said
that, after the Battle of the Boyne, King James
spurred hard to Dublin Castle with an escort of
Irish cavalry, whom he outstripped, arriving first
at the Castle. "How hard your countrymen
ride," he remarked to the lovely Lady Tyrconnell,
who came out to receive him, "Yes, Sire," was
the ready reply, "but you seem to have beaten
them hollow."

1695.

The Earldom of Essex gave the Commonwealth
of England many good representatives in Church
and State. There was a halo of romance and
chivalrous devotion to king and country in the
Devereux family, which, if it did not tend to great
personal prosperity, raises several of the tenants
of this title far above "the common people of the
Peerage," and identifies them with the history of
our Empire which they did their *devoir* in creating
and maintaining. When that noble family became
extinct the title passed to the Capells, of Suffolk
originally, and next of Hertfordshire, who seem to
have been masterful people, of strong convictions,

to which they clung courageously, even to the
scaffold. Two Capells were Lords Lieutenant of
Ireland, one from 1672 to 1677, the other was in
office in 1696. Their reigns were more remarkable for domestic or urban improvements than for
martial exploits or sensational achievements. But
that even the more peaceable and commercial
portions of the island had not yet settled down in
the ways of law and order is proved by the fact
that in the year 1671 there was a pitched battle in
the city of Dublin, between the apprentices and
the authorities, the former having undertaken to
destroy a wooden bridge not far from the Castle ;
which, though metamorphosed now into stone,
still bears the name of " Bloody," in commemora-
tion of this fray, in which several perished. It
was in this reign that Essex Gate (Dublin) was
erected on the site of Izod's tower, and that the
foundations of Essex bridge, since renamed
" Grattan bridge," were laid.

That Lord Essex was very solicitous to advance
the material interests of his Kingdom is evidenced
by his request to Sir Richard Temple to make a
report on the " means and ways he esteemed most
proper for the advancing of trade in Ireland."
This report, which is drawn at considerable length,
shows that Sir Richard Temple had formed a very

just estimate of the enormous capability of
Ireland and its soil if properly developed and
husbanded.   At this moment we can only make
an extract about his views as to the horse-breed-
ing capacities of Ireland, because the question of
cavalry remounts has lately occupied a large share
of public attention, and that something of a panic
has been created by the proclamation of a possible
or probable horse famine, and also because it
shows that a statesman and man of letters, as Sir
Richard Temple proved himself to be (he was
Swift's patron), can combine literature and art with
a due appreciation of the value of the noble
animal, and the place he should occupy in a well
regulated state.   " Horses in Ireland are a drug,"
he writes, " but might be improved to a com-
modity, not only by a greater use at home,
but also fit for exportation into other countries.
The soil is of a sweet and plentiful grass, which
will raise a large breed ; and the hills, especially
near the sea coasts, are hard and rough, and
so fit to give them shape and breadth and sound
feet.   The present defects in them are breeding
without choice of stallions, either in shape or size,
and trusting so far to the gentleness of the
climate as to winter them abroad, without ever
handling colts till they are four years old.

This both checks the growth of the common breeds and gives them an incurable shyness, which is the general vice of Irish horses, and is hardly ever seen in Flanders, because the hardship of the winters in those parts forces the breeders there to house and handle their colts for at least six months every year. In the studs of persons of quality in Ireland, where care is taken and cost is not spared, we see horses bred of excellent shape and vigour and size, so as to reach great prices at home, and encourage strangers to find the market here, among whom I met with one this summer that came over on that errand, and bought about twenty horses to carry over into the French army, from twenty to three score pounds price at the first hand.

"The improvement of horses here may be made by a standard prescribed to all stallions, and all horses that shall be used for draught; the main point being to make the common breed larger, for then, whether they have shape or no, they have ever some reasonable price both at home and abroad; and besides being not to be raised without wintering, they will help to force men into improvement of land by a necessity of fodder. But for encouragement of a finer breed, and in the better hands, some other

institutions may be invented, by which emulation
may be raised among the breeders by a prospect
both of particular honour and profit to those who
succeed best, and of good ordinary gains and
ready vent to such as by aiming at the best,
though they fail, yet go beyond the common
sorts.

"To this purpose there may be set up both a
horse-fair, and races to be held at a certain time
every year for the space of a week; the first
in the fairest Green near the city of Dublin,
the latter in that place designed by your
Lordship in the Park for some such purpose.
During this week the Monday, Wednesday,
and Friday may be the races; the Tuesday,
Thursday, and Saturday the fairs may be held.
At each race may be two plates given by the
King, one of £30, and the other of £20 (besides
the fashion), as the prizes for the first and second
horses, the first engraven with a horse crowned
with a crown; the second with a coronet, and
under it the day of the month and the year.
Besides these plates the wagers may be as the
persons please among themselves, but the horses
must be evidenced by good testimonies to have
been bred in Ireland. Furthermore, the Lord
Lieutenant may even be present himself, or at

least name a deputy in his room, and two judges
of the field, who shall decide all controversies,
and with sound of the trumpet declare the two
victors. The masters of these two horses may be
admitted to ride from the field to the Castle
with the Lord Lieutenant, or his deputy, and to
dine with him that day, and there receive all
the honour of the table. This to be done what
quality soever the persons are of, for the lower
that is, the more will be the honour and perhaps
the more the sport, and the encouragement of
breeding will by that means extend to all sorts of
men.

" In the fairs the Lord Lieutenant may likewise
be present every day in the height of them, by
himself or deputy, and may, with the advice of the
two chief officers of the Army then present, chuse
out one of the best horses and two of the best
geldings that appear in the fair, not under four,
nor above seven years old, for which shall be
paid to the owners of them, after sufficient testimony of their being bred in Ireland, one hundred
pounds for the horse and fifty pounds apiece for
the geldings. These sums, as that for the plates,
to issue out of the revenue of Ireland, and without
trouble or fee, and the three horses to be sent
over every year to the King's stables.

L.

" Both those that win the plate and those which are thus sold, ought immediately to be marked, so as they may never return a second time, either to the race or to the sale. The benefit by such an institution as this will be very great and various, for besides the encouragement to breed the best horses, from the honour and gain already mentioned, there will be a sort of public entertainment for one whole week, during which the Lord Lieutenant, the Lord Mayor of the city, and the great officers, both civil and military, ought to keep open tables for all strangers. This will draw a confluence of people from all parts of the country. Many, perhaps, from the nearer parts of England may come, not only as to a public kind of solemnity, but as to a great mart of the best horses. This will enrich the city by the expense of such a concourse, and the country by the sale of many horses into England, and in turn (or from thence) into foreign parts.

" This will make personal acquaintances among the gentry of the kingdom, and bring the Lord Lieutenant to be more personally known and more honoured by his appearing in more greatness and with more solemnity than usual upon these occasions—and all this with the expense only of two hundred and fifty pounds a year to the Crown, for which the King shall have the three best horses sold that year in Ireland."

This counsel of Sir Richard Temple has a true statesmanlike ring about it, as might be expected in a man so eminent, who was, moreover, the ancestor of a statesman *ejusdem farinæ*, Lord Palmerston, who commended himself to his countrymen by his courage and common sense, and who, moreover, was of a most "philhippic" turn, practically as well as theoretically. If Sir Richard Temple's spirit could have been transplanted for one hour or two to the premises allocated at Balls' Bridge to horses and horse culture, by the Royal Dublin Society—the oldest, by the way, in the kingdom of its kind (it was incorporated by charter in 1750), on any one of the four days in the last week of August, when the annual horse show is held—he would witness the realisation of his ideas and conceptions on a magnificent scale. He would see delegates and representatives from all parts of the world where horses are held in honour, collected together to witness more than a thousand hunters in *esse* and *posse*, with a few hacks, paraded in all their paces, and critically as well as scientifically judged. He would see the Lord Lieutenant of the time being with, perhaps, some of the royalties of the kingdom visiting the

L 2

show every day, and such an array of rank,
wealth, beauty, and fashion as no similar function
in the kingdom can congregate; and lastly, he
would see a number of thoroughbred sires collected together and examined as to soundness and
symmetry, prior to their distribution among the
farmers of the country, to encourage them to
breed horses on scientific rather than haphazard
methods. In a word, he would see the embodi-
ment or fulfilment of his aspirations.

1707.

Lord Pembroke was another Lord Lieutenant
who, without any claims to greatness, was a man
of some slight mark among the Viceroys, and
his literary eminence, superior probably to his
greatness as a Governor, is attested by his having
been elected a member of the French Academy
("the Immortals"), and having had the honour
of receiving the dedication by Locke of his
treatise on "The Human Understanding."

Swift and His Excellency seem to have been
great allies, and the Dean remarked that "he
first hit Lord Pembroke with a pun." Dr.
Delany, as quoted by Foster, relates how "the
Vicar of Laracor found the Viceroy listening to a

lecture from a learned physician on the valuable
qualities of bees, which in every other sentence he
called a commonwealth or a nation. ' Yes,' inter-
posed Swift, 'no doubt, and very ancient ; Moses
numbers the *Hivites* among the nations Joshua
was appointed to conquer.' Pembroke was de-
lighted, and punning became his great enjoyment
after that day." Within the last decade we, too,
have heard of apiculture, blackberry wine, tobacco
culture, and sericulture advocated as among the
panaceas for Paddy Land.

1724.

Lord Carteret, afterwards Lord Granville, was
among the ablest public servants who held the
Sword of State in Ireland. Though living in
comparatively peaceful times, it was not his lot to
gain the benediction, or rather beatitude, of the
Roman philosopher. " Beatos equidem puto
quibus deorum munere aut agenda scribere aut
scribenda agere, beatissimos autem quibus
utrumque contigerit." Even Horace Walpole, his
political opponent, styles him the ablest among
contemporary statesmen ; and, like his successor
in the Lord Lieutenancy, the Marquis Wellesley,
he never gave up the charms and cultivation of

scholarship. Of his punnings with Dean Swift, Foster has left us some good examples, and it is recorded that when Swift was in trouble about the Drapier's letters, he went to see Lord Carteret at the Castle, and having been kept "making anti-chamber," as the French put it, for an unconscion-able time, he lost patience, and wrote with his diamond ring on one of the panes of glass—

> "My very good Lord 'tis a very hard task
> For a man to wait here who has nothing to ask."

Lord Carteret, coming in soon after the Dean's departure, saw the couplet, and wrote under it—

> "My very good Dean there are few who come here
> But have something to ask and something to fear."

On the fall of Sir Robert Walpole, "the Grand Corrupter," he was made Prime Minister of England.

Lord Carteret was a special favourite of George I., as he was the only minister who could talk with him in German. He was twice Lord Lieutenant, and afterwards Prime Minister.

1745.

Among the universally lauded and lamented Lord Lieutenants in Ireland, no name suggests

itself with more spontaneity, so to speak, than
that of Philip Dormer, fourth Earl of Chesterfield,
though his reign was too short for great results,
or even for the fruition of the harvest, whose
seeds he had scattered on the good soil of his
satrapy. It was Chesterfield's privilege, in an
age of venality and corruption, to have had clear
hands and a clean conscience. He was not, perhaps, a great statesman, and war he never essayed,
but we know that he proved an able diplomatist ;
and it was, perhaps, owing to his exceedingly
clever conduct of contemporary affairs in Ireland
that the advent of the Pretender in the '45
created, perhaps, rather less excitement in a most
excitable island, than the more recent manœuvres
of the Mahdi, who in the Press and on the platform did not lack a strong body of sympathisers.
Lord Chesterfield was very much in advance of
his age in the spirit of toleration, as well as in the
infusion of the maxims and principles of common
sense into politics. He was, with that mythic
power of whom the Roman lyrist tells us, a
welcome guest at celestial banquets, and also—

" Gratus et imis,"

for to them he was considerate and kind—in a
word, *a gentleman.* An able Irish writer talks of

him "as holding the balance even between the
Catholics and Protestants, protecting the establishment, yet never wounding religious liberty;
repressing lawlessness, yet never chilling the
affections of a turbulent but warm-hearted people;
the arbiter, but not the slave of parties;" yet he
held office in the plenitude of the penal period.
Lord Chesterfield was born in 1695 and found
his way early to Cambridge, where he became a
devotee to classical lore and literature, skilled in
the ancients. St. German's, a borough that
perhaps gave Lord St. Germans his title,
found him a seat in Parliament, where he soon
showed that he did not mean to be a "muta
persona" or mere "candle - snuffer," for he
always held that speech-making, not less than
shoemaking, were arts acquirable *by all*, maintaining that only thirty members hearkened *to
reason*, while the rest were "*people*." He sat for
Lostwithiel in 1726, was sent as minister to the
Hague, and got the Garter for his services. We
next find him perorating as a patriot against
privilege, and his argument that by our constitution "the King could do no wrong, while he could
do any amount of good," was ingenious. He
spoke very ably against the proposal that the
King should be allowed to levy troops without his

Parliament, on the freedom of the stage, on the presence of pensioners in Parliament, on the standing army of 18,000, on Hanoverian soldiers being introduced into England, and so on. Neither Mr. Gladstone nor Mr. Shaw-Lefevre could have enunciated more " patriotic " sentiments than he did. For instance, talking of a statesman, he remarked, " I shall never advise him to pursue any measure that is contrary to the sentiments of the majority of his subjects. A free people must be treated like a fine woman. If she has now and then a little caprice, you must not flatly contradict her ; you must give way, or at least seem to give way, to her humour, till by good treatment and a delicate opposition you find an opportunity to give a turn to her temper. This is the only way by which you can clap a padlock upon her mind, and this, in my opinion, is the only padlock in which there is any security. A free people must be treated in the same manner, for if you do not clap the padlock upon their mind, you must govern them by force, which puts an end *to their freedom* and, in my opinion, *to your security*." Able, too, were his denunciations of *gin* as a medium of revenue (though the Bishops voted in its favour), and of perpetuating the penalties of treason, being very strong in his invective against *delatores* or informers, and the traducers of "the Bonny Traitor," alias the traitor who would *cut up* well! He married a natural daughter of George I., Melusina de Schulenberg, but his only family seems to have been by Madame du Bouchet, the mother of that son to whom he devoted his life and letters. He was nominated Plenipotentiary to the Hague and Lord Lieutenant of Ireland at the same time, and addressing the Parliament of Ireland with reference to the Roman Catholics, spoke of their "speculative errors as only deserving pity if their pernicious influence upon civil society did not require and authorise restraint." His first passion was to excel—αἰέν ἀριστεύειν καὶ ὑπερέκον ἔμμεναι ἄλλων— next to please, in which he greatly succeeded. His speeches, if a trifle didactic, like Bulwer Lytton's, were very argumentative and forcible. His essays in " the World " of that day would, we fancy, be welcomed in "the World" of this, though rather cynical and slightly Sallustian in tone. His Viceregal style was splendid, and he found the income very liberal, as he speaks of that place being one of much more pleasure and profit than that of Secretary of State. He beautified the Phœnix Park greatly, where the Chesterfield column and the fine avenue of secular elms attest his good taste. No poet, he could write good verses. Thus, in his advice to a lady in autumn, is the couplet—

"The dews of the evening most carefully shun,
The tears of the sky for the loss of the sun."

Dr. Johnson, whose stern criticism of the famous letters is well known, succumbed to the grace and graciousness of Lord Chesterfield's manner. In those libelled letters are γνῶμαι that will live long, perhaps as long as Rochefoucalt's—such as when *apropos* of foolish customs, he said, " Diogenes, the cynic, was a wise man for despising them, but a fool for showing it." " Be wiser than other people if you can, but do not tell them so." In spite of a milk diet contributed by an ass, a cow, and a goat, he died in 1773. His son predeceased him in 1756. He had seen him an M.P. and Minister to Dresden. His Lordship held London the best place to live in and to die in, or the most convenient, rather; like Archilaus, he held human nature to be invariably the same everywhere.

1767

Sir Nathaniel Wraxall, a chronicler of courts and courtiers, confirms what we have said about

Lord Townsend's comparative political impotence, which was shared by nearly all the Viceroys of Ireland henceforward.

"He was a nobleman of very considerable ability, but of great eccentricity of manners and character, which seemed sometimes to approach almost to alienation of mind. Cheerful in his disposition, void of all pride or affectation, communicative, affable, convivial, facetious, and endowed with uncommon powers of conversation, he was formed to acquire popularity. He eminently possessed the dangerous talent of drawing caricatures, a faculty which he did not always restrain within the limits of severe prudence, though he no more spared himself than he did others. It is well known that he drew his own portrait, habited in the state dress of a Lord Lieutenant, having his hands tied behind him, in order to show *how destitute he was of political* power, or of the means of conferring favours. This allegorical picture, I have been assured, was hung up in a private cabinet of the Castle at Dublin, and when solicited to bestow offices or rewards, over which he had no control, he used to conduct the importunate suitor into the room, at the same time asking him if he recognised the likeness and understood the application. In

Ireland, while administering the affairs of that
kingdom during five years, he gave general satis-
faction, and I remember Courtenay eulogising him
in the House of Commons in the language which
Horace uses to Augustus :—

> " 'Longas, O Utinam, Dux bone, Ferias
> Præstes Hiberniæ ; dicimus integro
> Sicci mane Die, dicimus uvidi,
> Cum Sol oceano subest.'

" Indeed, not one of the Viceroys sent over to
Dublin in the course of twelve years, between
1772 and 1784 could compete with Lord Townsend in the affection of the Irish. Lord Harcourt
was too grave and measured in his manners.
The Earl of Buckinghamshire had too cold, stiff,
and lofty a deportment. Lord Carlisle was too
fine a gentleman, *and too highly bred ;* the Duke
of Portland and Earl Temple, both, either from
disinclination, or from physical inability, observed
too rigorously the virtues of temperance and
abstemiousness, virtues by no means congenial to
the soil ; lastly, Lord Northington was too infirm
in his health to acquire general attachment in a
country where no qualities, however meritorious,
could recommend to national approbation, unless
accompanied by personal sacrifices and exertions

of various kinds. The Duke of Rutland, whom
Pitt sent over to the sister kingdom, early in 1784,
by the magnificence of his establishment, the
conviviality of his temper, *and the excesses of his
table*, in all of which particulars he resembled his
father, the Marquis of Granby, obliterated or
superseded Lord Townsend in their regard; but
he paid for the triumph with his life, falling a
victim, within four years, to his irregularities."

They entertained handsomely in Dublin in those
days. Witness the following account drawn from
the same reservoir as the last, of Sir John Irwine,
who held during several years the post of Commander-in-Chief in Ireland, with very ample
appointments and advantages, a post now held by
General H.S.H. Prince Edward of Saxe Weimar
with reduced pay and allowances.

" But, no income, however large, could suffice for
his expenses, which, being never restrained within
any reasonable limits, finally involved him in
irretrievable difficulties. The fact will hardly
obtain belief, that at one of the entertainments
which he gave to the Lord Lieutenant in the year
1781 at Dublin, he displayed on the table, as the
principal piece in the dessert, a representation of
the fortress of Gibraltar invested by the Spanish
forces, executed in confectionery. It exhibited

a faithful view of that celebrated rock, so dear
to the English nation, together with the works,
batteries, and artillery of the besiegers, which
threw sugar plums against the walls.   The
expense of this ostentatious piece of magnificence
did not fall short of £1,500, and so incredible
must the circumstance appear, that if I had not
received the assurance of it from Lord Sackville I
should not venture to repeat it in these memoirs."

The end of Sir John was ruin and exile, but it
is refreshing to read that the king was very good
to him in his low estate, and did not forget his
widow and orphans.

1782.

The Dutch House of Bentinck, which, after the
revolution, became naturalised in England and
well endowed by a grateful monarch with " lands,
tenements, and hereditaments," naturally gave
many soldiers and statesmen to his service.
Among the first was William H. L. Bentinck,
who begun his official life under the Marquis of
Rockingham (the only marquis of England at the
time it is said).   His honesty of purpose was
probably greatly in excess of his administrative
talents, for we read in Lecky's famous chapters on

Ireland, that when Lord Lieutenant in 1782, just after the Act of Emancipation, he was very urgent on the adjustment of the trade treaty between the two islands, suggesting that if this were not done, it might be better for England to abandon Ireland, thereby showing that his gift of prescience and forecast was very small. However, this Duke of Portland was ever a pillar of the State, for he was the prime minister of North and Fox's coalition government, and was made Chancellor of Oxford University. He subsequently took office under Addington. The Duke was an early advocate of a union between the two kingdoms.

1782.

Lord Temple seems to have been a thoroughly honest Viceroy, to have taken a good measure of the forces at work in Ireland, and to have advocated a policy loyal to the independence of the country ; hence he supported Flood's " Renunciation Act." In his reign the Order of the Knights of St. Patrick was instituted. He was Viceroy under Lord Shelburne, afterwards Marquis of Lansdowne.

1783.

Lord Northington's Viceroyalty was short, and rather uneventful ; the strides made in the Volunteer movement being its chief feature.

1784.

The Duke of Rutland's reign lasted for some three years, and was, on the whole, one of great prosperity. Foster's Press Bill, more coercive than anything in modern times, curbed the *effrenata audacia* of the newspapers, who had indirectly, perhaps directly, incited to crime. The Duke, who was a *bon vivant*, succumbed to fever, and Lord Temple, now Duke of Buckingham,

1787,

was again made Lord Lieutenant. The Duke of Rutland learnt by practical experience how careful a Viceroy must be in his goings-in and goings-out, for at the theatre " the gods " showed they were no respecters of rank. " When was the Duke at Pegg Plunkett's ? " exclaimed one supernal from one side of the house. " Manners, ye dog ! " was the antistrophe from the other. Now, " Manners "

M

was his own name, and that of a famous beauty
not unappreciated by His Excellency was Peg
Plunkett.

1787.

The Duke of Buckingham's reign was one
of peace and prosperity, though the Regency
question caused tension, relieved, however, by the
King's recovery.   The Duke of Buckingham was
not a popular Viceroy, though a most conscientious
one.   To him is due the breaking through of the
prescription by which a Chancellor for Ireland was
always imported from England. His appointee was
the able and eloquent Fitzgibbon, Earl of Clare.
Apropos of the Duke of Rutland, who seems to
have been a very merry monarch, it should be
added that one of his convivial crazes was to
knight some *bon camarade*, or survivor of the
fittest, in the small hours of the morning, with his
Sword of State, or its representative.   On one
occasion he was making a south-eastern tour in
Ireland, and happened to stay at Marlfield, the
residence of the Bagwell family, large landed
proprietors in the County of Tipperary, and the
owners of the greater part of its capital, Clonmel.
While staying here he was invited to some public
dinner, to which came all sorts and conditions of

men; amongst them a gentleman named Murphy (or whom we shall name Murphy, as it is more or less a "generic" name). This guest "had made his head" early in life, and could appropriately join in the song—

> "For still I think
> That I can drink
> With man that wears a hood, sir!"

and towards morning few were left in the fierce (liquor) fray save His Excellency, Mr. Murphy, and some seasoned casks on whom liquor had as much effect as water on a duck's back. The Duke admired him greatly for his "staying powers," and insisted on giving him the knightly accolade then and there. Morning brings reflection, and it occurred to His Excellency that he had knighted a subject who could hardly be described as chivalrous. So he sent for him, told him to consider the whole thing a foolish frolic; and seeing that Murphy hesitated, offered him a handsome douceur "to be off." But the latter replied readily, "I thank your Excellency very much; I do not care for titles myself; but the fact is, I told LADY Murphy of the honour you bestowed upon me, and for that reason *we* cannot forego it."

M 2

The Duke was by no means a water drinker, or "hydropot," to use the current slang, but they gave his name to a pump near the Royal Barracks, which has lately been disestablished and demolished. The Duchess of Rutland is said to have been a great beauty.

1795.

One of the most sensational scenes in the great Irish drama—a drama in which tragedy and comedy so constantly alternated—took place in 1795. The following rough outline of the situation will give some idea of the events that led up to the appointment of Lord Fitzwilliam as Lord Lieutenant of Ireland in that year. The Parliamentary wedge that separated parties in the English and Irish Houses of Parliament was the Catholic question, and its solution, whether by absolute or modified emancipation from the fetters that bound the many members of this religious denomination socially, financially, and politically. To a great extent, the bringing forward of this question at all was a declaration of war à *outrance* with the oligarchical system that obtained generally ; but this was chiefly felt in Dublin, where Protestant ascendancy was not only a spirited

slogan and rallying cry, but was also a source of
wealth and power to the fortunate few who probably conceived that the very examination of such
a question was as heterodoxical as the defamation
of Diana by a peripatetic preacher named Paul
seemed to the Ephesian silversmiths and shrine-
makers! However, the prophets of Emancipation
had great names on their side—amongst them
those of Pitt, the Duke of Portland, Lord Fitzwilliam, Lord Spencer, Edmund Burke, William
Wyndham, Grattan, the Ponsonbys (George and
William), Sir H. Langrishe, Sir John Parnell,
with many more. The inflexibles mainly relied
on the immense influence of Lord Clare and John
Beresford. Lord Clare was the great and eloquent
Fitzgibbon, the Irish Chancellor, Mr. Beresford
was the second or third son (Burke says second)
of Lord Tyrone, who had married the heiress of
the Powers, or De la Poers of Curraghmore, in
the co. Waterford, and was raised to the peerage
of Tyrone, which his wife's family had long represented. His grandfather had come over in the
reign of James I., as the Manager of the Corporation of Londoners, known by the name of the
Society of the New Plantation in Ulster; and
having a keen eye for advancement, or personal
progress, like many of his clever, enterprising

race, laid the foundations for the future fortunes
of his family, to whom Church and State alike
yielded rich revenues.   John Beresford, barrister-
at-law, was appointed in 1770 a Commissioner of
the Revenue in Ireland, and presided for many
years at the Board.   In two years he added to
this function the patent office of Taster of the
Wines in the Port of Dublin ; but whether by
conspicuous ability, dint of hard work, and well
directed industry, or by the extension of his personal and family influence, certain it is that his
civic greatness became, in many eyes, overweening ; and it was popularly said at the time that
Dublin was " a Beresford village."   His second
marriage to Miss Montgomery, of Magpie Hill,
N.B., increased vastly the number of his powerful
connections, and, in fact, John Beresford was
a power in Ireland who had to be reckoned with,
not *une quantité négligeable* by any means.

With a view of extending Catholic conciliation
Lord Fitzwilliam was sent over by Pitt to Ireland
as Lord Lieutenant; and what his exact powers
and instructions from the Prime Minister were is
not known, and probably never will be precisely
laid down : but we *do* know that Lord Fitzwilliam
received the warmest welcome on landing in
Ireland, and the national enthusiasm was kindled

to great heat. Almost his first official act was to break up what Burke called "the Junto," by dismissing Beresford and the law officers. "Surtout pas trop de zèle," was a motto not yet in common currency, perhaps not even coined—if Talleyrand was its real author. Certainly it was not adopted by the new Viceroy; and Pitt was so worked upon by the King's Protestant proclivities, and perhaps by Beresford's friends and supporters, that Lord Fitzwilliam was, in official parlance, commanded to execute the happy despatch by immediate resignation; upon which, Lord Clare, Foster, the Speaker, and the Primate, were appointed Lord Justices. Mr. Beresford, too, was reinstated in his office, and all the Catholic hopes and aspirations were dashed to the ground. It would be too long to dwell here on the demonstrations of unfeigned sorrow that marked the 25th of March in Dublin and its suburbs. All business was suspended, and a procession miles in length escorted the Earl to the place of embarkation for England; leading citizens yoking themselves to his carriage, and drawing it to the seashore! A national funeral to buried hope! Plowden tells us of an address on the subject from the Students of Dublin University to Grattan; to which the patriot replied, in the

stilted phrase of the period, commencing : " In-
genuous young men, for this effusion of the heart,
I owe you more than ordinary gratitude."

Thus far have we advanced into the bowels of
this great quarrel ; the curious sequel remains to
be told as briefly as may be.   Lord Fitzwilliam
had, it seems, printed for private circulation
certain vindications, or *pièces justificatives* of his
official career of a few weeks.   The reflections on
Mr. Beresford's character contained in the sentence : " because he was a person under universal
and heavy suspicions, subject to the opprobrium
and unpopularity attendant on maladministration
and much imputed malversation," led to a challenge from the inculpated officer of Revenue, to
which Lord Fitzwilliam replied thus :

" Sunday Morning, 28th June, 1795.
" (Delivered by Lord George Cavendish.)

" Sir,—I have the honour to announce to you
my presence in town.   As I could not mis-
understand the object of your letter, I have
only to signify that I am ready to attend your
call, and have the honour to be, Sir,
              " Your most obedient servant,
                  " WENTWORTH FITZWILLIAM."

Lord George Cavendish was Lord Fitzwilliam's second, Sir George Montgomery Mr. Beresford's in the absence of Lord Townshend, who was unable to come in time, and the ground was actually paced—a field beyond Paddington—when a magistrate intervened, and the duel was prevented. Lord Fitzwilliam subsequently apologised, and hands were shaken. It will be recollected that Sir John Perrot long ago had offered to decide matters with Desmond by the *duello*, which the latter declined. A few years later the Duke of Wellington fought Lord Winchelsea, and Canning and Castlereagh exchanged shots—these were the palmy days of duelling!

1795.

Lord Cornwallis' predecessor in office was Lord Camden, who had a very difficult part to play in leading up to the Union. He was the son of the famous legist who was raised to the peerage. His son gained a further step in the ladder of honour and dignities, for he was made a marquis. He was also given the Garter in recognition of his Irish services. Wraxall tells us how George III., when he learned that the

name of his new knight was to be John Jeffreys,
seemed half to repent the appointment, adding
that he had never given the accolade to any one
with such a name!

1798.

Charles Mann, the first Marquis Cornwallis, if
not one of England's greatest men in war or
statesmanship, stands very high on her list of
worthies as one whose predominant idea in life
coincided with that of the great Duke of Wellington, "how best to carry on the King's Government" (by-the-bye, it is something of a coincidence
that Wellington and Cornwallis each commanded
the 33rd regiment). Junius in his day made some
strictures on the brightness and vigour of Cornwallis' intellectual capacity; no one ever questioned
his integrity of purpose, his honour, or sincerity.
Like Sir Charles Metcalfe, who at the urgent
request of the Premier and Colonial Secretary of
the day, accepted the government, first of Jamaica
and then of Canada, at a time when he knew that
he was stricken by a malady from which recovery
was more than doubtful, he was always ready to
go to the post of danger and duty at the shortest
notice; and his unselfish acceptance, for the third

time, of the post of Governor-General of India,
when he might well have said, like the worn-out
gladiator, Veianuis, cited by Horace—

"Non eadem est ætas, non mens,"

and pleaded like him for a well earned rest, was
but a sample of the spirit that animated him
through a long and busy career, spent in the
service of the State.

Lord Cornwallis had, as we all know, his
brilliant successes and his dark reverses in his
American service ; but in India his progress was
one of victory, and thoroughly appreciated by his
countrymen and the East India Company ; but it is
as the Commander-in-Chief and Lord Lieutenant of
Ireland in very troublous times that we are just
now interested in Lord Cornwallis ; and it is in a
great measure due to the far-reaching wisdom of
men of his stamp, who could temper firmness with
humanity, and rise above the fury of faction, that
we owe that "auspicium melioris ævi," which,
though tardy in its coming, still makes sensible
progress ; and here Lord Cornwallis may be
bracketed with such master minds as Lords
Wellesley and Chesterfield (or Sidney before
them), who lent a deaf ear to the cuckoo cry,

"Can any good thing come out of Gallilee?"
and could descry merit even in an Irishman whose
faith did not quite conform to their own. "It is
said that your Lordship employs a Catholic coach-
man," wrote, according to tradition, or it may be
history, some great functionary in England to the
latter nobleman. "Well, what does it matter,"
was the reply, "so long as he does not drive me
to mass!" And something of the same spirit and
temper was in Lord Cornwallis at a period when
sects and factions were nearly as bitter and violent
as were those of the ill-fated Jews (from whom
some hold the Irish are sprung) at the memorable
siege of Jerusalem by Titus.

The danger that underlay the rebellion of
1798, which Lord Cornwallis was sent to quell as
Lord Lieutenant and Commander-in-Chief, was
that no one could precisely gauge its extent or
proportions, or say when the many men tainted
with disloyalty, and just then "sitting on the
fence," as a good many were, would think it
opportune to join the malcontents ; and then there
was the constant danger of French invasion when
the occasion offered. General Moore's successes
in Wexford, however, saved the Government
from present peril, and when it came to dealing
with the prisoners, Lord Cornwallis' combination

of great firmness with humanitarian principles proved most conspicuous. "*Catholicism*" had been generally substituted for "*Jacobinism*," and all his Excellency's efforts were now directed to mitigate the "odium theologicum," for, as he wrote to General Ross : "The violence of our friends and their folly in endeavouring to make it a religious war, added to the ferocity of our troops, *who delight in murder*, most powerfully counteract all plans of conciliation." His task was not an enviable one, or even satisfactory, as he tells us—"The life of a Lord Lieutenant in Ireland comes up to my idea of perfect misery, but if I can accomplish the great object of consolidating the British Empire I shall be sufficiently repaid." His opinion of the Irish Militia was not favourable : "They are totally without discipline, contemptible before the enemy, when any serious resistance is made to them, but ferocious and cruel in the extreme when any poor wretches, either with or without arms, come within their power; in short, murder appears to be their favourite pastime ;" in fact, like Abercromby, he held this force to be only formidable to their friends.

Like Pitt, he held the Union to be salvation to Ireland, as we find him writing confidentially

to General Ross: " People's minds are getting
cooler, and I have no doubt of their being
sufficiently manageable for all ordinary purposes,
but I do not know how they will be brought to
act on the great measure of all, on the event of
which the safety of Great Britain and Ireland so
much depends." The action of the Longford
and the Kilkenny Militia at Castlebar confirmed
Lord Cornwallis' diagnosis to the letter.   But
with the able co-operation of General Lake the
Castlebar calamity was soon effaced by the
capture of the entire French force, whose movements seem to have been singularly badly
planned by Humbert, who was most reckless of
life, unless indeed he was deceived in his expectations of Irish aid.

Early in the autumn Mr. Pelham resigned the
Chief Secretaryship, and the place was given to
Lord Castlereagh, a man who had quickly won the
complete confidence of Lord Cornwallis—by-the-
bye, Lord Castlereagh's appointment seems to
have been an innovation on the unwritten law
that prescribed that an Englishman only should
fill this important position.   Lord Cornwallis'
next year was spent in efforts to educate the
public mind towards the Union, but the more
violent of the victorious party were strenuously

opposed to him "as an object of disgust and abhorrence," at least in the opinion of Dr. Duigenan, their spokesman. According to the latter, Lord Cornwallis himself, through the odium he had acquired, was a bar to the Union by his very advocacy of it. Meanwhile, the Viceroy writes to General Ross: "How I long to *kick* those whom my public duty obliges me to court; if I did not hope to get out of this country I should most earnestly pray for immediate death." Death soon afterwards very nearly came to his rescue, as he was fired at by a sentry who challenged him and got no reply. The Union, after a long struggle, was at length carried in spite of the menace of civil war, and so convinced was Colonel Maitland of his Excellency's political foresight, that he wrote to Mr. Huskisson: "If his plans be hereafter steadily followed, Ireland will be a jewel—if changed, a thorn in the British Empire." Words somewhat prophetic! Here is Lord Cornwallis' opinion of the Act of Union: "This country could not be saved without the Union, but you must not take it for granted that it will be saved by it." After the passing of the measure came the apportionment of rewards. His Excellency was, he said, offered a dukedom, but declined it. One of Lord Cornwallis' last

despatches was to plead for clemency towards
Mr. Napper Tandy. His work being finished,
the Viceroy longed impatiently for what he styled
his release, but there was difficulty in finding a
successor for some time. He at last appeared
in the person of the Earl of Hardwicke, in
whose favour Lord Cornwallis retired for a
few days to the Lodge in the park to wind
up his business. At his recommendation Lord
Clanricarde was appointed " Master of Kilmainham," which implied the command of the forces
in Ireland.

It is a matter of history how all Lord Corn
wallis' hopes for the Union proving an entrance
gate to the penetralia of the Constitution for
the Catholics were frustrated. The general
opinion attributes the failure of pledges and pro-
mises to the inveteracy of His Majesty's obstinacy,
and danger to the stability of his mind by or
in urging Catholic claims. By some historians
Mr. Pitt's sincerity in the matter is questioned,
but there seems no valid reason for coming to
an unfavourable conclusion. No one, however,
can doubt Lord Cornwallis' candour and honesty
in the matter, and his correspondence confirms
this opinion.

1800.

To the Earl of Hardwicke was entrusted the
charge of the Province created by Pitt through
the Act of Union and incorporation.　He was
young and eminently handsome, with considerable
charm of manner and some felicity of expression,
and one of the acts of his earlier life seemed to
give some assurance that bigotry and intolerance
were foreign to his nature, for when in command
of his regiment of Militia (the Cambridgeshire)
in England, he had issued an order prohibiting
his men from joining the Orange Society, which
had its propagandists and missionaries in all
directions, with the view of creating a gigantic
and overwhelmingly irresistible association both
in Church and State.

Abbott, who was afterwards Speaker, and
raised to the Peerage as Baron Colchester, was
his Chief Secretary, and there was a general hope
cherished that even-handed justice and clemency
would tend to obliterate the horrors and atrocities
committed freely on both sides in the late rebellion,
for the Loyalists were triumphant and victorious
—the Catholics quelled and subdued, while their
aristocracy and leaders of position, though zealous
for emancipation from the fetters imposed upon

N

them by the victors, were very loyal to the Crown, and the bulk of the population followed them with an almost unreasoning fidelity. General Abercrombie's famous dictum, too, was freely quoted, namely, that the state and conduct of the Irish were just what the Government chose to make them—a dictum that threw a great weight of responsibility on the ruling powers. Lord Hardwicke, however, did not "train on," to use a racing metaphor. The Yeomanry were in high favour, and the Yeomanry were almost to a man "Orange." Banquets were exchanged between the Castle and the corps. Majors Sirr and Sandys were powers paramount at the Castle, and the notorious "Jemmy O'Brien," who had earned public execration by his "delations," was in full favour, till he was presently caught red-handed in a murder, and his great "public" services could not save him from the gallows— an execution most grateful to the masses, who attended it, not in their thousands but their hundreds of thousands. Meanwhile, Lord Clare, whose power had waned much since the Union, died from the effects of a fall from his horse. Mr. Abbott was made Speaker of the House of Commons, to be succeeded by Sir Evan Nepean, while the crack-brained conspiracy of Colonel

Despard in London showed the restless impatience of the public mind in England. In Ireland things tended no nearer towards a reconciliation and fusion of creeds and classes. Fifty thousand Protestant Yeomanry were anything but a despicable force, and whereas in the elder times the cry was against the *Irish enemy*, it was now raised against the *Catholic enemy*, and as *English* ascendancy was once the slogan of Loyalists, it now became changed to *Protestant* ascendancy! There was, too, an uneasy apprehension abroad that the *salus republicæ* required the crushing of Catholicism, because, it was argued, if a rebellion in three counties shook the fabric of the State to its foundations, what would be the issue if this rebellion became universal? So, as the poet puts it, "Timor addidit alas" to the intolerance and bigotry of a dominant and victorious oligarchy; nor did Lord Hardwicke smooth down suspicious anxieties on the part of the proscribed when it was found that, though he could put a curb on Giffard, he could also promote to a very lucrative post in the Excise Sir Richard Musgrave, who had not spared the Catholics in his history of Irish rebellions. Nor was the reputation for frugality of his government increased when a

N 2

new office was created, the Mastership of the
Rolls—a post which had hitherto been honorary,
and lately filled by Lords Glandore and Carysfort.
Then, too, the vindictive but abortive prosecution
of two judges, Fox and Johnson, by the Marquis
of Abercorn, to a certain extent discredited the
Government.

On the 23rd of July, 1803, and at 10 o'clock
at night, Emmett's "rebellion," which had been
hatching somewhat overtly for many months previously in Dublin, where warlike stores and
munitions for a campaign and siege had been
collected within the city, apparently without the
knowledge of the city police, broke out, and Lord
Kilwarden, his nephew Mr. Wolf, Colonel Brown,
and a few more, were brutally murdered, but
when it came to attacking the Castle, the rebels
shrank, and the rebellion collapsed ignominiously,
Emmett and his handsomely - uniformed staff
having to fly to the Wicklow Mountains. Lord
Hardwicke seems to have been endowed with
even a superfluity of spirit ; for though he heard
that the Lodge was to be attacked by a co-
operating party of conspirators from Kildare, he
drove out to dine there, escorted by only a
sergeant and twelve dragoons, though Marsden,
the Under-Secretary, sent a strong party out later

on, acting on his information. Emmett was soon
after taken, tried, and executed, his last speech
and dying declaration being an eloquent enuncia-
tion of the highest treason.

As an illustration of the lavish expenditure of
the Government of the day, it may be mentioned that the Yeomanry expenses amounted
to £100,000 *a month*. To a certain extent they
policed Ireland; and it is said that when Sir
Robert Peel introduced his Constabulary the
Yeomen formed the nucleus of the force, and
possibly led to its initial disfavour with "the
people." Certainly, in Lord Hardwicke's time,
the condition of Ireland could not be termed
satisfactory in any sense. The Emmet *rebellion*,
or riot, is said to have cost General Fox his
command in Ireland and Dublin. He was succeeded by Lord Cathcart. Motions for enquiry
into the condition of things were made by Sir
John Wrottesley and Mr. Hutchinson, who proposed that the Prince of Wales should go over
with a deputation, to judge for himself, and report
what he saw. Nor is the general public perhaps
aware that His Royal Highness constantly pleaded
with his father to be allowed to *work* in the State,
and not to be a mere hanger on. He recalled to
His Majesty that he was the oldest Colonel of

Dragoons in the Army, but got no further, while his younger brother, the Duke of York, was at the head of the Army. Sidney Smith declares that the characteristic of the modern sermon is *Decent debility*. Addington's government expired of the same complaint ; and then it became necessary for Pitt to return to the helm ; but Pitt was no longer *qualis erat*, and his power went with his energy. Lord Hardwicke deserves credit for opposing Pitt's attempt to increase the semi-sinecure office of Mr. Barrington from £800 to £2,500 a-year. Lord Hardwicke, a great stickler for etiquette, was not a popular Prorex ; and when Pitt died, and the Grenville Ministry came in, his departure did not cause much general regret. His successor was the Duke of Bedford, whom he received, then retired to the Pigeon House Fort, and returned to England, his long reign having extended over a very critical and important period in Ireland's history. One of his last acts was to reverse Mr. Rowan Hamilton's outlawry. The present Marchioness of Dufferin and Ava is the granddaughter of that gentleman.

Lord Hardwicke had secured for himself the reversion of the Clerkship of the Common Pleas, a sinecure of some £16,000 a-year.

1806.

When the Duke of Bedford accepted the Lord Lieutenancy of Ireland, he found Orangeism and Protestant Ascendancy *in excelsis*. The Orangemen were actually far more Orange than their great head, who was really, in many respects, most liberal. Thus, at Limerick he offered the garrison representing Catholic Ireland the free exercise of their religion, half the churches in the kingdom, and a moiety of their ancient estates; a proposal which the Orangemen would probably have scouted in 1807. A Russell is almost a Radical or an advanced Whig, *par droit de naissance*, and the first indication of his views by the new Viceroy was the dismissal of Sir John Mitford (afterwards created Lord Redesdale), the Chancellor, who had strong opinions on the other side, while he refilled the vacancy by the very liberally minded George Ponsonby. However, there is an old distich that declares that—

"As bees on flowers alighting cease to hum,
So Whigs when once in office soon grow dumb,"

or words to that effect; and there was a certain amount of disillusion in the public mind when they found the routine of the Castle system little changed. Curran, it is true, got the Mastership of the Rolls, though clogged with conditions, and hardly a congenial post, at best, to the great orator, wit, and patriot ; but the Verners were taught that the Law is no respecter of creeds (in Bedford's hands, at any rate), and the magistracy was weeded and reformed. The Excise and Customs were divided, and some thirty-eight sinecures were abolished.

The result of the debate on the Catholic Officers' Bill was a heavy blow to that interest ; and to illustrate the harshness of the system, it is mentioned that when Mr. Bryan, of Jenkinstown, co. Kilkenny, a Catholic, who was in the Foot Guards, being anxious to serve on the Staff of his friend, General Archer, in Dublin, applied for permission to do so, in the regular way, he was peremptorily refused ; and, on a second application, was gazetted out of the Service. The Duke of Bedford was liked in Ireland greatly for his good intentions, rather than actual performance, and when he was replaced by the Duke of Richmond, he was drawn to the place of embarkation by his enthusiastic admirers.

1807.

The Duke of Richmond, who succeeded His
Grace of Bedford, was the nominee of the
Portland-Percival Government, and may therefore
be supposed to have taken his colour, or political
complexion, from that anti-Catholic combination,
or coalition, but to his credit, be it said, he evinced
bigotry nowhere, and some of his sentiments and
enunciations might have been put into the mouth
of his predecessor, or even of Fitzwilliam, the
chosen champion of the Catholic cause. For
instance, when at Cork (on his Munster tour),
the toast of Protestant Ascendancy was given.
His Excellency declared that the only ascendancy
he wished to see flourish in his dominions was
the Ascendancy of Loyalty—brave words, but
hardly carried out in practice by "the system" of
which he was an integral part. At his accession,
or, to speak more correctly, on his arrival, he
found two great questions in occupation of the
public mind. One was the Catholic claims, more
especially in connection with the veto on the
appointment of their Bishops, claimed by the
British Government, and the state of the Prisons,
which was simply scandalous, and very different from what it is now—even for first class

misdemeanants, whose constitutions must have been wonderfully strong to have survived the treatment for any length of time. Sandy's Prevost, in the Castle Yard, and Trevor's cells, are said to have gained a bad pre-eminence among these jails. Sir Arthur Wellesley, who had managed to push on his Police Bill, was the nominal Chief Secretary to the Lord Lieutenant, but he was absent at the Convention of Cintra, already perhaps meditating the famous lines of Torres Vedras for his great base in the campaigns that so soon followed. So great was the avowed corruption in the House of Commons, that when a member—Mr. Maddox—brought charges of bribery against Lord Castlereagh and Mr. Quintin Dick, even the Opposition showed themselves most lukewarm in their condemnation of an offence so common and so venial, though venal. Then, too, as in the present Session of Parliament, tithes were a very burning question; for their incidence was fearfully unequal—the rich grazing tracts held by the gentry and middlemen being declared exempt, while the burden fell on the tilth of the small farmer, or cotter, who, to paraphrase Shakespeare, "No revenue had save his strong labour."

Then the balances allowed (corruptly) to lie

perdu (the word was sometimes prophetic) in the hands of well backed collectors of taxes and revenue, were nearly double those of England, and when a commission of enquiry was granted on the occasion of Mr. Beaucham Hill being appointed to a lucrative post in the Revenue, he confessed that when an Excise officer he had levied a tribute of 20 guineas from every still in his "walk;" while of 30 officers examined on this occasion 27 acknowledged that they were *Bribees*, driven to it by the smallness of their salaries. A writer of some repute sets down the robbery to the revenue at between one and two millions a year. Nor did the House seem much surprised at these revelations. A Government place must have been a fair berth in those days.

In his Munster tour, or "Progress" (to use a term of more Viceregal sound), the Duke of Richmond seems to have cultivated a tone of liberal impartiality; thus he was the guest at Limerick of a Catholic banker, Mr. Roche, whom he offered to knight, but Mr. Roche declined the honour. The Duke of Portland's resignation led soon to changes in the ministerial departments. Castlereagh and Canning, who had quarrelled and fought, were, for the time being, in a sort of quarantine; three Irishmen were added to its strength, namely the Marquis of Wellesley, Wellesley Pole, and William Croker, the rather eminent writer, who, the son of a Revenue officer in Ireland, had been educated at Port-arlington, and became a Protagonist in the Tory ranks.

We have thus had a few glimpses of the Duke of Richmond, who remained at the Castle till 1810 in his official capacity, and, as it were, in his robes of state, proclaiming " Tros Tyriusque mihi nullo discrimine agetur." Contemporary chroniclers maintain that he had a very jovial side, as the following excerpt from a county history, printed for private circulation only, will show.

" Lord de Blaquiere had been Secretary of State from the year 1772 to 1777, from which period, though he ceased to hold any employment, he enjoyed the confidence of the government, and was extensively engaged and employed in bringing about the Union, for which, besides various offices and pensions, he obtained his peerage. He purchased Portlomon, being part of the Pakenham property.

"Although having ceased to hold any Government situation, he by no means wished to relinquish his intimacy with the Castle, and continued to supply his Excellency with the choicest and most exquisite fruits from his hothouses. Upon several occasions he invited the Viceregal party to pay him a visit, but always without success, until at some period between 1807 and 1810 the Duke of Richmond, then Lord Lieutenant, very unexpectedly intimated his intention to accept an invitation to Portlomon, being extremely anxious to witness an Irish 'Pattern,' for which at that period Lough Owel was celebrated, and which Pattern was annually held on the first Sunday in August in the demesne of Portlomon. It is needless to say a word about the convivial habits of his Grace. The results were in many instances highly amusing, although they at times departed considerably from the dignity of a Court. At an advanced period of the night he has been known to confer the honour of knighthood for service performed, and to promote a humble clergyman to a rich deanery after a very protracted discussion of spiritual matters. On his Excellency's intention being made known to Lord de Blaquiere, he endeavoured to ascertain from some of the A.D.C.'s the probable duration of his Grace's sojourn at Portlomon, which was fixed, whether by authority or not, to extend two or three days. Lord de Blaquiere immediately made such preparations as the shortness of the period

would admit of, and furnished the cellar with what
he conceived would be an ample supply for the
duration of the visit which his Excellency proposed
paying. A hogshead of claret, and four dozen of
madeira, port, and sherry, all of the best quality and
finest vintage, were immediately forwarded and
stored in the cellars of Portlomon. His Excellency and staff arrived, comprising the usual number
of A.D.C.'s—a mischievous, reckless, and jolly set.
Sir Arthur Wellesley, afterwards Field Marshal
Duke of Wellington, was then Secretary of State.
Amongst other gentlemen of the county who were
invited to meet his Excellency was Admiral
Pakenham, from whom I heard the story. The
company next day was numerous, the wine excellent and plenty, the cooking varied and superior,
being the production of the Soyer of the day, the
fruit rare and delicately flavoured. His Excellency during the morning transacted his official
business and visited the different localities in the
neighbourhood. The fourth day arrived, and no
intimation of a break up. The claret was visibly
decreasing from the united efforts of the party.
The other wines were diminishing from the
exertions of the household. At the period of which
we write the intercourse between the country
and the city was not even as expeditious as at

present. Even now, with all our improvements, it is by no means certain when we arrive at the end of our journey, as persons leaving Mullingar at half-past seven in the evening by the railway to attend a ball in Dublin, do not arrive at the beautiful terminus in that city until half-past six next morning. An insurmountable difficulty therefore arose in procuring additional supplies of wine if required. Lord de Blaquiere was in a most woeful predicament. He therefore, in a fatal moment, and as a last resource, resolved to take Admiral Pakenham into his counsel and obtain his advice and assistance. He was no sooner made acquainted with the unfortunate state of the garrison than he gave the Lord a promise of a speedy relief from the exhausting party. This was too good a joke for the Admiral to keep it secret, and immediately communicated the entire to the Duke of Richmond, who instantly agreed not to budge one step. Every morning Lord de Blaquiere and the Admiral held a cabinet council, and the remaining stores were examined. It now became too late to get things from Dublin, and there were only two days' supply in the house. The next day being Saturday, his Excellency expressed his regret at being obliged to leave on Monday after seeing the 'Pattern.' The day of the Pattern arrived. His Excellency and his friends enlivened the scene with their presence, and at the accustomed hour sat down to dinner. Everything went on as usual, and late in the evening, but long before the Lord Lieutenant's usual hour for retiring, the circulation of the bottle became tedious, and ultimately entirely ceased. The dreadful truth must be told—the claret was out! His Grace affected considerable surprise, but told his host he would rather prefer some port. The household had unfortunately had the last bottle. Well! Sherry or madeira? All gone! Under such unexpected misfortunes, the Lord Lieutenant *really* preferred whiskey punch. But, alas! not a drop in the house. What was to be done? His Grace, in all horror of sobriety, appeared indignant at such unheard of treatment. The host was for a time speechless, and could not suggest anything. A supply from Mullingar was reported as too tedious, uncertain, and not drinkable if procured. The unfeeling and cutting remarks of the A.D.C.'s were insupportable. The regret and apologies of the host were neither received nor felt. His Excellency declared he could not stir without a supply of something ; he cared not what, but without it he should be ill. The Admiral, I suppose, by way of assisting his friend, said, 'Oh, sooner than your Excellency should incur a fit of illness, we'll sell by auction some of the fellow's furniture and send to Bunbrusna for whiskey. The devil pity him. He should not ask people here without the means of entertaining them!' This proposal was loudly cheered, but a difficulty still existed ; where shall we find bidders ? It was suggested that if any of the people that they saw at the Pattern were still there, they would be rejoiced at the opportunity of procuring bargains. Very few moments sufficed to assemble a number of bidders to constitute an auction. Some of the beds and other pieces of furniture were brought out before the hall door, and on a fine summer's night. The Admiral acted as auctioneer, under the superintendence of the Government ; the Chief Secretary as clerk. The terms were money down, for which a supply of ardent spirits was procured from the village of Bunbrusna. The company returned to bed highly pleased (with the exception of the host) with the last night ever passed by a Viceregal party at Port lomon."

Let me add that Portlomon has long since those days passed into the hands of the Greville Nugent family, whose hospitable head, Lord Greville of

o

Clonhugh, has a far less easily exhaustible cellar
at the opposite side of that inland sea, Lough
Owell.   It seems hard to understand how the
train from Mullingar to Dublin could be a whole
livelong night compassing some fifty miles!
Under Sir Ralph Cusack's improved management,
and metals, the journey now occupies not very
much more than an hour by the express trains
of the Midland and Great Western Railway.

1813.

To the Duke of Richmond succeeded Earl
Whitworth, a nobleman of sound judgment and
most varied accomplishments.   He had been
employed in several diplomatic missions, and
while at Paris had foiled Napoleon in his attempt
to brow-beat him in the *Salle des Ambassadeurs.*
In Ireland his reign was much troubled by distur-
bance and agitation, the result of the tithe collec-
tion, which was made sometimes with hardship,
while its incidence was unfair, the poorer tenants
being more severely mulcted than the wealthier
sheep and cattle farmers.   The peasant soldiers
in this campaign against tithe were known as
"Caravats" and "Shanavests," while in the
King's County the opponents of the system

adopted the abominable practice of "carding."
Hence it was necessary to renew the Insurrection
Act, and proclaim certain counties, as in the
present day. Meanwhile, the agitation for complete
Catholic emancipation was proceeding, but with
somewhat slow and irregular steps, though young
Counsellor O'Connell, who brought a combination
of Celtic energy and Celtic subtlety and considerable elocution and histrionic ability to bear
on the great question in which he himself had a
strong personal interest, was certain to accelerate
the movement, of which the cautious, courteous,
and most moderate Earl of Fingall had hitherto
been the fugleman. It was in Lord Whitworth's
time that the famous duel between O'Connell and
Mr. D'Esterre was fought at Bishopscourt, now
the residence of the Earl of Clonmell, but at that
time the property of Lord Ponsonby. The
Corporation of Dublin was then a very close
borough, and Mr. D'Esterre belonged to it.
O'Connell was never very guarded or self-
restrained in his choice of language (indeed, it
may be doubted whether he would ever have
acquired and retained his firm grasp of the
popular mind had his vocabulary been more select
and refined). He characterised the Corporation
of Dublin as "beggarly;" he refused to disavow

O 2

or qualify the language when called on to do
so by Mr. D'Esterre, and the consequence was
a hostile meeting, in which Mr. O'Connell's friend
was Major Macnamara, while Mr. D'Esterre's
second was Sir Edward Stanley. Mr. D'Esterre
fired first and missed his mark ; O'Connell's bullet
passed through his opponent's thigh, and the
wound proved mortal, for he died the next day,
the 3rd of February, 1815. Some chroniclers
relate that while arrangements were being made,
Mr. D'Esterre threw an orange in the air and hit
it with his pistol bullet, a proceeding properly
reprobated by Major Macnamara, who looked
upon it as a sort of intimidation ; but the story is
improbable in itself, and lacks all contemporary
confirmation. Mr. Greville in his valuable
" Memoirs," however, tells us that when O'Connell's party were driving back to Dublin they met
a party of dragoons coming along the road towards Bishopscourt. They had been sent by the
authorities, it adds, to protect D'Esterre in the
event of his killing his adversary, for it was
assumed that D'Esterre was sure to come off the
conqueror, and it was feared the country people
might commit some outrage or assault on the
overthrower of their idol.

Lord Whitworth's tenure of the Viceregal

office was saddened by a great domestic calamity
—the death of his popular young stepson, the
Duke of Dorset. The latter had been living in
Ireland for about a year and a half, and went on
a visit to Powerscourt, whose owner was his
friend, and had been his schoolfellow. According
to the "Annual Register," His Grace, accompanied by Lord Powerscourt and Mr. Wingfield,
joined some harriers who were drawing for a hare
round Killiney, a rough rocky district, full of big
boulders, where the fields were divided by rough
stone walls of irregular construction. In a run
that followed, the Duke jumped a small wall, but
the mare he was riding landed among some rocks
and fell, and in the struggle His Grace was badly
squeezed among the stones, and died an hour
after the fall, before Surgeons Crampton (afterwards the famous Sir Philip) and Macklin, who
had been summoned to attend by Lord Powerscourt, could arrive. The event cast a great
gloom over Dublin, as well as its Court and
Castle; for the Duke was only 22 at his death.
A monument of granite (the stone of the place)
was raised to his memory on the fatal spot,
and the following lines, believed to be the
composition of Baron Smith, were sculptured
upon it :—

When the Temple of Freedom by Liberty founded
   Was reared by her mandate on Britain's proud shore.
The ark of her glory our fathers surrounded,
   And enshrined in their bosoms the laws they adore.
'Twas then from the good, from the brave, were selected
   The nobles of England to pillar the shrine,
And bright from each column of her fane were reflected
   The rays of truth, honour, and freedom divine !
But mourn now, Britannia ! one column of thy glory
   Has fallen in the pride of its beauty and power,
While weeping Hibernia repeats the sad story,
   Responsively wailing the ill-fated hour !
'Tis not o'er the statesman or conqueror's urn,
   Nor yet for the chief who in battle has bled
No, 'tis not for these that the muse bids thee mourn—
   Oh, no ! but, alas ! 'tis thy Dorset is dead !
For his were endowments to claim admiration,
   High courage, pure honour, nobility, truth ;
Let the requiem of sorrow resound o'er the nation,
   For Dorset has fall'n in the pride of his youth !
Ah, never did Nature with proud emulation
   A heart with more virtue more honour adorn ;
And the bright rays of splendour that shone from high
     station
   Were the faintest of beams that illum'd his young morn.
Too early, alas ! has this bright promise faded,
   Too soon are we called to bewail his sad doom ;
While his relics with wreaths emblematic are shaded,
   The tears of his country shall fall on his tomb.
But be hush'd the loud plaint, and still'd the sad numbers
   Awake not the anguish a parent must feel,

As she mournfully bends where his cold form slumbers,
　　With grief more emphatic than words can reveal!
Be hallowed that grief, and be sacred the tear
　　That falls from a heart overcharged with woe;
Let the soul's warmest sympathy ever revere
　　The drops which the heart of a mother o'erflow.
May hope's brilliant lustre, dispelling dejection,
　　With time's lenient hand every sorrow remove;
And this truth cheer the heart of maternal affection,
　　Kindred virtues on earth are united above.

We trust his "law" was better than his poetry.

The following lines on the same sad theme are attributed to Lord Whitworth :—

Useless are all these trappings of the great
To him who sleeps in death, nor heeds their state;
To him who, lying in yon tower, alone,
Sees not the mother's tears nor hears the mother's moan;
Nor hears those mournful tones that sadly peal
Like the low murmurs of an evening gale:
Now straining into louder notes of grief,
Then soothing soft to give the heart relief.
These, may be, speak our sorrow. Can an ear,
Catching at angel choirs, such dull notes hear?
No! If a sound can reach him to yon skies,
'Tis the sad throbbing of a mother's sighs
That from a sorrowing bosom faintly break,
Heave her full heart and moisten her wan cheek.
Bright shone his morning—promising his days—
As Phœbus, glittering in meridian blaze.

Pure was his life, and affable, tho' great.
When Heav'n, in pity viewing mortal fate,
Quick as the lightning, by one fatal blow,
Snatch'd him in mercy from this vale of woe.

One of the Duke's ancestors had been twice
Viceroy of Ireland ; once in 1831, and the second
time in 1851. " Sackville Street " and " Dorset
Street," in Dublin, are memorials of this Viceroyalty ; the former, which has been styled by a
few patriots O'Connell Street, was originally
Drogheda Street, called from the Moore family,
then Earls, now Marquises of Drogheda. Some
say, however, that it was named Sackville, from
Sackville Gardiner. Lord Spencer, while hunting
with the Ward hounds one day, during his second
tenure of office, had rather a narrow escape of
being ridden on, and perhaps badly injured, by a
hard-riding horse-trainer, who probably could not
control the impetuosity of his young hunter, in
his eagerness to get over the fence after his predecessor—or *presaltator.* " I missed you, my
Lord," said the penitent pursuer, when apologising
to his Excellency afterwards, " by just the *black
of my nail.*"

The following extracts from contemporary
journals illustrate the formal entry of a Lord
Lieutenant into his dominions in 1773 :—

" Yesterday the great guns were sent from the Castle, to George's Key, to salute his Grace the Duke of Dorset on his landing here, which is expected to be Friday or Saturday next."—" Dublin Evg. Post, Sept. 11th, 1733."

" Yesterday arriv'd here from England, his Grace Lionel Cranfield, Duke of Dorset, Lord Lieut. and Gen. Gov. of this Kingdom ; his Grace has brought over with him, her Grace the Dutchess, the Rt. Hon. the Earl of Middlesex, the Rt. Hon. Lord John Sackville, two of his Sons, and the Rt. Hon. the Lady Carolina his only Daughter. They were received about 3 O'Clock at George's-key, by their Excellencies the Lords Justices, and several of the Lords and Nobility, from whence they were conducted by the Company of Battle-axes, a Regiment of Horse, and the High Sheriffs and Commons of this City, on Horseback to the Castle. The Rt. Hon. the Lord Mayor, Aldermen, and Recorder, as usual, received them at the upper End of Lazers-Hill, and deliver'd to his Grace the Keys of the City, at which time the Recorder made him an excellent Speech. After he arrived at the Castle, he went to his Grace the Lord Primate's to Dinner.

" There landed at the same time, the Hon.

Col. Ligonier, and George Bub-Doddington, Esq.,
Clerk of the Pells."—" Dub. Evg. Post, Sept.
18th, 1733."

1821.

Few phenomena are much more remarkable
in history than the manner in which hybrid
Hibernians, or Anglo-Irish, have moulded the
destinies of England. Lord Castlereagh is a
conspicuous instance of this plastic power, for
he was, for a time, the man endowed with the
largest share of political power not only in
England and the United Kingdom, but also in
Europe. Canning's meteoric career was cut
short by a premature death, but perhaps the
Colley-Wellesley family is the best instance that
can be adduced of a patrician *gens* that has made
itself as inseparable from the warp and woof of
our insular history as any of the great houses
that contributed to the supremacy of Rome.
Like Sir William Petty, the founder of the Lansdowne fortune and greatness, the ancestor of the
Colley family was a Surveyor-General or Land
Commissioner (to use the phrase in modern
vogue), and presently we find Sir Henry Colley of
Castle Carberry, in the co. Kildare, seneschal of

the King's County, and an army contractor, a circumstance which the Iron Duke perhaps forgot when he was so hard upon the contracting race in the Peninsula. Of Carberry Castle the gaunt ruins still remain, massive in their masonry. We hear little of these Colleys. They must have had a hard and exciting life on these marches, when the borderers were not unlike those of whom Sir Walter Scott wrote—

> "Let nobles fight for fame,
>   Let vassals follow where they lead,
>   But war's the Borderer's game."

A Miss Elizabeth Colley married Garrett Wesley, or Wellesley, of Dangan, co. Meath, and on his death *sine prole*, Richard Colley his cousin inherited the Meath property and took the name of Wellesley. He sat for the borough of Trim, where the statue of his descendant, Arthur Wellesley, *the* Duke of Wellington, is very conspicuous. He was raised to the peerage as Baron Mornington, and his eldest son subsequently became Earl of Mornington. He was a well known musical composer, and no less than four of his five sons had their names inscribed in the Libro D'oro of England. "Our affair" as the French idiom goes, however, is with Viscount

Wellesley, who rose to be Marquis Wellesley, one of the most famous Governor-Generals of India, " who doubled the revenue and more than doubled the dominion of the old East India Company." The tide of war carried out to the East his brother, Colonel Arthur Wellesley, whose career in India, unfortunate in its first essay, is one of the most brilliant illustrations of our military history.

Lord Wellesley, an autocrat by nature, never quite remembered that his younger brother, Arthur, was at least a co-partner in his fame, for to the last it is said he treated him with the superciliousness engendered by the presumed prestige of primogeniture, as well as by the consciousness of his own great gifts of intellect and beauty of feature if not of form, for he could hold his own even with such a sublime and scintillating scholar as Canning. With such qualifications it will be readily understood that the Marquis was through life " Richard le bien-aimé," but though twice married he left no son. As a Viceroy he proved rather a brilliant failure than a shining success. " Ce n'est que le premier pas qui coûte " was well illustrated in his first turn of Viceroyalty, for he misconstrued the throwing of a bottle into his

box at the theatre in Dublin into an attempt on
his life ; and the loss of dignity and prestige was
the natural consequence of his prosecution
breaking down, to the joy of the Orangemen, who
chorussed, "by Eldon" (the Lord Chancellor)
"'twas well done." He was again appointed
Lord Lieutenant in 1833, but though his views
were liberally statesmanlike, and even conciliatory,
he failed in conciliation. The autocratic satrapy
of an Oriental Empire was not a good school
for a constitutional Viceroyalty. However, Lord
Wellesley met a famine crisis ably, and maintained
law and order ; in the Peninsula he did good
service.

In the brief sketches we have presented of
Lord Wellesley's government of Ireland as Lord
Lieutenant, from which so much was anticipated
that the actual results seemed to contemporaries
somewhat disappointing, we tried to impress upon
the reader that the autocratic nature of the man
had been accentuated and intensified, so to speak,
by his tenure of power in India for so long a
period, at a time when the Governor-General of
our Eastern Empire, untrammelled by the modern
resources of science—fast lines of steamers and the
electric wire—was in many respects a more absolute sovereign than the Grand Monarque himself.

To descend from such a satrapy to the government of an island like Ireland must have appeared like undertaking an Ædileship at Rome after having filled a Proconsulship; a fall from a Grand Vizier-ship to a petty Pashalik; from having to write despatches about kings and kingdoms, to a chronicle of constitutional small beer, and the battles of kites and crows. But Wellesley would never fail to magnify his office and make it honourable in the eyes of men, as will be evidenced by a single fact. He had married *en secondes noces*, Mrs. Patterson, of Baltimore, so nearly related to Jerome Buonaparte. She was a Roman Catholic, while he was a Protestant who wor-shipped in the Castle chapel, and he always insisted on his wife being escorted from the Castle or Lodge to and from the Roman Catholic Cathedral of Marlborough Street, Dublin, by a troop of Dragoons, Lancers, or Hussars, a new departure that caused some little excitement at the time.

Lord Wellesley's attempt to remodel whole-sale the local magistracy was a grievous error in judgment and arrayed much of the gentry against him.

We have alluded to Lord Wellesley as a most accomplished scholar; indeed, it was in scholarship that the great consul and administrator of the easternmost and westernmost portions of our empire sought and found that *solatium senectutis*, which Talleyrand, according to the tale, attributed to Whist, for, when a young friend of the priestly *diplomat* admitted to him his total ignorance of, and distate for, the game, he remarked, " qu'elle triste vieillesse vous vous préparez." The " Greville Memoirs " tell us of the surprise felt among the Marquis's friends in England at the great vigour he threw into his Irish Government, when his energies were supposed to be somewhat sapped by his Oriental experiences ; but that vigour of mind was quite exceptional, for in his eightieth year we find him dedicating a small volume of Latin poems to his friend Lord Brougham, another intellectual giant. One of his Latin poems may be given in illustration ; the subject was a Weeping Willow which overhung the banks of the Thames, by which, not unmindful, perhaps, of " the schoolboy spot which we remember well, though there we are forgot "— Eton, to wit, he had selected his residence, Fernside, as a

" Modus lasso Maris et viarum militiaeque."

This willow had been brought from the

banks of the Euphrates—the real "waters of Babylon."

Passis mœsta comis, formosa doloris imago,
 Quæ flenti similis pendet in amne salix,
Euphratis nata in ripâ Babylone sub altâ
 Dicitur Hebreas sustenuisse lyras:
Cum, terrâ ignotâ, Proles Solymea refugit
 Divinum patriæ jussa movere melos:
Suspensis que lyris, et luctu muta, sedebat,
 In lacrymis memorans, te reverende Sion!
Te dilecte Sion! frustra sacrata Jehovæ,
 Te præsenti ædes irradiata Deo!
Nunc pede barbarico, et manibus temerata profanis,
 Nunc orbata tuis, et taciturna domus!
At tu pulchra salix, Thamesini littoris hospes,
 Sis sacra, et nobis pignora sacra feras;
Quâ cecidit Judica, mones, captiva sub irâ,
 Victricem stravit quæ Babylona manus:
Inde doces sacra et ritus servare parentum,
 Juraque, et antiquâ vi stabilire fidem.
Me quoties curas suadent lenire seniles
 Umbra tua, et viridi ripa beata toro
Sit mihi, primitiasque meas, tenuesque triumphos
 Sit revocare tuos dulcis Etona! dies
Auspice te summæ mirari culmina famæ,
 Et purum antiquæ lucis adire jubar
Edidici puer, et jam primo in limine vitæ,
 Ingenuas veræ laudis amare vices.
O Juncta Aonidum lauro præcepta salutis
 Æternæ! et musis consociata fides!

Felix doctrinâ ! divinâque insita luce !
  Quæ tuleras animo lumina fausta meo ;
Incorrupta precor maneas, atque integra, seu te,
  Aura regat populi, seu novitatis amor
Stet quoque prisca domus (neque enim manus impia
    tangat)
  Floreat in mediis intemerata minis ;
Det patribus patres, populoque det inclyta cives
  Eloquiumque foro, Judiciisque decus.
Conciliisque animos, magnæque det ordine genti
  Immortalem altâ cum pietate fidem.
Floreat, intactâ per postera sæcula famâ,
  Cura diu patriæ, cura paterna Dei.

1828.

After Lord Wellesley's departure from Ireland
for the first time, the Viceregal succession was
carried on by the Marquis of Anglesey, who was
of European reputation as a *beau sabreur*, a man
of great gallantry and intrepidity, who had done
the State good service as an infantry as well as
a cavalry leader, of clear head and fine judgment,
and a mind rather freer from political prejudice
than was commonly to be found at that time.
Lord Anglesey was the Prorex of Ireland twice :
once in 1828, and then again in 1830, the Duke
of Northumberland having held office in the
interval. Lord Anglesey's first term of office

P

was comparatively smooth, but in his second he had to encounter the whole weight of O'Connell's opposition, said, whether correctly or not, to have been envenomed by certain forensic appointments, as it was certainly accentuated by the legal victories of Mr. Attorney-General Blackburne (afterwards Lord Chancellor of Ireland) over the shifty efforts of Mr. O'Connell to circumvent the proclamations of the Lord Lieutenant against illegal assemblies. For a long time the historical individuality of the Viceroy has been eclipsed or overshadowed by his Chief Secretary, who manages the affairs of the island in the House of Commons, and is, therefore, constantly in evidence and action, while the Viceroy's official existence can only be gauged by reading his despatches. That Lord Anglesey, however, took the deepest interest in everything relating to his Proconsulate, and that his great aim was to hold the balance of justice between the warring factions, ever struggling for ascendancy, we learn from his letters. The tithe war, "bequeathed from bleeding sire to son," was carried on more boldly and audaciously in his reign than ever, and the murders, massacres, or victories, from whichever standpoint they are regarded, of Newtown Barry, in the co. Wexford, and of Carrickshock, in the co. Kilkenny, where a police inspector of the name of Gibbons, and a number of constables on their way to levy a distress for tithes due to the Rector of Innistiogue, were led into a sort of local Kyber Pass and stoned to death. were the precursors of the tithe settlement effected by the act of Mr. Stanley, the Chief Secretary to Lord Anglesey. The Cap of Maintenance does not enter into the daily costume of a Lord Lieutenant, but, I believe, the Anglesey Hat was generally esteemed by contemporary critics a masterpiece of art and design.

That his Excellency was a true patriot or lover of the land he had ruled is shown by a letter which he addressed from Rome to the Attorney-General, Blackburne, after his resignation of the Lord Lieutenancy. He is dilating on the solidity of the works of the Imperial city, which appear to have been "destined for eternity." "They would have made you a ship canal from Galway to your bay in a month. How a Roman Emperor would have smiled at the difficulty of forming one from Kingstown to Dublin!" A very wise and prophetic remark is added in this letter : " It is ecclesiastical wealth that will destroy Church establishments, and at no distant period."—Written in 1834.

1829.

The Duke of Northumberland, who was sand-wiched in between the two periods of Lord Angle-sey's government, ruled right royally—with a magnificent liberality—often, no doubt, deplored by less wealthy occupants of the Viceregal throne. He handed back £10,000 of his honorarium, hitherto £30,000 per annum, to the Treasury. Since then the salary has been £20,000.

As something of an illustration of the magni-ficent munificence of the Duke of Northumber-land's Viceroyalty, it may be mentioned that when he was leaving Dublin he sent an invitation to his Dublin tradesmen to pay him a visit at his Palace there and view the lions of London. The great majority accepted his hospitable suggestion, but one or two of the old-fashioned "stick-to-your business" sort stayed in Dublin, and when the travelled tradesmen returned to Ireland the "stay-at-homes" were very anxious to know all about the visit and how they had fared. One more outspoken than the others told them that nothing could have been better than their reception by his Grace, that they had had the best of every-thing, and every facility for seeing and enjoying "life in London;" but, he added, "in spite of all his Grace's liberality, the visit was a most costly affair, and for my own part I could have economised at a first-class hotel, so exorbitant were the expectations of the Northumberland servants, so large the gratifications given." It is just possible, however, that these gratifications were looked on as "commissions" by the household of the dispendious Duke.

1835.

The Viceroyalty of the Earl of Mulgrave, afterwards Marquis of Normanby, is viewed in very different lights by the extremists on either side in Ireland, by whom the temperate *via media* is seldom kept in matters political or polemical, for, like George Villiers, they prove—

> " So over violent, or over civil,
>   That every man with them is God or devil."

To the Protestant ascendancy clique, of whom the coryphæus in the House of Lords was the Earl of Roden, Lord Mulgrave appeared only a few degrees less abominable than the apocryphal beast. But to the great bulk of the inhabitants of Ireland, who were Liberal, because their hopes and expectations were based on Liberal support,

Lord Mulgrave was a right-minded and impartial Viceroy, who, while he put a curb on Orange violence, was equally unfavourable to secret societies—the Ribbon especially—on the other side. Hence the country party eschewed the levees and functions at the Castle, thereby throwing his Excellency still more into Catholic hands. O'Connell gave him his strenuous support, and for that reason probably the country, save for the tithe agitation, was restored to some temporary tranquillity. The wholesale gaol deliveries authorised by his Excellency on his progresses through the country, gave rise to no slight scandal; but almost anything seemed preferable to "the bloody assizes" so common previously. Lord Mulgrave's personal staff, which included Mr. Frank Sheridan, Mr. Bernal Osborne, Sir Thomas Burke, and men of that calibre, was very popular, and the Viceroy shared in its popularity. His Excellency, moreover, like Lord Anglesea, joined in the sports and pastimes of the country, particularly in racing, and as the Curragh was not then made quite so accessible by train as it is now from Dublin, the Lord Lieutenant spent much of his time at Normanby Lodge at its edge, which he either bought or rented for a sporting home in summer.

His Excellency was very fortunate in his Secretaries, for the Chief Secretary was Lord Morpeth, afterwards Earl of Carlisle, so long identified with the Castle and Viceregal Lodge ; while the Under-Secretary was Mr. Thomas Drummond, decidedly the ablest man, and, perhaps, the most earnest and devoted that ever filled that post. He may be said to have struck the hardest blows that ever were aimed at the odious oligarchical system of exclusivism, known as " Protestant Ascendancy," and to have done much to enlist the people to the side of government by the administration of unswerving and evenhanded justice. Mr. Drummond, who was the scion of a Scotch family almost as old as the Courtenays in England, began his career in the Royal Engineers, and very soon stepped out of the crowd by his clever invention of the limelight (of which the modern light is only an adaptation) for the scientific surveying and illumination of the coast. Lord Brougham introduced him to the political arena, and Lord Althorp persuaded him to become his private secretary. This, probably, led to his appointment as permanent Under-Secretary to the Lord Lieutenant of the time being. Some will say that his zeal for a still unenfranchised and half emanci-

pated peasantry led him too far in the opposite
direction, but no one ever doubted his philanthropic highmindedness and rectitude of purpose.
He was married to Miss Kinnaird just before
settling in the lodge in the Phœnix Park.
Whatever may be thought of Lord Mulgrave's
political views, he was not wanting in ability,
and he had the courage of his convictions.

Lord Normanby was Governor of Jamaica
prior to his Viceroyalty, and his son succeeded
him in that post.

1846.

The pestilence which "walketh in darkness"
and destroys human beings finds a replica in the
blight which sometimes in a mysterious and
sudden manner attacks the food staples of a
nation, and paralyses its industry. The vine is
especially subject to such a canker, but then
the vine, though it may minister greatly to the
wealth and power of a population, is not its sole
subsistence and stay, and so to speak its *raison
d'être;* but the potato in Ireland, the gift of an
English adventurer, fulfilled all these conditions,
and was practically the life of about four millions
of men, women, and children. In 1845 the

potato plant was struck with consumption, and the existence of millions was thus placed in jeopardy. Experts tell us that an improvident peasantry had brought this Nemesis on themselves by sowing bad seed year after year, and never changing or renewing it. They tell us, too, that Nature had given indications of the approaching decay some years previously, which were all unheeded, but the revelation of the potato rot, which extended all over Ireland, was as sudden and overwhelming as a shock of earthquake or the inroad of an overwhelming flood. Malthus' theories about the pressure of population, and the increase of the latter in a geometrical ratio, while the increase of the means of subsistence was only on an arithmetical scale of proportion, found no favour in Ireland, where politics, population, and potatoes formed an inseparable Trinity, the multiplication of forty-shilling freeholds to increase the political power of the landowners being the *fons et origo* of this perilous and precarious combination. When the emancipated freeholders refused to be driven to the poll like sheep, at least by their landlords, though they submitted cheerfully to the goad of "their natural leaders," secular and spiritual, these freeholders, on getting into almost inevitable arrear, were evicted freely, to swell the ranks of the lazy, listless loafers of the towns, who, like the ideal idlers in the market place referred to by the Evangelist, maintained that attitude because "no man had hired them." A system of cheap emigration had not then been devised, the Poor Law had not been introduced, and the clearance of a county side was then what it is *not* now, as asserted by Mr. Gladstone and his followers, something akin to a "sentence of death." Our Indian Empire experiences have taught us what it is to have a strong, capable, and humane Governor at the helm when a famine is threatened, or the industries of a population are suddenly arrested and paralysed. Fortunate was it for the United Kingdom that the Viceroy of Ireland—John William Ponsonby, fourth Earl of Bessborough—was an Irishman of heart and brains, who could master the situation and do his best to alleviate it, and who, moreover, was acceptable to the people he ruled and to their chiefs, while fully prepared to maintain the constitution and to respect the rights of property and the traditions of the Empire.

A Conservative Ponsonby would be something of a "rara avis" in politics—that is to say, a Conservative by public profession, for in practice the family are Conservative enough in many

respects, but in the Irish as well as in the English
Parliaments the Ponsonbys ever proved opponents to privilege and strenuous vindicators of
popular rights. The Prodigal Son is a typical
picture for all times, but fortunately the Ponsonby
family had few such erratic, if sublimely repentant,
members, and it seems to have been characterised
by prudence, policy, and common sense for
generations, since the Cromwellian Colonel pru-
dently purchased up the land debentures in which
the disbanded Parliamentary army was paid. In
Church and State, in war, and its image, the
chase, the Ponsonbys illustrate history and county
annals. We know from the Greville " Memoirs"
that the fourth Earl, while Liberal as any
hereditary Whig, was as opposed to anarchy and
lawlessness as—say Mr. Arthur Balfour or his
uncle Lord Salisbury. " He wants the Proclamation Act to be renewed ; the Conciliation Hall
has its agents everywhere, and governs Ireland
more than the Government does. If he had been
Lord Lieutenant he would not have consented to
divide authority with that body." Here is Charles
Greville's commentary on Lord Bessborough's
reign :—" In Ireland Bessborough has done
admirably well, with a mixture of wisdom and
firmness which has gained him great applause.

Even Lord Roden says he is the best Lord Lieutenant they ever had. The state of Ireland meanwhile is most deplorable, not so much from the magnitude of the prevailing calamity as from the utter corruption and demoralisation of the whole people from top to bottom. Obstinacy, ignorance, cupidity, and idleness overspread the land. Nobody thinks of anything but how they can turn the evil of the times to their own advantage. The upper classes are intent on jobbery, and the lower on being provided with everything, and doing nothing. It sickens and disgusts me, and it is necessary to bear constantly in mind how much we have to reproach ourselves for letting Ireland become so degraded and corrupt, to endure the spectacle with any sort of patience." Again, he writes :—" There is no doubt whatever that while English charity and commiseration have been so loudly invoked, and we have been harrowed with stories of Irish starvation, in many parts of Ireland the people have been suffered to die for want of food when there was all the time plenty of food to give them, but which was hoarded on speculation ; but what is still more extraordinary, people have died of starvation with money enough to buy food in their pockets. I was told the night before last

that Lord de Vesci had written to his son that
since the Government had positively declared they
would not furnish seed, abundance of seed had
come forth, and, what was more extraordinary,
plenty of potatoes ; and Labouchere told me there
had been three coroners' inquests, with verdicts
'*Starvation*,' and in each case the sufferers had
been found to have considerable sums of money
in their possession ; and in one, if not more, still
more considerable sums in the savings bank—yet
they died rather than spend their money in the
purchase of food." Without questioning these
eccentricities and hoarding hallucinations, the
awful nature and extent of the national calamity,
with the sequent pestilence, cannot be gainsayed.
The readers of Thucydides know that the combination of λιμός and λοιμός lead to strange
consequences and very moderate manifestations
of human nature.

It is something of a coincidence that the
deaths of Lord Bessborough and O'Connell took
place almost simultaneously. "The departure of
the latter, which not long ago would have excited
the greatest interest, and filled the world with
political speculations, was heard almost with un-
concern, so entirely had his importance vanished ;
he had, in fact, been for some time morally and

politically defunct, and nobody seems to know
whether his death is likely to prove a good or
an evil, or a mere matter of indifference. The
death of Bessborough excited far greater interest,
and no man ever quitted the world more surrounded by sympathy, approbation, respect, and
affection than he did—during his last illness,
which he himself and all about him knew to be
fatal, he was surrounded by a numerous and
devoted family, and the people of Dublin universally testified their regard for him, and their grief
at losing him.   He continued in the uninter-
rupted possession of his faculties almost to the
last hour of his existence, and he calmly discussed
every matter of public and private interest in
conversation with his children and friends, and
dictated letters to John Russell and his colleagues
at home.   He expired at eleven o'clock at night ;
at nine he felt his pulse, and said he saw the end
was approaching.   He then sent for all his family,
seventeen in number, saw them, and took leave
of them separately, and gave to each a small
present he had prepared, and then calmly lay
down to die ; in less than two hours all was over.
They say his funeral was one of the finest and
most striking sights possible, from the countless
multitudes which attended it, and the decorum

and good feeling which were displayed. Clarendon has kept the whole of Bessborough's staff
and household, with one exception, and he told
them that he kept them on account of their
attachment to his predecessor. The reputation
which Bessborough had acquired, which, at the
time of his death, and since his Irish administration, was very considerable, affords a remarkable example of the success which may be
obtained by qualities of a superior description,
without great talents, without knowledge and
information, and without any power of speaking
in Parliament. He had long been addicted to
politics, and was closely connected by relationship
or friendship with the most eminent Whig leaders.
His opinions had always been strongly Liberal,
and he seemed to have found the place exactly
adapted to his capacity and disposition, when he
became the Whig whipper-in of the House of
Commons; he was gradually initiated in all the
secrets of that party, and he soon became a
very important member of it, from his various
intimacies, and the personal influence he was
enabled to exercise. He had a remarkably calm
and unruffled temper, and very good sound sense.
The consequence was that he was consulted
by everybody, and usually and constantly em-

ployed in the arrangement of difficulties, the
adjustment of rival pretensions, and the reconciliation of differences, for which purposes some
such man is indispensable and invaluable in
every great political association. He continued to
acquire fresh weight and influence, and at length
nothing could be done without Duncannon, as
he then was; everybody liked him, and King
William, when he hated the rest of the Whigs,
always testified good humour and regard for
him. He took office and became a Cabinet
minister, and he continued to do a vast deal
of Parliamentary business, especially in the
House of Lords, and carry bills through Parliament without ever making the semblance
of a speech. In this way, by his good nature
and good sense, and an extreme liveliness
and elasticity of spirits, which made him a
very pleasant and acceptable member of society,
he continued to increase in public reputation
and private favour, and when the Government was formed last year his appointment to
the Lord Lieutenancy of Ireland was generally
approved of. He had almost always been on
good terms with O'Connell; indeed, he never was
on bad terms with anybody, and as an Irishman
he was agreeable to the people. In his adminis-

tration, adverse and unhappy as the times were,
he displayed great industry, firmness, and knowledge of the character and circumstances of the
Irish people, and he conciliated the good will
of those to whom he had been all his life opposed.
Lord Roden, the head of the Orange party, who
has all along acted a very honourable and patriotic
part, afforded ample testimony to his merits, and
gave him a very frank and generous support."

. After Lord John Russell had given up his pet
project of abolishing the Viceroyalty in favour
of a Secretaryship, there was some difficulty in
selecting a successor, the favourites for the post
being the Duke of Bedford, Clarendon, and Lord
Morpeth. Lord Bessborough's request to the
Premier was "*to appoint a man to succeed him
who shall be firm and bold, and, above all, who will
not seek for popularity.*" These were, indeed,
counsels of perfection.

Lord Bessborough's popularity in Ireland was
the spontaneous offering of all he came in contact
with, not sought by the usual arts and artifices,
much less by pandering to popular prejudices and
passions ; some of it, no doubt, may be accounted
for by the cordial relations between himself and
O'Connell, who was occasionally his guest, and by
his intimacy with that great benefactor of the

Q

people, Father Mathew; in fact, Lord Bessborough, in his largeness of view with regard to religious toleration, was almost as much in advance of his age as his predecessor, Lord Chesterfield, who, it is said, warned his Government to be far more afraid of *poverty* in Ireland than of *Popery*.

Lord Bessborough played Mæcenas to several Horaces (if not quite of the calibre of the great Quintus Flaccus). Fanny Kemble was among the *invités* to the Castle, and among literary *habitués* at his Court were Moncton Milnes, Mr. Abraham Hayward, and Eliot Warburton, whose "Crescent and Cross" is still of great and general interest. Of course, the social brilliancy of Dublin Castle was much eclipsed by the national calamity that cast its dark shadow over everything, but for all that the Levées and Drawing-Rooms were extremely well attended in the time of Lord Bessborough, whose death is attributed in a great measure to official anxiety and care.

1847.

Among the vigorous Viceroys of Ireland since the Union, the Earl of Clarendon must ever take a leading position. He may be said to have been

born in the purple of office, and his natural
acumen was sharpened by the various functions
which from an early age he was called upon to
perform. His very title suggests Constitutionalism
and political liberality, for " the constitutions of
Clarendon " are amongst the earliest bulwarks of
the State against the encroachments and aggres-
sions of sacerdotalism. They were passed in
1164, in a general council of peers and prelates, in
a park called Clarendon, near Salisbury, and had
their effect in shaping the destinies of England.

We are reminded of Dr. Johnson's sonorous
line—

"Is now no more than Tully or than Hyde,"

by the decay of the former tenants of the title of
Earls of Clarendon, to whom, however, the subject of our sketch was connected by a maternal
ancestress, his own family tracing their lineage
from the famous Duke of Buckingham. Lord
Clarendon was educated at Cambridge, and passed
into the diplomatic ranks after leaving the University, getting attached to the Embassy at St. Peters-
burg. From 1823 to 1833 he was a commissioner
of excise, and in that capacity he was sent to
Dublin to consolidate the excise boards, though

it is hinted in the Cloncurry memoirs that he had an even more important mission in preparing for the Emancipation Act. A commercial treaty with France was his next achievement, and then we find he was sent as Envoy Extraordinary and Minister Plenipotentiary to Madrid, where he acquired a thorough knowledge of Spanish affairs, as evidenced by his subsequent speech on the subject in the House of Lords. On the death of an uncle he succeeded to the Earldom, and we next find him in the Melbourne Cabinet as Lord Privy Seal, and temporarily Chancellor of the Duchy of Lancaster. These offices he held till Sir Robert Peel's ministry in 1841 ; when this was replaced in 1846 by Lord John Russell's administration, Lord Clarendon was given the Board of Trade, and on Lord Bessborough's death at the Castle (Dublin) he was sent to fill the Viceroyalty of Ireland. The times were critical, Chartism was rampant in England, with an Irishman, Fergus O'Connor, for its coryphaeus ; and in Ireland O'Connell, the champion of constitutional agitation, had been practically deposed and degraded by a more advanced party of separatists, headed by Smith-O'Brien, Duffy, Mitchell, and Meagher, who openly advocated violence or the sword as the only means of redressing the wrongs of Ireland. How the bubble burst at Ballingarry, without the intervention of a single soldier, is now matter of history, too trite to repeat; nor did the sanguinary retaliations that followed the Emmett *émeute* find any place consule Clarendon. The chiefs were banished, the followers were pardoned, and the anarchical scenes which deluged the continent with blood, and hurled monarchs from the thrones were unknown in Ireland; this happy consummation was due very much to the vigilance and boldness of the Viceroy, who only *struck* when it was absolutely necessary to do so, and proved himself a most efficient head of the Executive, never afraid of assuming responsibility when it was absolutely necessary in his opinion to act boldly, as in the suppression of certain prints whose patriotism tended to treason. It was during Lord Clarendon's term of office that Her Majesty Queen Victoria paid her first visit to Ireland with Prince Albert and the young princes and princesses. Their reception was enthusiastic, but unfortunately the stay of the royal visitors was limited to five days, during which there was a grand review of the garrison in the Phoenix Park, excursions were made to Howth and Carton, the chief institutions of Dublin were visited, and Her Majesty and the Prince Consort inscribed their

names in the Book of Kells at the Library of
Trinity College. Lord John Russell, it was well
known, was strongly opposed to the continuance
of the Viceroyalty, and Lord Clarendon certainly
considered himself the last of the tenants of the
Castle, but a great outcry was made in Dublin
about the proposed disestablishment, and the
institution has "brokenly lived on" ever since,
reminding one of Dryden's line in his poem "The
Hind and the Panther"—

"Still doomed to death tho' fated not to die."

In August, 1849, Her Majesty the Queen
granted a charter for the foundation of a new
university, to be called "the Queen's University
in Ireland"—of this Lord Clarendon was the
first chancellor.

Lord Clarendon's private secretary was the
witty Corry Conellan, whom Thackeray, in his
satire on the Viceregal office and its satellites,
described as "Corry, the bould Conellan." It is
said that on one occasion the Duke of Devonshire
paid a visit to the Viceroy at the Castle. Lord
Clarendon was at the moment of his announce-
ment absorbed in some affair of State that brooked
no delay, and he deputed Mr. Conellan to receive

his Grace till he could get a release from his preoccupying business. When this time came the Viceroy hurried to meet his Grace, and apologised profusely for his apparent neglect. "Pray make no apologies," said the Duke, "I have been entertained in your absence by a most kind, agreeable, and condescending gentleman, who made me feel perfectly at home." This was Corry Conellan, who, till he eclipsed himself for ever, was the ornament and despot of most dinner tables in Dublin. In 1825 (March the 2nd) Lord Clarendon left his capital on the resignation of his chief, Lord John Russell.

In Lord Clarendon's time the *entente cordiale* which for centuries had existed between the Irish or Castle Executive and the head of the Corporation of Dublin—its Lord Mayor—had not been severed by political antagonism; and the Mansion House in Dawson Street, bought in 1715 from the Dawson family, was a great meeting place for the leading citizens of Dublin, the Lord Lieutenant of the time being, and the nobility of the country. On the 21st of January, 1851, the then Lord Mayor, Benjamin Lee Guinness, entertained his Excellency at a banquet of unusual splendour. On the 1st of August of that year the Midland Great Western Railway of

Ireland was opened for traffic between Dublin and Galway—an event of higher importance, perhaps, to "the kingdom of Connaught" than any since Cromwell's "Plantation." Whether Lord Clarendon was offered the Premiership after his departure from Ireland we are unable to state positively, but his ability as Secretary of State for Foreign Affairs was most conspicuous. The gossipy Charles Greville tells us how, on his accepting the Foreign Office in Lord John Russell's ministry, Lord Aberdeen told him "that of all the new Cabinet, it was to *him* that the Queen and the Prince looked with the greatest confidence; they cared little for any of the others, but had a great opinion of him, and a great reliance on him, and mainly counted on his judgment and influence to make matters go on smoothly abroad. He said that Peel entertained the same opinion, and had said that Clarendon in the Cabinet was the best security for peace." It may be mentioned here that when Lord John Russell conceived that the death of Lord Bessborough gave him an opportunity of bringing in a bill for the abolition of the Viceroyalty and putting the government of Ireland into the hands of a Secretary, it was his intention to offer that Secretaryship to Lord Clarendon.

The Earl of Eglinton 1852 and 1858.

" Pour bien vivre," according to the Gallic proverb, which may bear the hall mark of Rochfoucauld or La Bruyère, or some such witty worthy, "il faut avoir mauvais cœur et bon estomac." There is a certain sardonic verity in the antithesis, however abhorrent to our better feelings, but we may lay down a cognate axiom, or law of life, for Viceroys in Ireland, that "pour bien vivre il faut avoir bon chef, et bon cru," and withal a largeness of hand and heart that are generally irresistible in the Green Isle. All these admirable qualifications were united in the handsome person of Archibald William, Earl of Eglinton and Winton, Knight of the Thistle, a Doctor of Civil Law, and an LL.D. Of his orthodoxy in jurisprudence much proof was never given or required by the world, so that the LL.D. may not be greatly insisted on in marshalling the titles and honours of this popular peer; but the possession of L.S.D. is, even in the Chesterfield code, no bad letter of recommendation when coupled with good looks, winning manners, a chivalrous spirit, and a ready wit. Ireland has a wonderful power of recuperation. Even in the Elizabethan age, after the scourgings and hostings of strong representatives of the Crown, when, according to contemporary chronicle, the low of kine was not to be heard throughout the land for many scores of miles, say from Cashel to Cork ; when wolves multiplied and waxed more and more audacious, as man their master began to wane, and the common kerne were fain to satisfy the cravings of hunger with such messes of pottage as the wild sorrel which the woods afforded, a few years of rest and respite sufficed to renew the face of the earth ; and now, in the second half of the 19th century, the potato-plague, the famine, and the pestilence and the financial disorganisation that followed, were being fast forgotten in returning plenty and prosperity, and society having supped full of horrors was fain once more to eat, drink, and be merry, and to look hopefully towards a better and brighter future. It was at such a time that Lord Eglinton was selected for the Viceregal throne in the Castle of Dublin by a Conservative premier, and Lord Naas, M.P. for Kildare, Coleraine, and Cockermouth in succession, was his Chief Secretary, while General Dunne, of an old Celtic stock, was the Permanent Secretary. Lord Eglinton came to govern a people for whom chivalry had not yet lost its charm, and in whom the passion for sport

is predominant. Horsemen by nature, and bred
up among horses, the Irish could not but feel a
leaning towards a nobleman who owned the best
horse of the century (so far), the Flying Dutch-
man, who had defeated another great rival, the
champion of the north, " Voltigeur," and who had
summoned his brother peers and paladins to a
splendid tournament at Eglinton Castle, where one
of the chief jousters was an Earl from Erin, another
a Milesian Marquis, Henry Lord Waterford ;
and the Queen of Beauty represented Irish wit
and Irish loveliness, while he himself wore a
cuirass inlaid with gold. Moreover, Lord Eglinton was indirectly connected with Ireland. At
Killester, on the road to Howth, about a mile from
Clontarf, was an Irish country house, not unlike a
French chateau, where were reared two comely
Irish maidens, the daughters of Lord Newcomen,
whose town house, just opposite the upper gate
of Dublin Castle, shows that architecture flourished
in Ireland at that period. One of these ladies
married Archdeacon Gould ; the second, Theresa,
after an Indian experience as the wife of Captain
Cockerell, R.N., became the wife of Lord
Eglinton. It is said that when Charles Kean,
the great son of the greater Edmund Kean,
came to Dublin, then as always a favorite his-

trionic hunting ground, he became devoted to Miss Theresa Newcomen, but her brother, a Captain Newcomen, gave the actor his *congé* in a rather summary fashion. Theresa seems to have liked her Charles, for 18 months after, she sent him a message to York to say she was going out to India *malgré*. He instantly left the stage where he was actually playing, and got leave to see his enchantress for ten minutes, and tried to persuade her not to sail, " But my trunks are all on board," she piteously pleaded. " Never mind, don't go ; " love laughs at locks we know, but trunks and locks prevailed in this case, and on the passage out she met Captain Cockerell, " her fate," and he became her mate. On his death she became a wealthy widow, and in time won and wore, though for a short time only, the coronets of Eglinton and Winton. Lord Eglinton married *en secondes noces* Lady Adela Caroline Harriet Capel at Dublin Castle.

Lord Eglinton's transition from the world of sport to that of politics was nearly as sudden as that of Lord George Bentinck, and if Lord Eglinton never attained the heights reached by the owner of Crucifix and Surplice, the terror of the turf, and the iconoclast of its brigands and ruffians, he developed into a graceful speaker

and an oratorical ornament of the gilded chamber.
" Happy the country that has no annals," said a
well-known writer ; and the history of Ireland
during the Eglinton *régime*, repeated as it was,
proved comparatively uneventful, and may be
summed up, in the language of Scripture, " The
land had rest." It was his privilege to lay the
first pillar of the exhibition of industrial art in
the Leinster lawn of the Royal Dublin Society,
and he lent his willing aid to the projects of Mr.
Lever for establishing a regular line of Trans-
Atlantic steamers between Galway and her nearest
western neighbour, New York.

But it was socially that Lord Eglinton shone
most brilliantly. It was in his day that the big
banquets that have ever since obtained at the
Castle were inaugurated, and that champagne
was discovered to be a capital solvent of political
and polemical acerbities. It flowed most freely
under his auspices, and all sorts and conditions of
men ate, drank, and were merry, which is, at any
rate, a better and a more hopeful state of things
than everlasting brooding over an impossible
past, or plotting for a more impossible future.
In fact, the order of the day was—

> " Dona præsentis cape lætus horæ, et
> Linque severa."

His Excellency's skill as a cueist (in which
he was almost unrivalled) was well and widely
known, but at racquets he was almost equally
good, and this manly game found great encouragement in his reign, and became quite the fashion.
One of the living ornaments and buttresses of the
Irish Bench is said to have owed something of
his precocious promotion to great skill and science
in the racquet court, where his tall figure was
almost as familiar as in that of Themis. He
failed, however, to win the beautiful pin, in which
a big pearl represented the ball, given by his
Excellency as a prize in a racquet tournament;
it was won by Mr. Alexander, of Carlow, who
belonged to a family always prominent in manly
sports of every kind.

On the resignation of Lord Derby's ministry,
Lord Eglinton, to the great regret of most Irishmen who had ever come in contact with him,
left Dublin Castle for the second time. This was
in June. In August we find the Lord Mayor
of Dublin calling a meeting of citizens at the
Mansion House to pay a tribute of respect to
the memory of a Viceroyalty conspicuous for its
efforts to advance the material interests of Ireland.

The idea took concrete form in the statue
erected in Stephens Green, which, however,

does scant justice to the manly beauty of Lord Eglinton, for, like Tom Bowling's—

> "His form was of the manliest beauty,
>   His heart was kind and soft,
> Faithful below he did his duty,
>   But now he's gone aloft."

1853.

Lord Eglinton's first successor was Lord St. Germans, the lineal descendant of the great confessor for liberty, Sir John Eliot. He, as Lord Elliot, had been Chief Secretary in Ireland, and had shown good aptitude for official business, having first proved himself in Spain a most able diplomatist; but the business side of Viceroyalty is, perhaps, the smallest, and Lord St. Germans, with somewhat slender means, was not capable of sustaining that splendid style that had characterised the reign of his predecessor.

> "Haud facile emergunt quorum virtutibus obstat
>   Res augusta domi; Eblanâ durius illis
>   Conatus."

For at Eblana, as well as at Imperial Rome, the style makes the man (*le style fait l'homme*), and a poor *prorex* is something rather anomalous! His Excellency had the honour of entertaining Her Majesty when she came over to visit the

Industrial Exhibition with the Prince Consort and the Prince of Wales. This exhibition was mainly the work of Mr. Dargan, the railway contractor; and another great work of his was the Dublin and Wicklow Railway, which in the reign of his Excellency was thrown open as far as Bray. In his Excellency's reign, too, was opened the Roman Catholic University in Stephens Green, involving in its title two inconsistencies, for " the Catholic " must have a wider sphere than Rome, while a University implies admittance to the general, rather than the particular.

1855.

Lord Carlisle, who as Viscount Morpeth had filled the office of Chief Secretary to the Lord Lieutenant under Lords Normanby, Fortescue, and de Grey, renewed his acquaintance with Ireland and the Irish as Lord Lieutenant, on the resignation of Lord St. Germans in 1855. Now Lord Morpeth had been an avowedly able Chief Secretary; his despatches were those of a thorough scholar and gentleman, as well as of a man of large and liberal views; but it does not follow that a first-rate Secretary should always develop into a first-rate Viceroy. The men of

Corinth complained that while St. Paul's letters were " weighty and powerful his bodily presence was weak," and the lack of power and dignity was possibly the one thing which prevented Lord Carlisle from being a model prorex or pro-consul, for he had great gifts, ample fortune, an un-impeachable pedigree, and a most kindly and genial disposition, combined with a power of happy expression that almost amounted at times to classical eloquence ; indeed, Lord Carlisle, whose nature it was to be happy and to confer happiness on others, was perhaps happiest when he was pointing periods and making felicitous allusions in his ornate orations, whether the occasion was the opening of a monster ware-house in Grafton or Sackville Street, or laying the foundation stone of the new College of Physicians. Lord Carlisle, too, was as hos-pitable as the typical Prelate as sketched by the Apostle to the Gentiles, and if the majority of his guests did not belong to the territorial aristocracy, whose supremacy in Church and State was contrary to all his notions, there was a tolerable blend of men and women of all creeds and conditions at the Castle and the Lodge. Every reign has been illustrated by " the might, the majesty of loveliness " in some

R

elected Queen of Beauty. Thus in the days of
Lord Chesterfield the universal toast was Miss
Ambrose, "the dangerous Papist," who after-
wards became Lady Palmer. Walpole has told
us of the remarkable trio of girls, the graceful
Gunnings, who were "Countessed and double
Duchessed." They were born at Castle Coote,
and became successively Duchesses of Hamilton
and Argyll, Countess of Coventry, and Mrs.
Travers; but beauty, grace, and that indes-
cribable fascination which we call "charm"
were united at the Carlisle Court in Miss Rose
O'Hara, who afterwards became Mrs. Forbes, of
Callender, N.B.

In Lord Carlisle's Viceroyalty the Queen and
the Prince Consort paid one of their angelic visits
to Ireland. Her Majesty reviewed the troops at
the Curragh, where H.R.H. the Prince of Wales
had been quartered for a few months, and, after a
short survey of Killarney, where the royal party
were entertained by Mr. Herbert, of Muckross,
and Lord Castlerosse, returned to England *via*
Dublin.

Lord Carlisle's affectionate disposition was
shown by the liberal legacies he bequeathed in his
will to several of the members of his personal staff.
He shares with Lord Eglington the posthumous

honour of a statue in the grounds of "the People's Park," part of the Phœnix Park. Lord Carlisle had great faith in the reformatory system which was carried out on an extensive scale in the vicinity of Dublin by Sir John Lentaigne. Sir John used to promote some of the "radically reformed" to domestic service in his own house, and when a wise and witty but agnostic official ventured to point out to the philanthropic reformer that it was hardly safe to entrust plate to such hands, Sir John indignantly asked, "Why not, when I can thoroughly trust them." "Because," was the reply, "you and his Excellency will very soon be the sole spoons left in the house." Lord Carlisle talked poetically and wrote verses, but he was no poet any more than Cicero, who claimed the double crown of poet and orator.

To show how urgent Lord Carlisle was in the cause of his many friends, the following letter to him from Lord Palmerston will serve for an example :—

"BROADLANDS,

"*April* 29, 1862.

" My dear Carlisle,

" I have received your letter of the 19th. I remember a sarcastic critic exclaiming, ' Here

R 2

comes Dudley Stuart with his eternal Poles.'
I shall parody the exclamation by saying, ' Here
comes Carlisle with his eternal X——;' but I
think the Poles better entitled to their freedom
than X. is to the Commandership, and so let us
adjourn the debate.

" Yours sincerely,

" PALMERSTON."

1864.

To the genial and generous Carlisle succeeded
a man made of somewhat sterner stuff, John
Wodehouse, third Baron Wodehouse, who attained to the Earldom of Kimberley in 1866.
Comparatively small socially (for his fortune was
unequal to the task of entertaining magnificently,
and on a sumptuous scale, like some of his predecessors in office), he was great administratively,
and proved a Viceroy of transcendant vigour
where strength of purpose and determination
were required for the safety of the State, seeing
that many thousands of American Irish—*désœuvrés*
since the enforced reunion of Columbia's provinces and "territories"—were banded together
to dismember the Empire of England, though
they had in most cases shed their blood freely for
the consolidation of America.   These men had

the advantage of numbers and military training, whether under Grant, Lee, or Jackson, and the friction between America and her Motherland, on account of the Alabama adventures, was availed of on the principle, first, I believe, enunciated by Grattan, " that England's difficulty or danger was Ireland's opportunity." Of course they had the support and sympathy of the thousands in Ireland whose chief creed was, " Anglia delenda est"—England must be blotted out—the same men who later on cheered for the Mahdi, and "hosannah'd" for Arabi. And so a dangerous conspiracy, in which it was hoped and believed some of our soldiers would join, was being hatched in Ireland and America simultaneously by men of action as well as by men of thoughts and ideas. Canada and Ireland were to be the prizes of victory. The standard of rebellion was unfurled on a cold night of March by the Fenian Executive on Tallaght Hill, a spur of the larger Dublin range that with the Wicklow mountains forms a long chain in which the O'Tooles and O'Byrnes found bases of operations and natural fastnesses in their long war with the English garrison in Dublin. A more foolhardy proceeding could hardly be conceived, unless indeed, as in the case of Hoche, strong supports, which were not forthcoming, had been promised and counted on. The police of the district were strong enough to cope with the outburst, for Lord Strathnairn and his staff represented the Cavalry of Great Britain on the occasion. The Fenian bubble burst when pricked ever so gently, and, as in the case of the Spanish Armada, when the storms in their courses fought against the invaders, "afflavit Deus et dissipantur." The spring snows and the want of necessaries extinguished the rising more effectually than arms of precision and gunpowder. Consul Kimberley was *not* decreed a triumph, but there was no doubt he had shown much promptness and decision, especially when he ordered the offices of " The People," an incendiary publication, to be entered and the plant of the paper seized forcibly. Next day a couple of commissariat wagons carted it off to some military store in Dublin.

Like his predecessor in office, Lord Kimberley was a fine scholar, and won distinction at Oxford, where his " First " was generally held to be a brilliant one, for, as everyone knows, there are firsts and firsts. It was in Lord Kimberley's "reign" that H.R.H. the Prince of Wales paid his first visit to the races of Punchestown — ever since then known as Princely

Punchestown. From that time the annual Vice-regal procession to these peerless plains, or rather undulations, has been *de rigueur*. Most Viceroys consider this portion of their duties among the pleasantest.

1866.

On the fall of the Russell Administration, tripped up by that talented tactician Mr. Benjamin D'Israeli, the Marquis of Abercorn came to the Castle of Dublin as Lord Lieutenant. If Her Majesty's Constitutional advisers had ransacked the realm they could hardly have found a subject better qualified to represent his Sovereign than James Hamilton, who subsequently became the first Duke of Abercorn. He had this advantage over many Viceroys before him and after him, namely, that he was a *persona grata* at Court, and honoured by the personal friendship of the Queen. An Irish nobleman, with a pedigree and quarterings that even the hierarchy of the Hofburgh at Vienna, who are apt to scoff at our bourgeois barons and parvenu peerage, must have respected, and an estate of very large acreage in Ulster (nearly 50,000 in Tyrone alone) ; he had great gifts of mind and body, one of the pleasantest and kindliest presences in the House of Lords or the Queen's

Drawing-Room, together with a happy art of expressing agreeably the ideas and conceptions of a busy brain. Of him in his early manhood it might be said—

> " Quid voveat dulci majus nutricula alumno
> Quam qui scit fari recte quæ sentiat, et cui
> Gratia, fama, valetudo, contingat abunde."

Lord Abercorn imbibed the atmosphere of Courts early, for we find him filling the official position of Groom of the Stole to the Prince Consort ; but most of his time was spent at his beautiful family place, Baronscourt, in the co. Tyrone, fulfilling the duties of a country gentleman and magistrate, being Custos Rotulorum for the neighbouring county of Donegal. The Duke (though we are anticipating his higher title) was not a gambler or the owner of a stud of race-horses, but he patronised with a liberal hand all country sports, and the shooting parties at Baronscourt were not only looked forward to as capital sources of sport but as opening the portals to the pleasantest country-house society, where the sister arts of dancing, singing, and the drama flourished greatly. " What has Lord ⸺ ever done ?" said a cynic one day to a friend of the noble Lord. " I don't know what he's done,"

was the reply, " but I know he's the father of the
most charming girls of our time." This might
have been said truly in the present case ; indeed,
few fathers or mothers ever had more reason to
be proud of their progeny, both men and women,
and here we may mention that the Duchess,
a daughter of John, sixth Duke of Bedford, was
a member of the Royal Order of Victoria and
Albert, a distinction that speaks for itself.

The Duke made his entry into disturbed
Dublin on the 20th of July, and took up his
quarters at the Viceregal Lodge. Lord Kimberley had boldly grasped the nettle conspiracy
in Ireland, and nearly crushed it as a national
effort. There were, however, a few hot-headed,
foolish Fenians who, unable to calculate the proportion of means to an end, resolved to strike a
blow for Ireland, and this they did at Tallaght Hill
on the 5th of March, a fact we noticed in sketch-
ing Lord Kimberley's Viceroyalty. The police
dealt with the belligerents. Lord Strathnairn, who
had had some experience of rebellions, dealt, it is
said, with the prisoners by ordering their brace
buttons to be cut off on the spot, so that they
were marched into Dublin without handcuffs, but
all fully occupied in the difficult task of preserving
personal dignity and decency by having to hold

up their trowsers as they marched along ; thus
the dangers incurred by a possible rescue *en route*
were minimised.

In this " reign " a great work, the foundations
of which were laid by Sir John Gray, was completed on the introduction into Dublin of the
Vartry water ; but the most splendidly successful
social pageant was the installation of the Prince
of Wales, in St. Patrick's Cathedral, as a Knight
of St. Patrick, in the presence of the Princess of
Wales, Prince Edward of Saxe Weimar, the
Duke of Cambridge, the Duke of Teck, and a
cloud of coronets.

Sir Bernard Burke, who has so happily illustrated the Court life of the Castle, must be heard
on the subject—" Ireland welcomed with acclaim
the Royal Prince, who makes himself loved
wherever he goes, and Ireland accepted as a
special compliment his enrolment in her own
Order of St. Patrick. The presence, too, of the
youthful Princess of Wales in all the pride of her
early beauty, 'glittering like the morning star, full
of life and splendour and joy.' gave a peculiar
charm to the event, and the popularity of the
Lord Lieutenant, then Marquis of Abercorn, did
not detract from the general excitement. The
knightly pageant brought all contending parties—

Celt and Saxon, Protestant and Catholic—into one mighty and friendly assemblage, and for one day, at all events, Irishmen, united by the patriotic and harmonious spirit of chivalry, cast every bitter remembrance away." A well known and accomplished writer, Percy Fitzgerald, catching the spirit of the scene, wrote with graphic pen a sparkling description of it, and concluded with these words, " Every knight passes to his stall ; in front of him stand his two esquires ; over his head his own banner and sword. Then the new knight is brought to the Grand Master and kneels before him while the sword is girded on, and the blue collar and robe are adjusted ; other blue mantles cluster round, and archbishops read the mystic forms. The most picturesque moment is when the esquire stands in the middle and unfurls the knight's gaudy banner, swinging it in defiance, and the trumpets twang out a cheerful blast, and Ulster, coming to the front, proclaims the style and titles of the most puissant knight. Then it begins to pass away.

" The tall knights and their esquires, the little blue pages, supplemented by more to bear up the new knight's train ; the dignified Grand Master, the three brilliant ladies in snowy white (the Ladies Hamilton), the pale lady in blue

(H.R.H. the Princess of Wales), who is most
interested, vanish in succession. It seems like a
soft dream, and we are sorry the spell has been
broken. It looks like going back to mediæval
times, and with so much poetry going out of the
world, it was pleasant to have such a relic left:
even a doctrinaire would have been moved. It
may have disturbed the grim ghost of the great
dead Dean, but to the crowd, Celtic and perfervid,
it was deeply and poetically interesting."

In the evening his Excellency gave a grand
installation banquet in St. Patrick's Hall, at which
were seen, besides the Prince and Princess of
Wales and the Duke of Cambridge, almost all
the Knights of St. Patrick, the Earl of Shrewsbury, who, as Great Seneschal of Ireland, had
precedence next to royalty ; the principal nobility
of the country, and Sir Benjamin Guinness, the
munificent restorer of St. Patrick's Cathedral. In
December, 1868, on the fall of Mr. D'Israeli's
ministry, Lord Abercorn was succeeded by Lord
Spencer. In 1872 the Duke of Abercorn returned
to the Castle, but resigned in 1876. Dublin
never knew a more splendid Court than that of
the Duke and Duchess of Abercorn. The capital
filled, for the gentry of the country took houses
there as in the old times of a College Green

Parliament, and a great impetus was given to local trade ; but it was the Duke's special glory to have laid the foundation of Ireland's splendid successes at Wimbledon, and to have assisted in transferring the Elcho Shield so often to Ireland.

1868.

With the turn of the tide political in favour of Mr. Gladstone, the Right Hon. John Poyntz Spencer, K.G., who had succeeded to the Earldom of Spencer on the death of the fourth Earl, came to the Castle as Lord Lieutenant, with all the prestige that large territorial possessions (17,000 acres in Northamptonshire alone), the high estimation of his uncle as a statesman and politician, and some personal prowess in the hunting field gained while Master of the Pytchley Hunt, one of the crackest packs and crackest countries in England, can confer. Added to this, he brought to the Viceregal throne a wife whose high-caste beauty and grace caused her to be styled by the wits of Dublin " Spencer's Faëry Queen," and who rivalled, if she did not actually eclipse, the loveliness of her connection by marriage, and predecessor at Dublin Castle—the Duchess of Tyrconnel, Count de Grammont's " la belle Jennings," sister to Sarah, Duchess of

Marlborough. All these advantages, coupled
with magnificent plate, which was kept constantly
bright by use, for his Excellency held that—

> " Nullus argento color est avaris
>   Abdito terris, nisi temperato
>   Splendeat usu,"

and a staff of sterling sportsmen made Lord
Spencer a most popular Viceroy at starting, while
every month of his reign increased his favour with
his subjects, gentle and simple ; for his Lordship,
while neglecting none of the details and minutiæ
of his office, which he determined to master
thoroughly, found time to join in the sports of the
country, to pay visits to country houses, and to
make several hunting progresses through his territory, acquiring a better insight into its wants and
capabilities than if he had remained in Dublin and
been satisfied with the reports of his subordinates.
In this way Lord Spencer was very often a conspicuous figure with the Meath, Louth, Kildare,
Queen's County, Carlow, Curraghmore, Ward
Union, and Kilkenny packs, while Mr. Burton
Persse, of Moyode Castle, gave him some good
gallops with " the Blazers," whom Lever has
immortalised. Lord Spencer was well mounted
and had a fine eye for country and the runs

of foxes, if not quite in the first class of cross-country Centaurs. In fact, Lord Spencer did much to raise the fame of the chase as conducted in Ireland all over the world, and it was mainly through his Excellency's representations and glowing eulogies that the Kaiserin of Austria came from Vienna to enjoy such sport as Ireland afforded, and which with a long and varied experience Her Majesty pronounced unapproachable in any part of the world. Lord Spencer, moreover, was not unfrequently accompanied in the field by Major Whyte-Melville, the poet of pursuit, who wrote several of his best known songs on Irish themes, and introduced Irish men, women, and horses into his fascinating novels. His Excellency, too, did his best to improve the breed of horses in Ireland by introducing a sire or two of promise and performance, while the Castle and the Viceregal Lodge were social centres, distinguished by a splendid hospitality. In his first reign the Castle was honoured by a visit from the Prince of Wales, the Princess Louise, the Marquess of Lorne, and Prince Arthur. The Dublin Exhibition of Arts, Industries, and Manufactures, originated by the Guinness family, was opened. New docks for Dublin were made, and the Gaiety

Theatre took the place of the Theatre Royal,
which had perished by fire, as so many theatres
have perished.　In 1874 Lord Spencer left the
Castle on the fall of the Gladstone Ministry.

1874.

On the resignation of the Duke of Abercorn,
John Winston Spencer Churchill, Duke of Marlborough, was sent to the Castle.　As his name
suggests, he was rather closely related to Lord
Spencer, though his hereditary politics (for
politics are often an heirloom in a family with
religions, pictures, and statues), reminding one of
the couplet—

> "And in another would as kindly go
> Had but his nurse or mother told him to,"

were different in title, at any rate.　His Grace of
Marlborough was a man of earnest religious
enquiry and thought, determined to do his duty
impartially ; but he had somewhat passed the
meridian of active official life, and with such men
the phrase "quieta non movere" becomes something of a cult—often a wise and sensible one,
and his Grace was wise and sensible.　He was
not a sportsman, save in the matter of salmon
fishing, of which he was as fond as John Bright,

and to get scope for this pastime, he took Black-castle-on-the-Boyne, as did Lord Spencer before him; but if he was no foxhunter, his son, Lord Randolph Churchill, who was his private secretary, was extremely fond of this *national* pastime, as was his accomplished wife, and his sister, the present Lady Curzon, who found nothing insurmountable in the severest lines of Meath and Dublin. The Duchess of Marlborough, a woman of talent and energy, played the *rôle* of Vice-Queen right royally, and patronised in every possible way the industries and arts of Ireland, showing, too, how strong she could be in the cause of humanity by the splendid service she did to the congested and famine-menaced districts of Connaught. In the Duke's reign Moore's centenary was celebrated with great pomp and pageantry as that of *the* national poet. Byron says something very strong and pithy as to the consequences of Platonism "to all posterity." "Mooreism" is probably responsible for much rebellion and revolt in Ireland. The poet had no idea of kindling anything of the sort, and his patriotism was of that lukewarm order that led him to settle in England, and maintain that Ireland was a very good country "to live out of." The Duke of Marlborough did not care much latterly for the

s

Viceregal Lodge, and leased the lovely Knockdrin, the property of the Levinge family, near the
midland town of Mullingar, as a summer and
autumnal residence—a rhododendron retreat, for
in few places on this side of the Himalayas are
rhododendrons more magnificently luxuriant than
there. It may be worth while here to relate a
personal experience which illustrates to some
extent the former condition of things in Ireland,
and shows what a germ of truth there was in
Mr. Forster's assignment of the greater part of
the crime and outrages of the country to "village
tyrants." Many years ago I was staying at a
country house close to Knockdrin, and left it for
a day or two to pay a visit in another part of the
country. On my return I found that a barbarous
murder had been committed close to the lodge
gates of both places. The victim was a bailiff, or
something of the sort, and what struck me more
than anything else was the matter-of-fact way in
which the bloody deed was spoken about and
commented on in the neighbourhood. It really
seemed to be a mere incident in every-day life.
I believe the murderers, though well known in the
county, were never brought to the bar of justice ;
but as murder and intimidation grew pretty rife
in the county, an Act giving the police further

powers was passed. The gang of village ruffians disappeared from the county, and the Knockdrin neighbourhood has remained ever since as peaceable and well disposed to law and order as any portion of Kent or Middlesex—"only more so," to quote a forcible bit of current slang.

1880.

The re-appearance of a Liberal Administration introduced Lord Cowper as Lord Lieutenant and Mr. Forster as his Chief Secretary, with Cabinet rank. Lord Cowper was a fair and fearless Prorex : he, like the Duke of Abercorn before him, showed no dread of the people, and mingled in crowds without police protection. It is a fact, I believe, that conspirators of an advanced pattern actually took a house that commanded the avenues to the Castle, and close to where Lord Kilwarden was done to death in the Emmett "rising," with the intention of shooting him—but no shot was fired. Lord Cowper supported his nominal subordinate most loyally in his efforts to restrain outrage and enforce law, but neither were supported by their chiefs in London, and, in

1882,

on their resignations, Lord Spencer and Lord

S 2

Frederick Cavendish took their places. The awful events of the 6th of May will long be recollected in Ireland, while in England the Commission Court has lately revived the ghastly memory. From an intended conciliator, Lord Spencer had the *rôle* of coercionist forced upon him. Mr. Campbell-Bannerman was his coadjutor in the Secretariat, and, after " the Invincibles " had terrorised Dublin for some time, one or two apparently trifling clues were gained as to the conspiracy and its members, and justice was done on the gang.

To commence a Government under such awful auspices was a severe ordeal; but Lord Spencer was equal to the occasion, and strengthened by the counsel and ability of his Lord Chancellor, Sir Edward Sullivan, and backed by the spontaneous support of all patriots in the island, whether Liberal, Radical, or Conservative, he managed to steer an even keel through billows and breakers. Lord Spencer at this time was a Satrap of whom any country might be proud. He inquired into everything, allowed nothing to pass by unnoticed, and lent the weight of his presence and support to every useful project— such as State-aided emigration—riding as long distances as Sidney, Bellingham, or Sir J. Perrot.

But "be thou pure as ice, chaste as snow, thou shalt not escape calumny," was as true of vigilant Viceroys as of the ideal Ophelia. Lord Spencer was overwhelmed with venomous vituperation by the Patriotic press, in which premeditated murder was one of the smallest offences laid to his charge, and the abominable conduct of one or two officials in Dublin handicapped the Lord Lieutenant considerably. It is a pity that Lord Spencer hunted during his second term of office; every time he went out a little legion of soldiers, police, and detectives were told off to keep watch and ward over the pursuing Prorex, who, rather ill-mounted, no longer rode over the peerless pastures of Meath and Dublin in his old form, and learnt the depth of several ditches by personal plumbing. His Excellency at this time was greatly esteemed by the gentry of Ireland, with whom he mixed very freely. This was quite reason enough for his cordial detestation by "the people," not that individually anyone particularly disliked him, but *obedience* even of thought, and the surrender of opinion was the *mot d'ordre* in the Patriotic ranks and the ukase had gone forth that Lord Spencer had offended the majesty of the people, and was to be abhorred by them, *ad majorem Hiberniæ gloriam!* It is a curious commentary on the

coercion of the country that its Press—pictorial
and printed—was suffered to lampoon, libel,
deride, and *pasquinade* the authorities of the land,
and Her Majesty's representative especially, in a
style that no other free country in the world
would tolerate. To disrupted Dublin, no doubt
with olive-branch intentions, came their Royal
Highnesses the Prince and Princess of Wales,
with Prince Eddie, and were Lord and Lady
Spencer's guests at the Castle. They were
magnificently entertained by their Excellencies,
and their reception throughout the country, in
whatever direction they went, was enthusiastic,
though in one or two places disloyal emblems
were displayed, and perhaps words were spoken
of unseemly purport; but, on the whole, to speak
in telegraphese style, " the great heart of the island
went out to them," while the Prince increased his
popularity by persistently refusing police protection, and insisting on being allowed to trust his
mother's subjects, no matter how *surexcitated*
their mood. The balls given in their Royal
Highnesses' honour at Dublin and Belfast were
a credit to the taste and public feeling of the
country.

Lord Spencer's *volte face* on retiring from
office was a painful surprise to many, who had

not observed that his leanings latterly had been towards Home Rule. It shows fidelity to his political or party leader pushed to very extreme lengths, and has, of course, alienated the majority of his old friends and allies, while, amongst others, it has gained him the support of Mr. W. O'Brien, who, having once blackened his reputation, now professes his readiness to blacken his boots; but if a strong administrator, Lord Spencer can hardly rank as a profound politician, as any one who reads his Preface to "The Handbook of Home Rule" will probably think. That Lord Spencer felt his position acutely is most probable. His looks for some time showed it, as the following contemporary couplet indicates :—

"Alas, poor Spencer's grown quite thin—his legs scarce fill his cords,
Quoth Mr. Pat whoe'er grew fat by eating his own words?"

One or two funny things happened in the hunting field during Lord Spencer's second occupation of the Castle. One of his Excellency's A.D.C.'s, a full-bearded and very jolly tar, who was about the same height, make, and shape as the Lord Lieutenant, was pursuing the fox with him and a number of sportsmen in Meath. A gallant gunner was among them, riding a hard puller

who was a little above himself, and was soon
above the lately-mentioned jolly tar, whom he
knocked over at a fence. The gunner, as soon
as he could pull up his fiery and untamed steed,
was profuse in protestations and apologies, and
thinking it was the Red Earl whom he had
temporarily disabled and very nearly stiffened,
he thought it necessary, after pouring forth his
regrets, to back out of the Viceroyal presence bare-
headed, as he might have done at St. James's!!

Lord Spencer originated the cross-country
races between members of his staff and escort,
which have since become most fashionable, and
afford one of the pleasantest reunions of the year.
The idea enlarged has led to some very exciting
competitions, of which perhaps the most memorable
was between a battalion of the Grenadier Guards
and the 16th Lancers, ending as it did very
nearly in a dead heat, though the 16th just won
it. It should be mentioned, however, that one of
their best horses met with a fatal accident in the
race.

Lord Spencer left Dublin on the retirement of
Mr. Gladstone's Government and the advent to
power of that of Lord Salisbury, who sent Lord
Carnarvon to the Castle. It was *not* a felicitous
choice, and a very able, if crotchetty, public

servant was placed in a position for which he was
not fitted either by nature or training, though not
a few of his ancestors had been Lord Lieutenants
in Ireland. Mr. Parnell has reiterated his state-
ment that Lord Carnarvon opened negotiations
with him, or proposed to do so, with reference to
Home Rule. His Lordship has denied it in his
place in the House of Lords, and so the matter
stands at present, but the mere fact of the charge
being made shows that the Earl must have been
a little incautious in dealing with a question that
should not have been touched by him at all. Then
Lord Carnarvon disregarded the canon that a
Viceroy *must* have a first-rate cook and cellar ; and
his speeches in his progresses through the country
were more erudite and archæological than apposite.
The Dons of Trinity College, I believe, maintain
that his scholarship was absolutely unimpeach-
able, and they ought to be able to form a good
opinion, but scholarship and statesmanship are
very different entities. There can be no doubt
that his Excellency meant to devote himself to the
welfare of Ireland, but he hardly understood the
subject. Dr. Whately declared that Englishmen, as a rule, in his time fancied they could
solve the Irish problem after the briefest study ;
in five or six weeks they began to grow sceptical

of their ability, and ultimately abandoned it in despair, as incomprehensible as the Schleswig-Holstein mystery or the Eastern Question.

1886.

When Lord Salisbury's Government was turned out of office on Mr. Jesse Collings's amendment, popularly known as "three acres and a cow," Mr. Gladstone, whose followers had severely called the Conservative Cabinet to task for not renewing the Irish Coercion Act, was made Premier, and his friend the Earl of Aberdeen became Lord Lieutenant, with Mr. John Morley for Secretary. The latter gentleman was mainly an absentee from Ireland, but the terribly violent riots in Belfast, that caused civic blood to be shed freely, recalled him to the Lodge, and to the more active administration of his important office. Meanwhile, Lord Aberdeen felt that the Fitzwilliam mantle had fallen upon him, that he was the Lieutenant of General Gladstone, the chosen champion of the Irish people, and in all his acts and words he manifested a decided wish to foster this feeling of intense faith in Gladstone government, and its administration by himself. Indeed, his severer

critics maintained that he made it far too evident
that he was rather Mr. Gladstone's Viceroy or
officer than the Queen's representative ; but be
these strictures just or unjust, certain it is that
he gained the undivided affection of the masses,
while the classes, as a rule, held somewhat aloof.
Lady Aberdeen, a clever, enthusiastic lady with
some talent and much inclination for practice in
public speaking, seconded his Excellency's views
with much power and persistence ; nor will the
afternoon Garden Party which they gave at the
Lodge, when national woollens and silks of St.
Patrick's special hue, all, of course, of native
manufacture, were worn, fade from the recollection
of those who attended it for years.

The Home Rule Bill for Ireland introduced
by Mr. Gladstone was so distasteful to the House
of Commons that it was thrown out by a majority
of thirty. This led to a dissolution, and the
eventual "disruption and dismemberment" of
the great Liberal party, the "Unionists" con-
ceiving that in such an Imperial crisis it was
their duty to forsake a leader who in their
judgment menaced the disruption and dismemberment of the Kingdom. In the meantime, Lord
and Lady Aberdeen left Dublin Castle, and for
some days before this event it was known

throughout Dublin that the occasion would be made use of for a leave-taking such as no Viceroy since Lord Fitzwilliam had ever received. The procession of the trades and guilds of Dublin City reminded the spectator of the imposing pageantry of the O'Connell Centenary celebrated eleven years previously, and even the carmen and jarvies of the city formed an imposing mounted escort to do honour to the departing Vice-King and Vice-Queen.

1886.

On the 18th September Lord Salisbury's new Viceroy, the Marquis of Londonderry, with his Marchioness, made their public entry into Dublin and took possession of the Castle and the Viceregal Lodge. There was no popular demonstration of joy or welcome, though the Conservative element in the city cheered the carriages as they passed through the thoroughfares, but the tone of the "National" and Radical press soon made it apparent that, no matter what his personal merits might be, the new Viceroy was not to be considered a "persona grata" to the Hibernian race. Had he not borne in early life that title so abhorrent

THE MARQUIS OF LONDONDERRY. K.G.

to national aspirations—"Castlereagh," which had
been that of his talented kinsman—

> "That Castlereagh
> (Who) stole the Union away;"

and the fact that he was eminently popular in
Ulster where he had been one of the representatives, in the Lower House, of his county,
was rather an argument for the negation to him
of the "popularis aura" in the other provinces of
his pro-Consulate; while his good reputation as a
rider across country, and his liberality as a sportsman and encourager of one of Ireland's most
famous products—high class horses—was turned
to his disparagement, and one hebdomadal oracle
likened him to Heliogabalus, meaning, probably,
his predecessor on the throne of the Cæsars,
Caligula, a most Philhippic Prince! Considering
the great ability in organisation shown by the
National party in Ireland, and the professed
liberality of their cult, it must be admitted even by
their own partisans, that they injured their cause
considerably by such pettinesses as the proscription of fox-hunting, whereby if a certain amount
of punishment was inflicted upon a few landlords
infinitely severer punishment was inflicted upon a
number of hard-working, meritorious men to whom

this popular pastime was a source of livelihood. After a few years the fatuousness of such proscription became evident, and it was discontinued, but a special exception was made against the venatic Viceroy, who individually had conquered prejudice and conciliated esteem and regard. His Excellency, feeling that the chase should always be regarded as a permissive pastime, at once abandoned pursuit, in which he had ever manifested his thorough confidence in the honour of the people, by coming out without any escort or protection. Such conduct was the direct antithesis of that of his great Gladstonian predecessor, in whose case the chase was made, at least in its external presentment, something more than "the image of war."

Lord Londonderry showed on several occasions that he could take broad and statesmanlike views, and that he could enunciate them in clear, well expressed language. He performed all the duties connected with his office punctually and fairly, but with a Cabinet Minister for Secretary he felt that it was his duty to leave the government of the country mainly to him, and so cause no loss of power by any possible appearance of divergence of views. Hence, to a certain extent, the Viceregal policy was one of unselfish self-effacement, in the interests of his Queen and country. How well, how right royally, the social side of the Castle rule was conducted Lord Londonderry's many visitors from England and his Irish guests will all admit. His court will take rank with those of Lord Eglinton, Lord Spencer, and the Duke of Abercorn, while Lady Londonderry kept up the stately succession of Vice-Queens, who were Queens of Beauty as well as social leaders. In September, 1889, Lord Londonderry left the Castle of Dublin (where he had held office for some months, only at Lord Salisbury's special request), for his estates in England imperatively called for his presence. The undress Levée of their Excellencies was more largely attended than any similar previous one, and the procession from the Castle to the railway station was cheered lustily as it passed through Nassau Street. In fact, Lord London-derry's popularity had grown greatly in his three years of office, if unacknowledged. To show how completely and cordially his Excellency and Mr. Balfour pulled together it may be here mentioned that he lent the Hall of St. Patrick to his Secretary when the latter wished to entertain a larger number of guests than the Lodge in the Park could accommodate. The ball proved a thorough social success.

1889.

Sir Laurence Dundas, Earl of Zetland, who, at a time when, owing chiefly to the immense depreciation in landed estate and the silent decrement of agricultural produce, there was some little difficulty experienced by Lord Salisbury in finding an adequate successor to Lord Londonderry in the Viceregal office, came forward manfully to fill a post which his predecessor's splendidly lavish liberality had made a more costly *corvée* than ever, belongs to a family who have been conspicuous for official ability through many generations. His Excellency and Lady Zetland are not unknown in Ireland, for they were frequent guests of Lord and Lady Londonderry, and Lord Zetland occupied a leading position in several good gallops with the Meath hounds during two seasons. It seems a little hard that what is called (rather curiously) by one or two leading Radical prints "his first official act," namely, the purchase of an Irish jaunting car, should be attributed to the most paltry and pitiful motives. "Noblesse," in his case was "obligeante;" all his tastes and interests prompted him *not* to go to Ireland. Lord Zetland is connected with the old and honourable family of Talbot in Ireland.

CHAPTER VI.

A SELECTION OF SECRETARIES.

"Lives of great men all remind us
   We can make our lives sublime,
   And departing leave behind us
   Footprints on the sands of time."

LONGFELLOW.

With the progress of civilisation comes the division of labour in all its departments, material as well as intellectual. In the earlier times of the Viceroyalty, the holder of the Sword of State, or "gladius authoritatis," had to fill many parts. He presided at Parliaments and "Star Chambers," and in the Law Courts; led the Army against the foe, and in one or two instances was expected to be, like his sovereign in England, "fidei defensor," a propagandist and evangeliser, in fact he had to fill as many functions as occasionally fall to the lot of the Chief Justice of Sierra-Leone, a British Consul in remote regions, or the Deputy Governor of that turtle territory, the island of Ruatan!

T

When Ireland became more or less assimilated to England (in theory if not absolutely in practice), this plurality of functions was found impossible, and Presidents of the Provinces at first relieved the Lord Lieutenant of the time being from a portion of his heavy burdens. Then when Parliament became *the* Power, and the bureau and desk supplanted the guard room and parade ground, there arose a necessity for the creation of Departments or " Portfolios," whose holders were responsible to the Viceroy, though each Chief of Department was tolerably absolute within its pur-views and limits. A Commander-in-Chief administered the forces of the island; Religion had its Hierarchy; Law its chancellor, judges, and official exponents; but for the actual administration of the affairs of the island, the Chief Secretary had to answer to Parliament, on which he depended for his " supply."

It seems now almost impossible to fix a date for the creation of the Chief Secretary's Department. It is very possible that in comparatively remote times the Lord Lieutenant of the time being desirous of having a representative in the House of Commons got his Private Secretary returned for some borough or other that was amenable to Crown influence; but this is only a conjecture.

However, there is an actual record of the office in the year 1623, when, however, it had not become *a* power much less *the* power in Ireland, seeing that patronage, the chief lever available, was entirely vested in the Lord Lieutenant. In 1798 Lord Castlereagh, I believe the first Irishman appointed, held the office on the resignation of Pelham ; Charles Abbott held it in 1801 ; Mr. Wickham in 1802 ; while in a few cases we find that the Secretariat was the portal to the Vice-royalty, as, for instance, in the case of Lord St. Germans, Lord Camden, and Lord Morpeth, afterwards Lord Carlisle. Of these men Lord Castlereagh was *facile princeps*, and to show the confidential nature of the office which was always before his time entrusted to English hands, it may be mentioned that Lord Camden, in writing to Lord Castlereagh prior to the appointment, says "there appeared to be every inclination in *his* (*i.e.*, Lord Cornwallis') mind to overcome the prejudice which is felt here against the Secretary being an Irishman in your favour, and he felt all the delicacy and responsibility of your situation now, as deserving every attention hereafter." We know the great work that Castlereagh accomplished in effecting the union of the islands ; we know, too, how " he who

T 2

stands upon a slippery place makes nice of no vile hold to stay him up." He had to deal with " Patriots "—he knew them well—and he acted according to his estimate. At the Congress of Vienna Lord Castlereagh was perhaps the most powerful subject in Europe. As an intrepid clear-headed official, capable of immense toil in the service of the State, he will ever be a conspicuous exemplar.

Another Irishman who filled the office of Chief Secretary with great ability—an ability not to be wholly measured by his speeches in Parliament, though some of them were powerful and per-suasive too—was Lord Naas, afterwards Earl of Mayo, who died in discharging the duties of Viceroy of India.

The Earls of Mayo and Marquises of Clan-ricarde claim a common ancestor, and Mayo was one of the titles of the Clanricardes. Richard Southwell Bourke, the eldest of a band of brothers who have one and all fought the battle of life bravely and well, was not born titularly noble or rich, and as he owed his early education, as well as his academic teaching, to Ireland, so he may be said to have remained a thorough Irishman, and racy of her soil, all his life ; for he dearly loved his native land, of which he was proud, and

THE LATE LORD MAYO.

which he strove to benefit, advance, and improve according to the light that was in him, though that light may seem tenebrous to some who arrogate for themselves and their co-thinkers a quasi-patent of patriotism and Hibernian heroism. After travelling for some months through Russia, Mr. Bourke—a Conservative by profession and tradition—wrote an account of his experiences in the land of the Tzar, which might be termed by many Radical in tone, but which is perhaps a proof that true liberty is the basis of the Conservative party, which, avoiding declamations on the natural rights of man, and such sickly sentimentalities, proved itself the friend of liberality and progress on many occasions, though perhaps it occasionally made shipwreck on such rocks as Protection, both in Church and State.

The generous and liberal views enunciated by Mr. Bourke brought him into some notice, and his pleasant personality did the rest ; for it made him hosts of friends wherever he went, and his good judgment, solid sense, and attention to detail marked him for future office. His great uncle, the Earl of Mayo, had given him a commission in the County Militia—the Kildare Rifles —a *corps d'élite*, composed, for the most part, of the *fine fleur* of the noblemen and gentlemen of that aristocratic county. Lord Heytesbury had attached him to his Staff as "gentleman at large," which was a pleasant introduction to the best Dublin society, in a becoming uniform, whose light blue facings found much favour, 'tis said, with the belles of the period; but farming was his trade when the potato blight set in, and made every man, woman, and child in Ireland an almoner to relieve the surrounding distress. In this labour of love Mr. Bourke did yeoman's service, and, though Conservatism was not popular in Kildare, he gained the suffrages of his countrymen in an election for its representation in the House of Commons, in spite of strong opposition.

On his father's inheriting the title of Mayo, Mr. Bourke became Lord Naas, and soon after his entrance into the House of Commons found his fate in Miss Blanche Wyndham, who proved a true helpmeet in all his triumphs and difficulties. When Lord Derby came into office in 1849 he offered him the post of Chief Secretary—a signal compliment to a comparatively untried man— he accepted it; and getting returned for Coleraine represented it for five years, when Cockermouth made him her M.P., and retained him for eleven years in her service.

Lord Naas was fortunate in his chief, the Earl of Eglinton, as well as in the permanent Under-Secretary, Sir Thomas Larcom, who may be compared to the solicitor who gets up all the facts of the case for the counsels' opinion and review. Lord Derby's ministry was not long-lived, but it returned to place and power in 1858, and again Lords Eglinton and Naas filled the same official positions with the same complete harmony. Lord Naas' liberality of views is proved by his having anticipated Mr. Gladstone in his efforts at land reform and compensation to tenants for improvements, but his views proved premature then. In 1866 Mr. D'Israeli came into office, and with the Duke of Abercorn for chief, Lord Naas was again the occupant of the Chief Secretary's Lodge, where Lady Naas' great social talents found splendid scope, and her reunions were universally voted delightful. The Fenian rising at Tallaght Hill was promptly put down by a Government that was well-informed and could hardly be taken by surprise; but if the feeble Fenians had not been quickly crushed at the first hostile movement, an insurrection might have grown out of the attempt, and the tragedies of '98 been repeated. However, the constabulary and the climate promptly gave it the *coup de grâce*.

With the complete crushing of this Fenian fiasco, which took its origin and colour from the greater Ireland in America, Lord Mayo's (for his father's death had put him in possession of the first title) official connection with Ireland ceased, as he was offered the Governor-Generalship of Canada, or the reversion of the Viceroyalty of India, by the Premier, and he accepted the latter. It is a matter of history how, in the midst of a most successful administration of our Oriental Empire, Lord Mayo was assassinated by a fanatic while inspecting some prisons in the Andaman Islands, his Lordship having ever taken the deepest interest in prison discipline and prison ameliora- tion as a system. The enormous crowds that attended the funeral of one who to many was a political opponent, attest the estimate formed of him in his native country. His remains rest in the old cemetery overlooked by an ivy-mantled ruin—once a church—at the Gate of Palmerstown, his Kildare residence.

> " The dust of some is Irish earth,
>   Among their own they rest ;
> And the same land that gave them birth
>   Has caught them to her breast."

As a sportsman Lord Mayo was quite in the

first rank ; he took the Kildare hounds at a time
when the finances of the Hunt were at a very low
ebb.   He showed splendid sport, though a welter
weight, and left the association to his successor
in a flourishing financial condition.   He was as
earnest in sport as he was at his official work.
" Omnis in hoc sum," his motto ; he wished, as an
M.F.H., to win the Kildare Hunt Cup, and he
won it with a horse called Hornpipe.   The Peel,
known as " Archie," rode him.

Another Conservative Secretary to whom
the Chief Secretaryship was a step in the
official ladder was Sir Michael Edward Hicks-
Beach, who twice filled the arduous office and
very nearly lost his eyesight from too close
attention to the business of his office.   Modera
tion is often voted Laodicean lukewarmness when
political passion is at fever heat ; we know
by their unseemly exultation at Sir Michael's
affliction (an exultation, we trust, confined to a
very small circle) that the Nationalists did not
love him, and as a body the Irish landowners did
not regard him very highly, because they considered that he did not lend them sufficient armed
force to enforce the decrees of the law in their
favour ; no one, however, ever questioned Sir
Michael's assiduity and anxiety to do right under

circumstances of extreme difficulty. Sir Michael
was a member of the Cabinet while Chief Secretary. He hunted while in office, and rode hard
and straight. His successor, the Right Hon.
Arthur James Balfour, stands forth on the page
of contemporary history as having earned more
odium from the Nationalist party in Ireland than
any of his predecessors in office, by his unswerving enforcement of the law under all
circumstances, and his total disregard of the
angry voices of citizens *prava jubentium;* he has
not sought popularity, and he certainly has not
gained it, but his subordinates admire him greatly
because they feel confident of his thorough support
if they endeavour to do their duty. He has not
done anything for the landowners save in the way
of support of legal claims, but they feel the strength
of even that support, moral as well as physical,
and rally round him. Whether "post hoc" or
"propter hoc" comparative prosperity has returned to Ireland. Under his firm sway coercion
is in reality felt to be emancipation from tyranny
by many thousands, and no law-abiding subject
has as yet suffered from its administration.

Among great Chief Secretaries the Right
Hon. W. E. Forster certainly merits mention.
No braver man ever kept the Privy Seal or

THE RIGHT HON. A. J. BALFOUR, M.P.

endeavoured to serve Ireland more heartily or
effectively. He had earned the gratitude of
thousands in the west by his liberality and
philanthropy in the famine years, but politics
know no gratitude. In 1880 he accepted the
appointment of Chief Secretary to Ireland, from
an innate belief that he understood the needs
of the nation, and could bring her back to the
paths of law and order. Armed with coercive
powers more anti-constitutional than had ever
been claimed before, he suppressed the Land
League, imprisoned the leaders of the National
party, and filled the gaols with men whom he
"suspected," though sometimes without any
rational cause whatever. These high-handed
measures brought on him the intense hatred of
the more advanced politicians, and his life was
often in great danger, his escapes marvellous,
for he took no precautions and recklessly risked
his life, hardly knowing the meaning of the word
fear. His chief was Lord Cowper, a most intrepid
Governor, and when his Excellency and his Chief
Secretary found that they were not supported, as
they expected, by the Government, they resigned.
Mr. Forster took an early opportunity of vindi-
cating his official conduct in Parliament, and his
indictment of Mr. Parnell in the House was

Ciceronianly strong. That Mr. Forster was quite right in his diagnosis of Ireland, and that the rank and file of her countrymen were misled by what he called "village ruffians" seems true, but his methods of meeting the evil appears questionable and pedagoguish. He was a brave statesmanlike man, most liberal in hand and heart, in purse as well as in profession, "integer vitæ scelerisque purus," a Quaker with the virtues of "the Friends" and few of their faults.

Another historical Chief Secretary was Edward Geoffrey Smith Stanley, who did much towards settling the terrible tithe war, and establishing mixed education in Ireland, noble monuments to statesmanship, but almost eclipsed by his subsequent share in the great measure of negro emancipation. O'Connell and he were rival orators and fierce Parliamentary foes. Perhaps his fame as Lord Stanley was even greater than that which he gained as Lord Derby and Premier of England twice, but Lord Derby had many crowns, and was as eminent in literature as in politics. With the Chief Secretaryship of Sir Robert Peel, one of the ablest and honestest statesmen of the century, will ever be associated the establishment of the Irish Constabulary, a body that has done almost more to civilise Ireland than any other, and which has ever proved a credit to the country. His eldest son and successor, Sir Robert Peel, was also Chief Secretary in Ireland during Lord Derby's Administration. He was popular with many, and "the Rollicking Robert," as he has been called, left many friends in Ireland, where he was very outspoken and liberal in hand and heart.

It may not be generally known that the preliminaries of a duel were actually arranged between Sir Robert Peel and Daniel O'Connell, to come off in France or Belgium, and that both belligerents were on their way thither, when the latter was arrested in Jermyn Street, London, and, of course, bound over to keep the peace.

Lord Carlingford, better known as Chichester Fortescue, was another eminent Chief Secretary, and his wife, Lady Waldegrave, a queen of society.

In connection with Lord Naas' Secretaryship it may be mentioned here that he was constantly threatened, and that his friends feared that in his nightly rides between his office at the Castle and the Lodge in the Phœnix Park he might be fired at, but he took no precautions beyond riding at a brisk pace, and had no police protection.